BOAT DOLLIES

Joyce Holland

BOAT DOLLIES

WORLDWIDE ®

TORONTO • NEW YORK • LONDON
AMSTERDAM • PARIS • SYDNEY • HAMBURG
STOCKHOLM • ATHENS • TOKYO • MILAN
MADRID • WARSAW • BUDAPEST • AUCKLAND

To my husband, Tony, for his enduring faith in my ability.

Recycling programs
for this product may
not exist in your area.

Boat Dollies

A Worldwide Mystery/February 2015

First published by Deadly Alibi Press Ltd.

ISBN-13: 978-0-373-26933-4

Copyright © 2000 by Joyce Holland

All rights reserved. No part of this book may be reproduced
or transmitted in any form or by any means, electronic or
mechanical, including photocopying, recording or by any
information storage and retrieval system, without permission
in writing from the publisher. For information, contact: Deadly Alibi
Press Ltd., PO Box 5947, Vancouver, WA, 98668-5947.

This is a work of fiction. Names, characters, places and incidents are
either the product of the author's imagination or are used fictitiously,
and any resemblance to actual persons, living or dead, business
establishments, events or locales is entirely coincidental.

® and TM are trademarks of Harlequin Enterprises Limited.
Trademarks indicated with ® are registered in the United States
Patent and Trademark Office, the Canadian Intellectual Property Office
and in other countries.

Printed in U.S.A.

Acknowledgments

To Graeme and Cathy Jones for their patience through countless readings. And to all my friends and family, especially my sister Penny Lester, who writes much better than I do—when she writes. To the Emerald Coast Writers' Guild members, Laverne Brigman, Vicki Hinze, Ginny Winn, Cindy Holbrook, Mickie Phipps, Lorna Tedder and Beverly Suarez-Beard. To Earl Staggs and Donna Nigon, my online sources for confidence. To the memory of my parents, Oliver and Babbette Knapp. And finally, to my "Sunday Champagne Crowd," for helping me celebrate long before I was published!

ONE

THE MARINA DOCKS were closed for the night to all but the live-aboards, and even those hearty souls hovered below decks, annoyed by a howling wind that dropped in like an uninvited guest and stayed for dinner.

The shadowy figure of a man prowled the deserted docks. The wind stretched his nerves with its eerie whine and tried his patience with long tense moments of silence. He checked his watch. Two in the morning. Sooner or later Rita would have to show.

Like the answer to a prayer, Rita suddenly appeared in the labyrinth of catwalks connecting the boat slips, so drunk she could hardly walk. Long hair shrouded her shoulders in darkness, and only a wisp of it, tugged by the breeze, reflected its true golden beauty in the dim harbor light. She clutched anxiously at a tall post to steady herself and staggered dangerously near the water's edge. She hung there for a few minutes staring down into the black depths. Her slender body etched against the gray horizon through her flimsy, gauze dress looked like an artist's silhouette done in moon tones. He followed Rita's progress with fervent interest, keeping out of sight behind the long row of upright storage lockers. He'd already singled out a boat to borrow from among those nestled tightly together near the ferry pier. He'd moved it into position earlier. The purr of a small engine would barely be heard above the angry wind and lapping waves.

He flinched when Rita lurched forward again, tacking

her way along the dock from piling to piling. "That bastard," she cried. "That lousy rotten bastard, I'll show him. He'll be sorry! Oh…God. Why?"

Rita stepped forward into empty space and fell heavily into the forgiving softness of the rubber dinghy. She leaned toward the pier and freed the painter and unshiped the oars, her actions wholly instinctive now. They had to be, she was too high on booze and cocaine to receive any coherent messages from her brain.

The little yellow dinghy slipped quietly away, its bow aimed at the harbor entrance. The strong breeze, pungent with the odor of rain-drenched sugarcane, absorbed the sound of her weeping.

He watched the dinghy's progress and followed, occasionally putting the engine into neutral so he wouldn't close on her too quickly. Patience would ensure his advantage. The farther out their altercation took place, the better. Since the wind blew through the channel, he would tow her out to sea past the harbor entrance no matter what. It wouldn't do to have her found too soon.

Rita stopped rowing and he could no longer hear her sobs. Her oars dangled loosely on their own, caught now and then by a wave. Soon only her head was visible, pillowed against the inflated rim of the raft.

It wouldn't be long. He used the time to fashion a noose of sorts to slip over her fortuitously proffered head. Fortuitous, because the knife he'd brought along for the killing would no longer be needed. It lay on the seat beside him. He didn't want to get blood on him anyway. This would be much cleaner all around. He smiled as he watched the little dinghy bob on the waves. *Rockabyebaby, Rita.*

The knife glinted in the sporadic moonlight, drawing his attention once more. It still might come in handy. Maybe he should use it to sink the raft, that way they might not look for her for days, figure she had gotten drunk and gone to one of the other islands. She'd done that before. On the other hand, the hell with it, let them find her, it would close the chapter for him.

His boat, pushed by the choppy waves, bumped Rita's dinghy, causing her head to loll from side to side. He held his breath. She was always getting drunk. Getting drunk and running her mouth, threatening him. Well, her pretty pouting little mouth would soon close for the last time. He should never have let her live this long. She knew too much.

Rita struggled briefly when he slipped the noose over her head. Her hands clutched at the coarse rope. He pushed them away roughly, not wanting to feel Rita's touch in her dying moments, the touch of death.

She stopped moving. He plucked at the knot at the back of her neck, but it refused to loosen and only grew tighter with his efforts to undo it. Frantic, he picked up the knife and slashed wildly at the knot.

From out of the night came the sound of another boat approaching. He focused on the harbor entrance in front of him. A large sailboat loomed. It bore down on the two small boats and the ghastly scene. He froze for a moment, unsure what to do. On the bow of the offending craft knelt a woman, crouched over, her attention devoted to something at her feet. The anchor, she was readying the anchor. He must move quickly before she saw him. He pushed Rita's limp body down into her raft, reached for the throttle and revved his engine ever so slightly.

The noise startled the woman on the sailboat. She stood and looked straight at him. He felt her eyes bore into him. No, she couldn't possibly see him. Surely the glaring spreader lights on her mast would make it impossible. Still, he could swear her eyes met his and held them for an instant. The boat slid quietly through the channel, steering straight toward him. He could even read the name inscribed on its bow, Sere Dina. *Another boat, another dollie, another threat. Damn*.

Snatching the dinghy's painter, he moved to the cover of darkness, and once clear of the sailboat, out to sea.

Safely away from prying eyes, he edged Rita's lithe body over the side, all efforts at removing the rope from around her neck abandoned. The dinghy drifted beside her like a watchdog, tethered by the rope tied around her neck. The hell with sinking it. He stared, entranced as Rita's lifeless body floated in a rhythmic dance. Her long dress rippled out like angels' wings on the waves. Soon, the sea Rita loved so passionately would take her to its bosom, swallowing her misery and her dreams with an undiscerning gusto.

TWO

UNSECURED HALYARDS SLAPPED noisily in the distance, stirred by an early morning breeze that swept cool air into the picturesque little harbor. The raging tempest of the evening before left little or no trace in its wake. The clear blue sky held only powder puff clouds now and gentle waves caressed the palm-lined shore.

The sleepy island village came slowly to life, like a morning glory unfolding its petals. The roar of the first seaplane of the day roused the pelicans from their dock perches. Hand carts rattled over the cobblestone waterfront as their owners arrived to set up shop for the day. Their happy voices mingled with those of the excited tourists arriving on the island ferry. Excited perhaps, because the ferry's reputation for speed and daring was legend. Arriving safely was an accomplishment.

Sally slept through all these noises. It was the incessant chugging of an outboard passing near the stern of their boat that finally woke her up. She uncoiled with the stretching motion of a cat, automatically reaching for Pete, but her arm met empty space. She rose to a sitting position and inhaled the rich aroma of coffee wafting from the galley. Confused for a moment, still not fully awake, after all, Sally took stock of her situation.

Then she remembered and fell back on the pillows again. No wonder her body betrayed her, it had taken them thirty-six hours to cross that wretched passage. What seemed like square waves, whipped into fury by the relentless winds, had assaulted them from two directions. Not exactly a warm welcome to paradise. Somewhere in the wee hours of the morning, Sally swore never to set foot on a boat again, if they made it. It was not the first time she made such promises.

And speaking of welcomes, she could still see the outline of a boat in her mind's eye. Could see, no feel, someone's eyes reaching out to her across the water last night when they'd entered the harbor. Pete insisted her imagination played tricks on her because she was overtired from their harrowing trip. Well, she had been too tired to argue the point. She took a deep breath. A new day called for new thoughts.

She smiled. The whole world seemed different once you made safe harbor. Even the harsh rattle of the anchor chain became the loveliest music. She snuggled against the pillows, luxuriating in the gentle rocking of the sailboat as it persistently nosed its sleek bowsprit into the wind, like a bird dog scenting prey. She patted the hull affectionately. "Good girl, Old Tub. Sorry I doubted you for a while there."

Pete appeared in the hatchway blocking the morning sun. He looked fresh and rested which seemed grossly unfair. "Is this a private conversation?" he grinned. "Or can anyone join in?"

"Yes it is," she replied. "It's private. At least until I have my coffee. Besides, I'm not sure I want to speak with anyone miraculously rejuvenated after two days of terror at sea. *You* are a masochist!"

"Life is for the adventurous. Coffee's on deck, so come on up. Oh, and please do not refer to Sere Dina as 'Old Tub' on shore today, it embarrasses her."

"Nonsense!" Sally hollered after him. "She loves it, and no one knows what Sere Dina means anyway. Some weird Fijian chant," she mumbled. She quickly threw on a bikini and a knee-length T-shirt and followed Pete topside.

"Should have come up earlier," he teased, handing her a steaming mug. "Girl on the next boat took a nice loo…ng bath on deck."

"Really? Surely not unclothed, Peter?" Sally resisted rising to the bait and smiled instead.

"Oh, yes indeed. Stark. In. The. Raw. Naked," Pete continued, apparently quite pleased with this revelation.

"Grow up, will you, Pete! Honestly, sometimes I…"

The sound of an approaching launch drowned out her words. They both looked up automatically to see if their customs' flag was in place. It flapped dutifully in the breeze, indicating they had not yet checked in with the local customs' official and could not visit or be visited until they did.

The boat and uniformed black occupant appeared unquestionably official, even though the government emblem on the port bow lacked definition and the agent's dark blue uniform had seen better days.

Behind his weathered boat he towed a small rubber dinghy. Maneuvering with practiced expertise, he cut the power on his engine and drifted into position alongside.

"Morning, mon," he said to Pete. "What time you come to harbor, mon?" His dark eyes swept the boat from bow to stern but studiously avoided Sally's tall, slender presence.

"Around three or four this morning."

"You happen to see this boat anytime, mon?"

Pete glanced at the trailing dinghy with the large bundle draped across its only seat.

Sally followed his gaze. The bright yellow rubber craft lent a cheerful note to the sunny morning. Then she leaned over the side for a closer look and gasped as it dawned on her that the cargo was a body. Long golden tresses escaped the tarpaulin bundle and snaked lazily in the pool of blood-red water trapped in the bottom of the dinghy.

Sally opened her mouth to speak, but caught Pete's brief frown in her direction and stifled the impulse. She wanted to mention the vague shape of a boat she had seen in the night. Pete would only discount her story though. He avoided complications. Sally recalled the vision vividly and even remembered the distinctive sound of an outboard motor. The sense of someone there.

"Truthfully, we were too tired last night to notice much of anything," Pete said in a serious tone. Frown lines creased his forehead. "A whole fleet could have passed in review and not have bothered us."

The man nodded. "Okay, mon. You want to clear customs you better get your boat and follow me now. I'm going to be a busy fella today." His ebony eyes studied the body for a moment, then centered on the distant sea.

Sally searched the sky, half expecting some sort of answer to be emblazoned across the horizon.

The official turned back to Pete. "Rough out there last night, mon?"

"Rough as a cob, mister."

The man squinted in confusion.

"Sorry," Pete corrected. "I mean yes, it was very rough out there last night."

"I think so too, mon, I think so. Come on, I got a lot of work to do. The lady, she don't need to come. You got anybody else on the boat, mon?"

"Just the two of us. I'll get our passports and a shirt and be right along."

KNOTTING HER LONG dark hair into a bun, Sally pinned it to the top of her head. Beads of perspiration dotted her nose, her aristocratic nose. That's what her mother always called it anyway. You could, according to Mother, tell a lot about people by their noses. They reflected the personalities of their owners. Shallow noses—the cute, ski-jump ones Sally envied—indicated shallow minds, her mother maintained. It therefore followed that strong noses spoke of superior minds. But then her mother had strong opinions on every-thing and everyone. It wasn't until she grew up that Sally realized she actually sported a fairly ordinary nose, but her mother possessed a dilly wizzer.

She patted her face dry with a cloth. The day would be a scorcher.

Sally tidied the bunk area. Pete's gun lay on the shelf above his pillow. Loaded, of course. She hated it being there, but didn't consider the issue worth an argument. He insisted there was no point in having a gun if you didn't have it handy. Sally slid it gingerly out of the way, cover-ing it with Pete's pajamas. Another gun lay tucked away in the lazarette. It too was loaded. Things could be worse. He could carry one around all the time.

She could hear their dinghy returning. Pete would be hungry. Breakfast options were in order. Although it was only nine o'clock in the morning, the tropical sun would rapidly turn the harbor into a steam bath. Fruit and cold cereal seemed the best bet.

"What a charming introduction to the Caribbean," Sally announced, as she went topside with a tray. "Storms and dead bodies! One thing is for sure, things can only im-prove from here."

Pete nodded in agreement. "I hope you're right. And speaking of the body, it was a young woman, late twen-ties I would say."

Sally tensed. He might say more. He might even say a woman Becky's age. Or the age their daughter would be if she were alive. Then she sighed, certain he wouldn't mention Becky in relation to a dead body. The last thing Pete would do is bring up Becky. Sally wanted to talk about her, but the wound was too fresh and too deep. She grimaced at the thought.

"You saw the body? Why?"

"I didn't mean to. A fellow from the neighboring boat volunteered to identify it as soon as we hit the beach. I was just there. Believe me, I would rather have missed the experience."

"Oh, really? Our neighbor? Would that be the one with the naked bather?"

"The one and only. Anyway, he said the dead girl was the cook off a boat called Sunawind or Summerswind, something like that." Pete ran his fingers through his hair, spreading the dark curls in an attempt to cover the bald spot that plagued him. "It seems a lot of people were looking for her last night. She and the captain, her boyfriend, had a parting of the ways because of another girl."

"So what does that mean? Are they saying she committed suicide? Do you think that's the boat I saw last night? Shouldn't I tell the customs official?"

"Last question first. No, you shouldn't tell the customs official, or anybody else for that matter. I hate to tell you, but this was no suicide. It looks as though somebody strangled her and then did some weird knife work on her neck, to boot. Besides, you didn't really see anything."

"Weird knife work? What do you mean, mutilation?" she shot back, ignoring his disclaimer of her sighting. "Please tell me you don't mean mutilation." Sally pushed her cereal away and gave a perceptible shudder.

"Well, I could be wrong, perhaps the guy just wanted to get his rope back. On the other hand, he may have decided to sever her spinal cord to make sure she couldn't swim to shore."

"You said guy. Why did you say guy? Do they have a suspect?" Sally twisted her cloth napkin into a tight little ball.

"No, I said guy because it doesn't seem the sort of thing a woman would do, the strangling and the knife and all. Don't women usually poison people or club them from behind or something?"

"I'm going to assume you're suggesting those methods because women lack the physical strength for other means, not because you think they lack the courage, right?"

"We're not having an argument, are we? The only woman I know well enough to make judgments about would never knife anyone, if that answers your question. Anyway, getting back to the girl, I heard a few snide remarks concerning her habit of overindulging a bit on booze and drugs."

"God, I thought we had left all that behind us with the soap operas and lawn mowers, but I guess it's everywhere." Sally made a face.

Pete reached out and squeezed her shoulder. "From what I've seen in our first few hours, you're right. Oh, by the way, I invited the neighbor over for a drink later this afternoon."

"Wonderful, darling. Shall I undress so she won't be too uncomfortable?"

"*Him*, Sally, I invited *him*. But come to think of it, that might be a nice gesture on your part. Show him we're regular boat people and all. Yeah, great idea." He smiled and poured some fresh juice.

"Always the perfect host, aren't you, Peter? But what say we just test the ground this visit. See if we really want to get quite that close first."

Sally turned away, putting an end to their silly banter. Her attention was drawn to a nearby boat. Someone in a small runabout dropped anchor nearby, some total klutz who didn't know beans about boating. The man's head snapped in her direction, causing her to glance away, embarrassed to have witnessed his ineptitude.

Sally chose to ignore him and stared into space, recalling the mutilated body in the dinghy. Closing her eyes, she tried to recapture the whole of the vision from the night before. Had she witnessed a murder? The events were related, had to be. The question was, what to do about it? Pete's position of never getting involved, complicated the problem.

THREE

THE NEIGHBOR'S NAME was Jeff. His hair was long, sun
streaked and blond. And, Sally noted, very shiny. Clean
people, these neighbors. Jeff stood around five foot ten. He
reminded her of one of those pictures in anatomy books,
the ones designed to show all the muscles in the body. Most
people would call him wiry, really wiry. At close to thirty-
something, she wondered what he did for a living. Sally
panned the harbor studying the dozens of boats moored
there. What did they all do for a living?

Sally sat up straight for a minute, her attention again
drawn to the fisherman who had anchored on their port
side. If he was a fisherman, she would need to revise her
views on the hobby. Only an idiot would brave the tropical sun in a black shirt and long pants. And he grasped his
fishing pole with both hands extended before him, grip-
ping the rod like a weapon. With his slicked back hair and
dark glasses he appeared sinister. Nuts, she thought, the
dead girl's body inspired weird suspicions, goosing her
imagination into overdrive.

Sally and Pete were there to finally deal with the loss of
Becky. In their twenty years of marriage, Pete had managed to be gone for all the important times. That explained
his singular burden of guilt. Deep down, Sally knew she
was wounded so deeply she might never be capable of discussing Becky. But ignoring memories of Becky like Pete
did was like having her die all over again. There seemed
no safe middle ground. Pete had taken a sabbatical in an

effort to help her get past her grief. Physically they had never had a problem, so at first, the seafaring life had been like a second honeymoon. But they still avoided discussions on the subject of Becky. The Caribbean was new to them and only time would tell if they would be happy here. Only time would tell if they would be happy at all. She glanced at the palm trees on the golden shore, at the wispy clouds forming over the lush green hills, at the vivid, blue green water, what was not to like? Sighing, Sally brought her attention back to Pete and Jeff.

"Just another boat dollie," Jeff said.

"Excuse me," Sally interrupted. "What's a boat dollie?" Something in the way Jeff said the words gave Sally the feeling she was not going to enjoy the definition.

Jeff appraised her, a curious look on his face. "Sorry, I sort of figured you were longtime live-aboards. We saw you settle in last night and you maneuvered like naturals."

"Thank you, Jeff," Pete said. "I take that to be a compliment. Actually we've been weekend sailors for twenty years or so, mostly in the northern lakes and bays. You don't meet many live-aboards there. We've been really moving for a month though, and I don't have to tell you, sailing down the east coast in the Fall can teach you a great deal in a hurry. I hope we didn't wake you when we came in last night. We didn't get here until almost three in the morning."

Jeff's expression was part serious and part amused. "One of the first things you need to learn if you're going to stay in this part of the world any length of time, is to check it out when anyone drops anchor near you, day or night. There are a lot of people who rent their boats to tourists because the money is great. Trouble with tourists is, even if they know about boats…well, let's say they tend to party a little more here than they do at home." He laughed and raised his eyebrows.

"And these *boat dollies*," Sally coached, not wanting to lose the thread of their original conversation, "are they the girls on the tourist boats having a vacation fling or something?"

Jeff blushed. "Ah, no, ma'am. I think I know what you're getting at, but no, ma'am. That's not what a boat dollie is, no way."

Sally blushed. She turned toward Pete instinctively. He sported a barely discernible smirk.

No one spoke for a moment.

"But maybe that's how a boat dollie gets started." Jeff pinched his chin between one thumb and forefinger. "Honestly, I never thought of it before, but I guess it could be. Anyway, a real boat dollie is a full-time kind of thing. They have to be on boats."

Jeff had a very expressive face, with bushy eyebrows and a lot of smile lines. Something had obviously occurred to him because he lit up like a Christmas tree. "I've got it! They're like baseball Annies, fanatics. Or groupies, in the music world. Only with dollies, it's boats."

"And this girl who was killed, you're saying she was a boat dollie?" Pete asked.

"Rita? Yeah, an absolute for sure boat dollie. It's unreal she was killed, man. She used to just get out of it on booze and stuff. Last night she went really gonzo. I mean, I could believe it if she fell out of the stupid boat or something."

Jeff's face revealed his puzzlement. He seriously could not absorb the idea of Rita having been murdered. Sally studied him with new interest.

"Rita," he continued, shaking his head, "always went for a boat ride when she got upset about something. Normally, she would have been fine the next day. Shoot, she could have crewed on any boat in the harbor. She was good looking as all get out. She cooked like a professional chef and she handled a sailboat better than most of the captains in the harbor."

Sally felt a small ache settle somewhere deep within her for the boat dollie named Rita. Where had she come from? Did she have family? Why was she always going out for a boat ride alone when she was upset? Didn't she have any friends? To die as "just another boat dollie" seemed a singularly empty epitaph.

"What about her friends, couldn't she talk to someone when she had a problem?"

"Some dollies make friends, but most don't. At least not with other boat girls. You see, they're all the time trying to move up to a better boat. Rita was always afraid of another girl getting her place. And who can blame her, it happens all the time. But I don't believe anybody could have ousted Rita in the long run. She was the best crew in the harbor. The only one who didn't know that, was Rita. You get it?" Jeff didn't sound malicious, he sounded honest.

"Yes," Sally sighed. "Unfortunately, I get it."

"Hey, I'm sorry." Jeff's expressive face glowed with sympathy.

Sally studied him, awed by his facial dexterity. The man was a living, breathing chameleon. But she liked him. There was something wholesome about his flighty sensitivity.

"I didn't mean to depress you," Jeff explained. "Really I didn't. You get a few like Rita, but for the most part, boat people are the happiest people I know. Wait till you've settled in a while. You'll see."

He directed a question to Pete without pausing. "Did Joseph say who he thought had done it?"

"Assuming that the official I spoke with on the beach

is Joseph," Pete said, "the answer is no. And to tell you the truth, it's like I told Sally, I wish I hadn't been there. I certainly wouldn't want to start any false rumors. Besides, you heard everything I heard."

"Yeah, that was Joseph," Jeff replied. "He hardly ever talks to people from outside, by the way, unless it's business, and I guess this was business all right. It's unbelievable. Why would anybody want to kill Rita?"

"Well, the woman is dead, after all," Sally said with resignation. "Somebody must have felt there was cause. Don't they have to do an autopsy or something before anyone can say anything about how she died?"

Pete and Jeff both looked at her strangely this time.

"We know how she died. There was a rope around her neck," Pete protested.

Sally gave him a hard look, picked up her rum punch and stirred it noisily.

The conversation soon turned to sailing stories and local island lore. Sally only half listened, still saddened by the fate of the boat dollie named Rita. And death, all deaths, brought fresh memories of Becky. It had been over a year and a half and still the pain ate at her soul. Would that last horrible night of Becky's life haunt her forever? The cruel words they'd exchanged echoed across time and like icy daggers dropping from eaves, and always caught her unprepared. Pictures flashed through her mind. Becky, standing on the porch in tears, screaming at her, telling her goodbye. She would marry Dean no matter what. "Great," Sally had told her, "just great." What foolish last words those were. Last words should be momentous, said with feeling not resignation. But how was she to have known Becky would die that night, from injuries suffered in a fiery crash? How was she to have known that Becky was pregnant? Because she was her mother, that's why.

Sally longed to exorcize the memories. What were Rita's mother's last memories of her daughter? She hoped they were better.

After Jeff left, Sally and Pete spent the afternoon adjusting the boat for harbor living. Pete spread the huge awning that doubled as a rain catcher for their fresh water supply. He stashed the extra sails under the V-berth. It took several hours to get everything scrubbed down and shipshape. They took a break around three and gorged themselves on bread with butter and sharp cheddar, washing it down with some hearty red wine.

Sally cupped her glass, looking over its rim as she scanned the surrounding water for the out-of-place fisherman. He was farther away now, but he was still there, leaning over in the confines of his small craft. Sally watched as he reached for something. Binoculars. He raised them to his face and trained them on Sere Dina. Sally resisted the urge to wave. Was this guy for real? He swept the boat from bow to stern, but when he spotted her, he immediately dropped them into the boat and turned away.

"Pete, I think that man is watching our boat." She pointed.

"Why would he be?" He shrugged and studied her for a moment. "Oh, I get it, your phantom boat last night and now a dead girl. Well, when he starts following us I'll take it seriously. Let's not get involved in any murder investigation, okay?"

"Right." Sally sighed, but kept her eye on the boat in the distance and poured the rest of the wine into their glasses. When she looked again, she saw the fisherman pull up his anchor. He must have caught her stare, letting him know she saw him too.

"While you were busy watching that innocent fisherman, Jeff suggested we join him at a little beach bar around six to meet some of the boat crowd."

She gathered their plates onto the tray "Sounds good to me. I'm anxious to meet the locals. And innocent fishermen don't focus binoculars on people."

She stole one last glance at the man, before going below. He glanced at her again as he motored away. The hell with it. She was the one who didn't belong here. But she really didn't want to go home, either. The ghosts at home haunted without letup.

FOUR

"THE OFFICIAL NAME of this bar is Reefside. Unofficially it's the Chamber Pot; that's what Jeff told me anyway." Pete helped Sally into the dinghy. "It was named by an old salt who sailed these waters for twenty years. He doesn't own the place, or even have an interest in it, but there's a bar stool with his name on it, and he still comes in once or twice a week."

"My, you really were soaking up the local lore while I was daydreaming." Sally sat on the wooden seat of the small craft and propped her feet on the extra gas can.

"The old salt's real name is Jake and he originally named the place the Piss Pot Saloon, for reasons no one seriously wants to know. He's a crusty sort who takes delight in insulting the tourists, even when they're customers on his charter boat. Supposedly, most of them revel in it. His day charters are always booked solid for weeks in advance. Jeff says an insult from Jake is a sought after badge. I guess if this guy doesn't zing you occasionally, you're too boring to know."

Sally rested her crossed arms on her drawn-up knees. "Sounds like my kind of character." She pushed her hair back as Pete turned the small craft into the wind.

"It gets better. The romantic side of you will like the next part." Pete smiled and stared at her briefly, as though measuring the depths of her attention. "Then one day a lady, as in real lady, came along," he continued. "To everyone's surprise, she not only took Jake's subtle remarks with a smile, she dealt them back double barbed. Jake spent ten minutes with her and was totally smitten. The lady had come for a week but stayed six months. She jokingly said one night, that the least they could do to upgrade the place was to call it The Chamber Pot or something.

"Jake pitched a fit and swore to boil in oil the first man who did. The last thing the Piss Pot needed, he said, were more bloody, shrimp-skinned tourists. And here's the good part, he swore to marry her in the Piss Pot Saloon. And if that wasn't good enough for her, then the hell with her, too."

Sally scowled. "Is this going to have a good ending? You're watching me too closely. Something terrible is going to happen to someone in this story, right?" She turned as they approached the seawall. Bad endings seemed to track her like predators lately.

Pete cut the power to idle. "Chapter two after we get tied up." He tossed her a fender, then fed the tender through a seawall cleat.

"You didn't answer my question about the happy ending," Sally prompted, as they walked along the sandy path toward the beach bar. The heavy aroma of fried seafood assaulted them, permeating their clothing and hair. Sally waved her hand in front of her face.

Pete raised his eyebrows but didn't speak.

"Okay, so just tell me the rest of it!" She wouldn't beg, but she was getting nervous about the ending.

"Well, the lady accepted Jake's bizarre proposal right then and there. That started a party at the Piss Pot, the wildest one ever. It lasted several days, in fact a major hotel registered numerous complaints on behalf of their guests. No charter people could be found on the docks the next morning and some of the whining tourists almost had sun strokes waiting for them. There also seemed to be a rather inordinate number of drunks passed out on the beach in front of the Piss Pot, some with glasses still in their hands."

Pete touched her arm. "The bad part is coming."

"I knew it!" Sally pushed his hand away. "I hope that fish smell isn't coming from where we're headed." She lifted her eyes to meet Pete's and sighed. "Go ahead, finish it."

"The lady was killed the following day in a freak accident on one of the ferries. An accident that remains unexplained to this day, since falling off a ferry is no easy trick. Jake refused to believe the news and insisted on seeing the body for himself. Everyone tried to talk him out of it, but Jeff insists he is as stubborn as he is crusty and was eventually led to the makeshift morgue. According to the locals, Jake has never been quite the same since. He still insults the occasional tourist, but not with the same cheerful enthusiasm."

Sally grimaced, her head bowed. "Now I know why I didn't pay attention while Jeff was cheering you up. That's it? Story time is over?"

"Not quite." Pete slipped one arm around her shoulders. "Finally, apparently heartbroken, Jake boarded his boat and wasn't seen for several months. When he reappeared at the bar he was quite drunk. He carried a large piece of driftwood with the name Chamber Pot carved in it. He ceremoniously nailed it to the center post. Then pouring a straight shot, he toasted his lady and took his usual seat at the bar. End of story and just in time, we have arrived." Pete stopped and stared.

"So what is the place called now, I'm confused."

"None of the names stuck, apparently it's just called *The Pot*."

Sally studied the beach shanty ahead of them with an

eye to deciding if it were the sort of place she wanted to spend any time. Pete could manage anywhere.

The bar was basically more outside than in, with a thatched roof and long sweeping eaves all around. The walls that served to close the bar at night were tethered to an old mast that served as the center post for the building. There were tables and benches under the palms on one side of the huge thatched hut, but most of the customers sat in little clusters around the weather-beaten bar.

The group appeared ordinary enough at first glance. A couple of beach bums in the crowd, but she expected that. Some were well dressed, some casual. The thing they all had in common was suntans. Probably not a tourist in the bunch. The place spoke to her and she loved it immediately. A beach bar in the tropics ought to look exactly like this. Every inch of surface supporting the building sported nautical decorations, fishing floats, nets, shells, sea fans and a thousand other things.

Jeff spotted Pete and waved them over. A slender girl next to Jeff spun to face them. She was plain except for her blue green eyes and she had the longest eyelashes Sally had ever seen. Her hair was a mousy brown, cut to shoulder length.

The girl extended her hand. "Hi, I'm Mae. Rotten name, but what can I do? It was my aunt's and my grandmother's, so I'm stuck with it." When she smiled she was no longer plain, she was stunning and she exuded a certain innocence. Sally felt her motherly instincts surface. On impulse, she squeezed Mae's hand and drew her close for a brief hug. She was surprised when Mae responded by hugging her firmly in return.

Pete missed the encounter, too busy studying the others at the bar, which was fine with Sally, since he had already examined Mae quite thoroughly at her morning bath. Pete was not given to voyeurism, but when a lovely young woman undressed just fifty feet away, he would watch. He'd claimed that the experience hadn't been even subliminally sensuous, that she had really just been taking a bath. Meeting her now, Sally could almost believe him. There was a childlike aura about Mae.

Sally turned her attention to some of the others. Directly across from her sat an unbelievably handsome young man. She guessed him to be in his late twenties. Bright blond hair framed his tanned face, setting off his ice blue eyes like jewels. He was movie star material. Next to him sat a very attractive brunette.

Mae tapped her arm. "The Apollo's name is Lance and the girl on his left is Lisa."

Sally almost choked on her drink. "Lordy, how did I know his name would be Lance, or Rock, or something equally suggestive?"

Mae gave her a sly grin. "It gets worse. His last name is L'Amour. Has a ring to it, don't you agree? Lance L'Amour."

"Nooo…you're making this up," Sally groaned.

Jeff led Pete farther down the bar to meet some of the other boaters, probably to get away from their silliness.

The topic of conversation at the bar concerned Rita, Sally noted with interest. Everyone seemed truly sorry she was no longer among the living. But why did *she* feel such empathy for Rita, a girl she had never known? Perhaps it was seeing her dead body draped so haphazardly across the seat of a dinghy. Or perhaps, because like Becky, she was somebody's little girl, forever lost to them now. Would she be sitting here talking with these people at the bar if she had known Rita?

"I think we should have a service for Rita tomorrow, on the dock or a boat," someone suggested. "Maybe a wake."

If these other girls are boat dollies, Sally thought, this probably *is* Rita's wake.

Sally watched several reactions to the suggestion. On the surface Jeff's expressions as he considered this proposal were varied as though channeled through a kaleidoscope. They appeared almost comic in their intensity. And Mae seemed less concerned. There was no doubt that Mae was a listener and a thinker. She sensed a gentle quality in both their personalities.

Suddenly, Sally was alerted by an inner sense of something vying for her attention, not the transmission of emotion she recalled having experienced the night before, but something. She surveyed the crowd. No new faces. Perhaps Pete was right and she was imagining things.

Still, she felt decidedly uneasy. Someone watched them, she could feel it.

FIVE

JEFF AND PETE returned from the other end of the bar with a couple in tow. "Lyle owns a forty-three foot charter sailboat named Lift Off and Elaine is his first mate, cook, et cetera," Jeff announced by way of introduction.

Sally noticed Elaine stiffen at Jeff's description. Was this Jeff's way of signaling Elaine was a boat dollie?

Like the other girls around the bar, Elaine was very pretty. A petite, rather fragile-looking blonde. Sally marveled the girl was physically strong enough for the rigors of boat life. And evidently et cetera covered quite a bit of territory in the boating world, Sally concluded. If these women reflected the standard of boat dollies, then two of the criteria were looks and great bodies. None of the guys were exactly throw aways either. But then, youth was so gorgeous in general.

After a few pleasantries Sally turned back to Mae. "Were you a friend of Rita's, Mae?" she asked, still puzzled by the girl's distant attitude on the subject of Rita.

"As much as anyone, I guess," Mae replied with a frown. "It's kind of hard to explain, I mean Jeff told me you're new to the boat world. It's like this. We may not all be close, in fact, most boaters are pretty independent, but when it comes to outsiders we stick together. Somebody killed one of us, so we all feel it. If you mean am I sad? Yeah, I guess I am. Yes and no would say it best. Rita tried to make friends with me, probably because we were so different, she thought I would be safe."

"You were her friend or not? I don't understand your answer."

"Oh, I would spend some time with her once in a while, but I never really became her friend because she was so wild, wild in a way I'm not. I don't think I was better than her or anything. It's just that I don't drink and do drugs the way she did. She wasn't a bad person. We just weren't the same type."

"I think I see," Sally said. "You feel bad because you weren't able to be the confidant Rita evidently wanted or needed?" Sally didn't expect an answer. Mae's cool attitude regarding Rita's death now suggested a familiar ring of guilt, a ploy Sally knew only too well. "Don't be so hard on yourself, in time you might have been able to be the friend she needed. Seriously, don't take on the burden of her death. Someone else deserves that punishment. It will all come out, you'll see." The girl's eyes started to tear and Sally patted her reassuringly.

"Well, at least you don't think I killed her," Mae said. She tucked her hair behind her ears like a child chastened after a scolding.

Sally found herself baffled the girl would say such a thing. But then why not consider Mae a suspect? In essence, she knew little about Mae.

"Mae, do you know why anyone would kill Rita?"

"No, I haven't thought about it much, really."

"Did anyone you know truly dislike Rita enough to do something so gruesome?"

"Jeff thinks...." Mae fiddled with her glass. She rolled the edges of the napkin that held it. "...Jeff thinks maybe she was killed by accident, in an argument or something. She could make people really mad, especially when she drank a lot, like last night. She stayed so messed up most of the time, I hardly paid attention anymore."

"Well, she wasn't killed by accident, there's no doubt on that score. And people don't normally go out in dinghies armed with knives to have arguments, right?" Sally raised her eyebrows for emphasis.

"Wait a minute, though," Mae countered. "Boat people do carry knives, almost always. On a sailboat, you never know when you're going to need one to cut a line in an emergency."

"So, you're suggesting it could have been an argument that went wrong and the knife was handy? No, think about it. How do you get someone to turn around so you can stab them in the back of the neck?"

"You're right there," Mae agreed. "And then why bother with the rope, or the other way around. God, I hate to think of Rita's last moments."

"So do I. But let's consider another angle." Sally pursed her lips and continued. "What if there was no argument? Say this person didn't have anything against Rita. What if it's some sicko who killed her for sport or whatever? Is there anyone new or suspicious on the island?"

Mae looked at her and nodded. "Yes, you and your husband." She stifled a laugh. "But if you're guilty, you've certainly thought of a clever way to throw suspicion off yourself."

"Miss Marple I'm not, I guess." Sally shrugged.

Mae smoothed her hair.

Sally ordered another drink and used the sudden break in conversation to scan the crowd, to look for the fisherman in the group. She didn't see him, but still sensed someone out there watched her. She tried to analyze the sensation. It was different, not really like last night. Could someone grip you with their eyes? That's what it felt like. She wanted to stand back, to look at the gathering from the outside, to focus on the source of this strange malevolence.

"Point me to the ladies' room, Mae," Sally said.

Mae indicated a long narrow building under the palms. "I'd join you but it's not exactly a powder room. You'll see what I mean. Hope you don't need a mirror."

Sally slid off her bar stool and made her way across the open stretch of sand, glad the sun had not quite set. Still, the low angle of light made for strange shadows. She crossed the open area and casually looked back when she reached the corner of the building. She still felt someone held her with their eyes. If she had to pin it down, the source of her discomfort came from the palm trees surrounding the row of shower and bathroom stalls. Was there movement in the semi darkness? Or was she paranoid? Phooey! Enough of the melodrama, she decided. But she might as well use the facility while she was here.

Sally entered one of the stalls, disturbing a cloud of mosquitoes. Mae was right, this was no powder room. The tiny windowless chamber was dark. She felt the wall for a light switch, running her hand all the way to the corner. Her fingertips raked a huge spiderweb free. She jumped back with an involuntary shriek and fought the sticky mess from between her fingers with her free hand. She prayed the web's occupant was busy elsewhere.

Exploring the other wall, more gingerly this time, she found the switch and flicked it gratefully. Nothing. Her eyes adjusted to the half-light. Sally slammed the door and locked it, determined to make the best of it.

Insects hummed around her head. She flailed at them. The purse hanging from her shoulder thumped against the wall. She heard another thump. Someone else must be having the same problem. Funny though, she hadn't seen anyone else outside the stalls. Maybe someone was in there when she'd arrived.

"Hello?" she called out, but received no response. Goose bumps rose on her legs. There might be a guy in the next stall for all she knew. But so what? "Anyone out there?" she called loudly once more. The silence was broken, but not by an answering voice. She could hear heavy breathing outside the door. The tiny stall was no place to be trapped. On the other hand the door remained locked. And Mae knew where she'd gone. Had Pete seen her leave? Sally quickly stood and buckled the belt of her shorts. The rasping sound from outside changed. Was it human? A dog maybe? She pressed her ear to the door, then quickly drew back when another thought occurred to her. Someone could easily press a knife through the thin partition.

The breathing grew distant, then quieted altogether.

Was her tormentor frightened by a new arrival? She had to get out. Now! She pushed the door roughly and laughed aloud when nothing happened. Of course nothing happened, the door was locked. She unlatched the eye hook and pushed gently but firmly this time, trying to remain calm. The door wouldn't budge. Probably gets stuck sometimes, humidity and all that, she thought. Sally pounded on the door with her fist. Then her shoulder. "Help!" she hollered on the third try.

The door burst open on the fourth hit and Sally dropped to the sand outside when it gave way. She quickly glanced around, expecting to see the person who had held the door, the someone she'd heard breathing. The surrounding area revealed no predator, human or otherwise. A weathered board lay beside her. It must have barred the door. Was it leaning against the frame when she'd entered? She didn't recall, she'd been studying the trees behind the building. When she hit the wall with her purse, could she have dislodged the board from its resting place, causing it to bar the door? But the sound of breathing had not been a figment of her imagination. Someone real did this.

She would keep the details of this incident to herself, however. Pete would want to move on down island right away, afraid for her safety. Or more afraid she would get involved. Sally wasn't leaving. She would watch and wait. Besides, if someone targeted her, what was to keep him from following if they did leave?

SIX

SALLY TOOK A final look at the dark area behind the stalls. She walked toward the beach bar, her eyes fixed on her goal. Look for bogeymen, she chided herself, you find bogeymen.

She ordered ice for her diluted drink. Her hand shook. That door hadn't accidentally jammed, someone had deliberately barred it. Someone who meant to scare her. Whoever did the deed could have hurt her if they'd wanted and she had foolishly placed herself at their disposal with no one around to observe. Someone must believe she presented a threat, a witness to something in the dark harbor last night? What? She'd seen only a glimpse of another boat and heard the sound of an outboard. God, whoever it was probably managed a great look at her though. She was all but on stage beneath the spreader lights. The only important thing that happened last night to Sally's knowledge was that someone might imagine she was witness to Rita's murder. Had she been? Had she caught someone in the act of strangling Rita out there in the night? She shuddered at the thought.

Mae interrupted her dark recollections as she shook her arm gently and pointed.

Sally came sharply back to the real world. "See that fellow way down the beach?"

Sally followed Mae's gaze and saw a portly man standing amidst the palms. From what she could see of him in the shadows he looked like a tourist, loud, flowered, and mussed by humidity. He moved forward and Sally examined him as he approached. He was no boat person and she seriously doubted his red nose was the result of solar exposure. His general appearance suggested blatant dissipation. She glanced at Mae for a clue.

Mae's lovely face pinched into a tight snarl. "That's Doug. Watch him, he's really a creep. He paws all the girls at every opportunity."

"Then why do they put up with him?"

Mae tossed her head. "Oh, they all laugh at him and think he's just a harmless old guy."

"But you don't, I take it?"

"No, I don't," Mae repeated firmly. "And before you even suggest it, I'm not accusing him of murdering Rita, either. He just makes my skin crawl. See, he's looking over the crowd. He'll make a subtle pass at anyone. But it's Ruth he's looking for."

Sally watched Doug with new interest after Mae's venomous description. She knew better than to accept another's judgment so readily, but his eyes actually did seem a tad beadier than they had a minute earlier. He scanned the group, apparently in search of someone in particular. Quite by accident, his glance met Sally's. She flinched and looked away.

"I give up," she shrugged. "Who's Ruth?"

"She's a nurse, but she's more like a nun."

Sally peered at Mae from lowered brows. "Say what? Excuse me, but did you say nun?"

"Well, she's not really a nun. But she was going to be one once, only her parents were so upset by the plan, she became a nurse instead. Anyway, she lives near here and sort of looks after all of us. Tells us how to treat minor problems and when it's time to see a real doctor. She's taught everyone all kinds of first aid and stuff in case something happens to one of us at sea." All of this was said in a rush.

Sally pursed her lips in doubt, but Mae continued.

"She really should have been a nun. She lives like one. She goes to church every day. She never dates anyone and she always helps people. You know what though? Ruth really loves sailing. That's why we consider her one of us. It's how we pay her for all she does for us. Whenever we have an empty seat on a charter, we all call Ruth."

"*She really loves sailing*?" Sally quoted. "You say that as though sailing were a sin."

"Did I? I didn't mean to," Mae replied. She dug for something deep within the confines of her purse.

Sally turned her attention back to Doug, determined not to let her opinion of him reflect Mae's disclosures, but it was hopeless. She knew the type too well. Why was it that the more depraved some people became, the more they sought to defile the truly pure? To bring them down to their level? Because nothing else could satisfy them? Sally didn't know the answer and wasn't sure she wanted to anyway.

"What about Doug?" she asked Mae. "What's his story?"

"His full name is Doug Wilson. He runs a small restaurant on the other side of the island. Thank goodness, otherwise he would camp out right here." She waved her arm in a sweeping gesture. "He has the idea all boat girls are easy marks." She turned and stared deeply into Sally's eyes. "A lot of people share that opinion."

Sally placed her hand on Mae's arm and returned her stare. "Mae, I do have strong opinions, so if you ever want to know what I think, just ask me plainly. For starters, I know nothing about boat girls, boat dollies or whatever." What Sally didn't say was that she had quit judging people, all people, when Becky died. Becky would have been twenty-one this year. She looked around once more. All these girls were probably in their twenties.

Mae turned her eyes aside briefly, then smiled at Sally. "Okay, that sounds fair enough. Anyway, I only wanted you to know we're not all bad. So, getting back to Doug, he's been here a few years. Doesn't look like it though, still dresses as though he just stepped off the plane." Mae shuddered and rummaged even deeper in her oversized handbag.

Sally could not imagine what was wrong with the girl, but quickly realized Doug was almost upon them. She watched the expressions of those nearest her and noted a wave of avoidance tactics come and pass in Doug's wake. How fantastic, she thought, that one seemingly innocuous human being could have such an emotional effect. Doug was abreast of them now and Mae appeared ready to climb inside her handbag.

It didn't work.

Doug sidled in between them and slipped one hairy arm around Mae's tiny waist. "Hello, Mae, you little honey. Who's your friend?" he asked. His eyes swept over Sally, lingering on her breasts.

Fortunately, no answer or conversation was required because a disturbance down the beach caught everyone's attention.

It was music, raucous, vibrating music.

Sally and Mae casually pushed Doug to one side and stood on the rungs of their bar stools for a better look at what was happening.

A group of islanders approached. Steel drums hung from their shoulders by straps. The staccato beat of their music sent shivers down Sally's spine. It was wonderful, light, emotion-inspiring music.

A tall man brandishing a cane led this bizarre entourage. He waved the cane in the air as though conducting. Dressed like a refugee from a desert island, his once blue shirt was bleached by time and his threadbare cutoffs were barely of a piece. His beard was white on white and lines etched his tanned face like a road map.

"Sally, Sally!" Mae screeched in her ear. "It's Jake. I can't believe it. I've never seen him like this, he can hardly walk straight. I swear he's drunk! And Jake doesn't get drunk!"

Sally's reply was lost in the tumultuous thunder of the drums. The musicians were only yards away now.

Suddenly with the grace of an acrobat, Jake leaped into the air and executed a full spin to face the crowd. His brilliant blue eyes captured the attention of those before him like shrimp mesmerized by a beam of light. They were captive to his performance. Jake swung the cane into position over his head. The music stopped abruptly. A painful silence followed, one taut with expectation. Sally could hardly breathe. Seconds stretched into a minute and Jake held them riveted with his maniacal grin and incandescent eyes. Then, into the silence Jake let out a bloodcurdling scream. "Ri…taa…Ri…taa…Rita," he bellowed, "this one's for you!"

From somewhere a glass magically appeared in Jake's hand. He raised it up and forward as though in reverent salute, then closed his bright eyes and downed the drink. The drums started again. Slowly at first, then built to their previous crescendo.

Sally had goose bumps down to her toes. So I was right, she thought. This is Rita's wake. She felt the tears behind her eyes. Not an empty epitaph at all.

Mae pulled at her. Tears ran down her cheeks. She pressed Sally's drink into her hand and drew her into the crowd that marched round and round the Chamber Pot.

When Jake and his followers finally trooped away across the sand, Sally felt weak. Their exit left her as breathless as their arrival. She watched in awe as Jake led them across the sand into the fiery sunset.

Rita would not be forgotten.

Rita. Dear God, who was Rita and what was a boat dollie? These were questions Sally planned to explore and no jerk in the palm trees would scare her off easily.

She turned to Mae. "I think I saw Rita's murderer last night."

Mae whirled around, her face a study in shock. "You saw the murder?"

"She didn't see anything," Pete said, appearing from nowhere. He reached out and took Sally's arm. "She thinks she heard another boat in the dark last night, that's all." He roughly drew Sally away. "Come on, we're out of here."

SEVEN

SALLY PEERED OUT Sere Dina's porthole. Could the fisherman be out there? The darkness held onto the answer. She tiptoed around, afraid she would wake Pete. She made hot cocoa and toast and carried it topside and forward to her favorite spot near the bow. The half-light of dawn crept like a cat over the imposing black mountains, mountains that would later turn to brilliant green against an azure sky. The tropical nights on the water made sleeping a new experience. A gentle breeze always blew in from the sea. She wore a flannel pullover and lightweight cotton deck pants, the warmest clothing she would need in this part of the world.

She scanned the horizon. No fisherman. She took deep breaths of the crisp morning air. Her primary mission was to enjoy whatever time she would have in the islands. Pete balked at settling in for any extended period of time. Two months, three. Did she dare hope for longer? She doubted it. Pete's wanderlust plagued him. As an anthropologist, traveling dictated their past. Would it dictate their future? If they had a future. Before they had reached the islands, he'd talked about an Atlantic crossing, perusing charts and articles on the inland waterways of Europe. Sally shared that particular goal, but it would be nice to stop and smell the tropical flowers along the way.

Maybe it would be best to keep traveling and let time settle their future, but like tea leaves in the bottom of an empty cup, Becky's ghost settled with them wherever they went.

Sally wanted to hang around long enough to find out more about *boat dollies*. Telling Pete she thought someone might have locked her in the bathroom last night would have been a stupid move. She was glad she hadn't. He would have whipped the charts out looking for the next island. She rather liked this one. It was time for new rules. Even if she saw the fisherman today, she wouldn't tell Pete. He'd pitched a fit last night when she'd mentioned the imagined boat to Mae. They had fought for an hour, then made love. It always came to that, she thought. But their lovemaking had changed. There was a raw, sad edge to it now. A desperation at first, but Sally always ended up weeping inwardly when they were through. Perhaps there were some things you could never go back and recapture.

The black mountains loomed in front of her like huge hovering phantoms. A peculiar rustling sound distracted her from further reflection. A flock of egrets converged overhead. She'd watched them many times on their journey south as they completely blanketed tiny islands, turning dusky mangrove foliage to stark white.

Sally gasped in awe as the sun rose over the mountain. Its piercing shafts of light outlined the delicate birds, like halos around angels.

The vision of angels finally brought her thoughts back to Rita, the boat dollie. Was Rita with the angels? Would she be forgotten now? Was there some crazed killer out there on the loose? Or had Rita made an enemy so angry that murder was the only recourse? What made Rita a boat dollie? Sally didn't know what the designation really entailed. Was Mae one? She could hardly ask the girl and risk insulting her. On the other hand, she still wanted to ask Mae a lot of questions.

Sally heard a splashing noise near the boat and turned to locate its source. Mae was taking her morning bath in the sea. Sally envied her lack of inhibition, in bathing anyway. It looked so exhilarating!

Mae submerged herself, surfaced, shook her hair as naturally as a mermaid. She hauled herself up to perch on a swing-like affair hung from the ladder and pushed the hair from her face, then soaped down with something from a squeeze bottle as she turned toward the bow of Sere Dina. She waved.

Sally waved back.

Apparently taking this to be an invitation, Mae plunged into the water again and swam toward Sere Dina.

"Hi, Sally." She popped up not ten feet away. Her smile was infectious.

"Great looking day," Sally said.

"Yeah, but then it always is in this part of the world. People who have lived here a long time say things like, 'oh no, not another beautiful day.' Funny, isn't it? Even I look forward to a stormy day once in a while. But the truth is even bad days are beautiful down here. Wait until you see a storm roll in across the island. The sea turns black and boils, and the rain falls so heavily you can't see your outstretched hand. Then suddenly it's over and the sun breaks through. Everything glistens and a frilly mist rises off the green hills like newborn clouds."

Sally turned to Mae as she delivered this poetic vision. "Why, Mae, what a lovely description. You actually have me looking forward to a lousy day!"

Mae laughed. "I'd better get back to the boat and finish my joy-bath. Want to go to town and look around? I'll pick you up in my dinghy in a little bit."

"Sure, why not? I'll buy you brunch or whatever and

you can tell me what a joy-bath is." And maybe a few other things, Sally told herself silently.

Sally made coffee and brought it to Pete. "Wake up, lazy bones, the joy-bath is over, and guess what? One of these days I do believe I'm going to take one myself."

"What? What in the world are you taking about, woman?"

Sally narrowed her eyes. "I really don't know, but when I finally get proper instruction, I bet you'll be pleasantly surprised. Oh, by the way, I'm off to explore town with Mae this morning. I see her heading this way in the dinghy. You should probably check with Jeff if you're going in later, since he will be boatless for the morning. I suspect he'll swim over in a little while anyway. Bye now."

"Oh, sure. Don't worry about poor ole Pete or anything. Noo…he'll be fine."

Sally smiled sweetly. "Why, thank you, ole Pete, I won't then." With that she went topside to board the waiting dinghy.

"I love you," Pete called after her.

"I know," Sally called back. "I'm trying," she whispered under her breath.

EIGHT

SALLY CHECKED OUT the boats Mae passed, searching for the guy in black, the fisherman. She doubted he would be dumb enough to dress the same way again which was too bad, since she might not recognize him, otherwise. And unless he was really, really dumb, she doubted he would even sit nearby in a boat again. Why should he, when he could sit comfortably on shore and wait for her to come to him?

She and Mae rode to shore in silence. The brief ride refreshed Sally and in no time they were tying up at the seawall near the center of the picturesque little town. Sally watched Mae produce a heavy chain, then lock and secure the small boat to a metal ring in the wall.

"Dare I ask?" Sally said with a frown.

"You're kidding? This chain surprises you? You tie up with a regular line, right? Well, now our shopping spree has a goal. We will definitely visit the marina after I've shown you what the tourists come thousands of miles to see. The marina is a great place to have lunch, too. Not as cool as the Pot, but I think you'll enjoy it."

Sally surveyed the village buildings with wonder. They were pale turquoise, lime and pink, like the fade-over colors in a rainbow. The architectural style defied classification, incorporating subtle touches of the many cultures that had influenced the island throughout its tumultuous history. The one unifying element common to all the structures, she noticed, was ornate wrought iron. It trailed up stairways, blanketed windows and enclosed balconies like a grapevine. Flowering plants hung in profusion from ceilings and posts. Every courtyard was shaded by forests of potted palms.

The merchandise inside the stores had less allure than the buildings that housed them. Tourists would buy a few local handicrafts, but most just bought something extravagant to take home to show Uncle Whosit, so they could brag about their bargaining techniques. Never mind that it cost them two-thousand dollars to get there and several hundred a day to eat and sleep.

Sally happily absorbed the overall exotic effect. Souvenirs left her unimpressed. She wanted to experience every aroma and sight, to feel the pulse of island life.

The locals, she noticed, smiled in spite of the rudeness of the tourists. They probably went home and compared stories at the end of each day to determine who encountered the worst tourist. Sally certainly would, for comic relief. And with the tourists making fun of the locals and the locals making fun of the tourists, there was something for everyone.

They wandered up and down shaded streets and back alleys for more than an hour while Mae pointed out the shops Sally would explore on future excursions. There was a canvas and sail store, a laundry, several food markets and a plethora of secondhand shops, all hidden on little side streets, away from the daily tidal surge of tourists.

"Jeff said you're not sure Rita was murdered," Mae declared in a loud voice as they strolled along. "Then, last night you asked me if I knew anyone who would want to kill her. And why did you say you thought you saw Rita's murderer? You shocked me."

Sally came to a stop with a slight tripping motion, as though she had just run out of gas. "You certainly have a strange way of introducing a subject, Mae, I'll say that for you. I didn't say I didn't think she was murdered. I'm sure she was murdered! I said we won't know *how* until there's an autopsy. And we won't, will we? Has anything official been said yet? Let's face it, she could have died from being strangled, stabbed or drowned. And about the boat, I saw what I thought to be a shadow of a boat beyond the loom of the spreader lights. It could be nothing. I swear I heard the purr of a small engine, though."

Mae cocked her head sideways. "The person in the other boat had to see you then, with the lights on and all." She gave herself a small hug. "Too creepy, if it was the killer. Back to Rita though, if somebody drowned her, why add the rope and the knife wounds?" Mae hunched her shoulders. "I heard some talk after you left the Pot the other night. Claudette, she's the big black gal behind the bar, was saying the doctor suggested there was something funny, or wrong about the body."

"I'll say. Rita had a rope around her neck, not to mention assorted knife wounds." Sally rolled her eyes.

"I guess we knew that," Mae acknowledged. "Well, if I hear anything else, I'll tell you," Mae said, ending the discussion as precipitously as she had begun it.

The marina, as Mae had so subtly put it, was different. Marinas the world over, where live-aboards are allowed, tend to have as residents a higher percentage of eccentrics than would be found in a normal population. According to Mae, this ratio doubled in the Caribbean.

The marina clubhouse stood on high stilts overlooking the harbor to the west. From its upper deck Sally could see the tall, varnished mast of Sere Dina in the distance, towering proudly over the boats nearest her.

Tim, the marina manager, was single, in his mid fifties, and starting to run a little to fat. His fast moving eyes flashed signals to Sally, signals that spoke of things done in the night. She felt somewhat abashed at his obvious admiration.

Tim stood in front of a huge table that dominated the room. The table was round, probably an inch and a half thick and at least fifteen feet across. Sally doubted there was another like it anywhere. Dozens of captains' chairs surrounded the monster without the slightest hint of crowding. She examined the poured resin surface, which must add another hundred pounds to the table's unguessable weight.

"What is this thing, a stage?" Sally asked.

"It has been used as one a couple of times!" Tim laughed, moving to where Sally bent to check the underside.

"There's a cluster of posts in the center that hold this thing up," Tim continued. His hand rested briefly on her shoulder. "The cluster is more than three feet thick and two circles of posts spread out from there. So what you have here is major support. Not only that, but all the posts go through the building and into the ground."

Sally squatted down for a better look and to give herself breathing room. Someone had enclosed the underside a few feet back. Sally saw hinges to a door as the wall curved away from her.

Tim crouched beside her. Their knees touched for a moment. "I walled it in a while back 'cause nobody wanted to crawl underneath to clean. Can't blame them much. We use the area for storage. Now, before you ask me any more questions about this table, I'll be honest with you. I don't know the answers. I've been here for two years and the guy I replaced died. What I'm saying is, it beats the hell outta me why somebody built this thing. One thing I do know, come a hurricane, this baby and this building ain't going nowhere." He shrugged and stood up.

Sally rose with him, taking a moment to assess him at arm's length. He was a little less than average height. She could see the top of his balding head. His eyes were set deep in their sockets under heavy brow ridges, giving him a somewhat Neanderthal look. But his warm friendly smile softened his overall appearance, making him more teddy bearish than tough. She doubted Tim would appreciate her description. But he did two things Sally found disturbing, things that unsettled her. He locked eyes with her when he spoke, never even blinking, and he operated inside what she considered to be *her space*.

Tim started to say something, but Mae diverted his attention by motioning from an open doorway across the room.

Sally quickly moved forward and joined her.

The room they entered was stocked to the ceiling with marine equipment. Mae wrestled a few feet of line from a large spool. The core of the line was heavy gauge wire. "Now this is what you need," she said in a soft but determined voice. "Unless you want chain like I have, and I wouldn't if I were you. I keep telling Jeff it's too heavy for me."

"Oh, come on, Mae, you can't be serious!"

"Yes, I am. Dinghies disappear in the islands on a regular basis. If you're standing on the shore and someone steps into your dinghy and drives away, what are you going to do, swim after it?"

"Out of all the dinghies I saw at the seawall this morning, I doubt there were five that were locked up."

"Then make yours the sixth, because she's right," Tim interceded, closing in on her again. "Dinghy theft is a major problem in the islands. You could almost call it dinghy swapping, except that someone sells them at either end. They steal a few dinghies from one island and sell them at the next, to people who lost one the day before in a similar fashion. It's a nasty business, but boat people can't swim in for groceries. Even the wire line doesn't guarantee you won't be ripped off. The industrious thieves carry wire cutters. But they mostly like to hit at night while your dinghy drifts peacefully behind your anchored boat. It's the inflatables they prefer. They break down into neat little packages which can be easily stashed on the inter-island cargo barges or fishing boats. The best thing to do is to pull your dinghy up in the air at night, or better yet on board."

"Remember this advice when you buy your sixty-foot yacht, Sally," Mae said. "Get real, Tim. Most of us just snug our dinghies up alongside as best we can. If we pulled ours up, it would fill the cockpit."

"Can't the authorities do anything about the situation?" Sally asked.

Tim shook his head. "The authorities can do a lot of things, but they face priorities. There is a great deal of crime that goes on in this part of the world. Crime the tourists never hear about, or perhaps I should say that the locals don't want the tourists to hear about."

Sally sighed. "You mean like at home?"

"Right. Everything, just like at home. Child abuse, rape, mugging, murder, the whole gamut. The major problem though, and probably the root of all the others, is drugs. Just like at home. Geographically we couldn't be in a worse place. We're a perfect stopover for the guys running drugs from South America. I am speaking about the area in general, by the way. Our little island here really does have less crime than most, mainly because we are so small and everyone knows everyone. Still…." He rapped one hand on the countertop.

"Okay, enough of the down side," Mae insisted. "You still have to buy the line though, Sally." She gave the spool a tug and the line slowly coiled at their feet like a snake.

"Exactly," Tim agreed. "Think of it this way. If you have to put up with all that crap most everywhere, why not do it in paradise?"

Sally made a face. "Because it doesn't follow, that's why. Paradise?" She glanced at the coiled line. "And I have to buy my own serpent?"

Tim winked and moved to intercept another customer.

Sally considered Tim's lecture about drugs. She turned to Mae and spoke softly. "Jeff told Pete that Rita used drugs on occasion. And you said the same thing. Maybe she was murdered in a deal gone wrong? The problem is, I don't know anything about Rita. Damn." She frowned.

Mae patted Sally gently. "Let's ignore Mr. Doom and Gloom and get on with lunch. We'll talk about Rita another time."

Lunch was a singularly unusual affair, a do-it-yourself situation in the small corner which served as the kitchen. Two walk-in refrigerators tempted the customers with everything from steaks to breakfast cereal. A detailed price list was on the wall outside, and it was reasonable. Customers made out tickets and presented them to Tim with money or signatures.

"An unusual concept in food service," Sally said. Then, eying Mae's plate, she put her hand to her heart. "Are you going to eat that? Seriously, do you only eat once a week, or what?" Sally had constructed a simple Swiss cheese on rye, but Mae was busy layering a foot-long loaf from every cold cut available.

"I'm going to cut it into thirds and bring one to Ruth and one back to the boat for Jeff. Do you mind if we go by the hospital for a minute? I told Ruth I would if I got a chance. We'll stop by here later with the boat and pick up your new line. Or better yet, we'll have Tim get someone to take it down to the dock for us."

"Fine, I'm looking forward to meeting Ruth. I've never met a pseudonun. Now is as good a time as any." Sally sliced pickle wedges and put some on both their plates. She glanced up as the fragile little blonde Sally had met at the Pot approached. The one Jeff had suggested was a boat dollie when he'd said, et cetera.

Mae smiled. "Hi, Elaine, want to join us? We can't stay too long, but you're welcome."

"Thanks, I will if you don't mind."

"Super," Mae said. But a strange expression replaced her welcoming smile. "Tim will be happy to have his audience grouped for a change." She turned to Sally. "Tim tells atrocious stories."

"Couple's name was Brewster," Tim was saying as they seated themselves at the table. "John and Dottie Brewster. I used to take great delight in spelling her name D-O-T-T-Y on their bill. She used to come in here screaming and waving that bill.

"Anyway, when they originally sailed in here I didn't pay a whole lot of attention. They seemed to be normal people for the most part. Had a nice boat and paid as they went. So when the complaints started I naturally took them to heart. No kidding, I honestly thought we had some weirdo running around peeking in the ladies' shower room and just generally following Dottie around. She was an attractive enough old broad."

Mae and Sally exchanged looks, but didn't interrupt.

"She was in her late forties, early fifties and she kept her body in good shape. So the first time she came in hysterical, insisting some man had been peeking at her over the bathhouse wall, I believed her. For a while, her husband, who was usually too busy, or I, actually stood guard when she took a shower. But that building also houses the toilets and I couldn't be there every time she took a pee. Well, sure enough, every time I wasn't there, this phantom guy would show up to watch, according to Dottie.

"I didn't want to call in the locals, there were enough stories going around about the marina as it was. Some mornings I got up early to do a little jogging. I covered the whole marina looking for strangers. Nothing. Until the morning I took my last lap past the bathhouse on my way to the office. Dottie planted herself in front of my desk five minutes later with a detailed description of the peeper whom she'd almost caught in the act. She sketched a short, fat, balding man wearing a gray sweat suit, who ran kinda funny, like a warthog, in little spurts and dashes. In other words, me. I knew as I sat there with my jacket zipped up over my gray sweats that she was as dotty as they come."

Sally watched Elaine while she listened to Tim start another story. The girl was nervous, there was no doubt about that. It was as though she were ready to spring up and run at a moment's notice. Her small hands alternately gripped the chair, then the table edge. Fragile, that's how someone would describe Elaine, Sally decided. Her heart went out to the girl. There must be some way she could help her. She turned to see if Mae noticed Elaine's peculiar behavior.

Mae sent her signals, signals not related to Elaine, however. She pointed at her watch, then nodded in the direction of the door and rose from her chair. "Time to go," she whispered.

Sally followed reluctantly. She glanced back as they neared the door. Elaine stared after them. Something was definitely wrong here. On a hunch, Sally beckoned for her to join them. The girl pushed herself back from the table, then waved and shook her head negatively.

ARMANDO FOLLOWED THE two women from the marina, wondering if he should call the boss. See if the plan had changed. He didn't mind scaring this broad off the island, but how bad was he supposed to scare her? Should he hurt her a little? On the other hand if he didn't ask, the plan might stay simple. One of these days the boss was going to hand him a hit job. This one could be it. No point in calling then. He wasn't ready for the big time. If he could scare her bad enough, she would vamoose. Nothing was said about hurting her. Nothing about not hurting her either, though. So he'd hurt her a little. What the hell, if he scared her bad enough to leave the island he might be saving her life.

Where were they headed? He'd expected them to return to the dinghy, but they started up the hill behind town. It would have been easy to follow them on the crowded waterfront. Well, they would return there sooner or later. Whatever he did, he would do it on land, like the bathroom business. No more of that water shit for him. He'd gotten the message. She'd stared at him all day. Locking her in the stupid stall hadn't done much. It was time for a stronger message.

NINE

"I ENJOY TIM'S STORIES," Mae admitted as they climbed the steep hill leading to the hospital. Beads of perspiration dotted their faces. "He's been in the boat business most of his life and probably has enough anecdotes to fill a book. But the only stories he tells are the ones with himself as the fool. That's kind of nice, don't you think."

Sally agreed. "I could have done without the old broad who was fiftyish."

"I wonder what was on Elaine's mind," Mae said.

"Does she have to have something on her mind to join you for lunch?"

"Yes, she does. I always ask the others out of politeness. No one ever says yes. Except Ruth, but she's not a boat...a boat person."

"You were going to say *boat dollie,* weren't you?" Here was her opportunity to learn more on the subject of boat dollies.

"I was, but Jeff said you didn't understand what a boat dollie was, so I decided not to."

"All right. Then why don't you explain it to me?"

"Give me a minute to get it right," Mae frowned.

Sally could feel a cool breeze against the back of her damp shirt. It provided small relief from the heat rising off the pavement. Several women passed carrying baskets on their heads. They were tall sleek black women. There was something ethereal about them. They moved without effort, each step undulating up their graceful bodies like curling smoke. Yet the baskets seemed to travel on a flat plane, uphill or down.

"Well, let's start with me," Mae began. "I'm a boat person, but I'm not a boat dollie. Now you. Let's say that you and Pete decided you loved boat life and planned to live on your boat permanently, you would be boat people. If he decided it wasn't for him but you couldn't leave the boat world and left him for another boat. You would be a boat dollie. That's pretty simplistic, sorry."

"No, it seems quite clear to me, it's a priority problem. In this case it seems to be an obsession with boats, the boating lifestyle. It happens in other areas of life. *Music groupies*, or *baseball annies*, sounds like the same kind of thing. Jeff did pretty much say that."

"That's close enough, but there's more to it than that. It really is an addictive lifestyle. Getting back to Elaine though," Mae continued." Maybe she's not a boat dollie. I don't know. They haven't been here very long. Could be she's just a loner. Anyway, something changed her usual aloofness today. With Tim telling stories there was no chance of finding out what her problem involved."

Sally had a sudden inspiration. "Could it be connected with Rita's murder? Maybe she saw or overheard something. Loner or not, I think she wanted to tell us something."

"Can you believe it? I never even thought of that!" Mae said. "But why come to us? Personally, I thought she looked like she didn't feel well."

"She was in a state, that's for sure, but I don't think it was her stomach that was upset." Sally stepped aside to make way for another woman carrying a huge basket.

THEY WERE HEADED for the hospital, Armando decided. They had to be, it was the only public building on the street. He could be wrong of course, they could turn in at any house on the way up. A calculated risk. He could beat them to the hospital if he hightailed it.

Armando turned the corner and broke into a run. The hospital was a great place for an accident. He smiled at his own joke. His slick black hair stuck to his head as he jogged. Sweat ran down his angular face, dripping onto his good silk shirt. He had a hard body from working out. He passed a house. A young girl cocked her head at him from a front room window. He pushed out his chest and tightened his buns. *Eat your heart out, baby. I got work to do.*

A large group of locals overflowed the hospital entrance. It was fate. Armando reached down to caress the outline of the switchblade in his hip pocket, then merged into the group to wait.

A POSTER ON the hospital door advised all personnel to take note of a tropical depression off the coast of Africa. Mae dutifully took pencil and paper from her purse and wrote down the coordinates.

Sally followed Mae through a mass of sweating bodies in the reception room. The people in the crowd spoke in a high-pitched, melodious patois, their gestures animated by a visible climate of tension.

Everyone pushed and shoved. Sally became separated from Mae. Finally, she stood on her toes and pushed like everyone else. Where did the girl go so quickly? An altercation broke out next to her. Voices rose. Hands flailed the air. Mae waved at her from down the hallway, beyond the melee. Sally's only hope of escaping the pandemonium was to wade through the combatants. She took a deep breath and crossed her arms in front of her, elbows out. Sally lurched forward, helped by a firm shove from someone behind her. This could get serious. Anger took the place of fear. She decided to fight back. A woman directly in her path saw her dilemma and extended her hand toward Sally indicating with a nod for Sally to grab hold. Why not, she wasn't getting anywhere this way. Sally clasped the offered hand in her own and moved three magical feet in an instant as the woman snatched her from the crowd.

Sally heard a woman scream behind her and turned to look back at the space created by her own sudden exit. The screaming woman clutched at her right buttocks, moaning. Blood seeped between her fingers and dripped, creating Rorschach patterns on the white tile floor. They ought to let that poor woman through, Sally thought, she's been wounded somehow.

"Thanks, you're a lifesaver," Sally said to the regal black woman who had come to her aid. She stole a last glance at the crowd.

Mae took her arm and they made their way down several hallways before entering the staff lounge.

"Phew! What a zoo," Mae exclaimed. "What's going on out there?" She directed her words at a dark-haired woman seated on a couch.

The woman rose. Her hair was parted in the middle in the style of the sixties. No makeup. Attributes that fit very nicely with Sally's mental picture of how Ruth should look. Her voluptuousness scrambled the illusion, however. She could have stepped right out of a Vargas calendar. Her demure nurse's uniform did little to dispel the overall effect of sensuality. She would be totally miscast in the role of Florence Nightingale but perfect in "Nurse Nancy does Newark." And this was the girl Mae had described as 'sort of like a nun?'

"Evidently, a rumor has started concerning an epidemic of dengue fever and it's creating a bit of a panic," Ruth told them, in a decidedly husky voice.

Oh great, a voice to match the body. Ruth would have done a favor to all womankind if she had donned a heavy black habit and become a nun.

"Is there anything to it?" Sally asked.

"And what exactly is it?" Mae finished.

"It's a pretty insidious disease and fortunately the rumor is false. A case or two is always going to pop up from time to time, this is the tropics. But I don't think we're looking at an epidemic here," Ruth answered.

Sally noticed the other person in the room with them, a man in a doctor's coat. Large horn-rimmed glasses weighed down his fine, angular nose. He was of medium height, had rather ordinary brown hair and a schoolboy face with rosy cheeks. He took in Ruth's every movement with adoring eyes while she explained the dangers of dengue as though she were reading great literature.

"It's carried by mosquito. Actually, a specific type of mosquito known as Aedes aegypti. And there's more than one form of dengue. And yes, epidemics and sporadic outbreaks do occur here occasionally. However, we generally know when to expect them, after a hurricane or enough heavy rains to cause flooding. Unlike other mosquitoes, the Aedes aegypti likes to deposit her larvae in fresh, clean water. No swamps or stagnant pools for this little jewel. It starts as a virus. If the mosquito bites an infected person at a certain stage in their illness, the first three days, it's transmitted to the mosquito for life. After a short incubation period, everyone the mosquito bites will be infected. It's the same mosquito that carries yellow fever and a few other nasty illnesses around the world."

Sally resisted an urge to scratch the mosquito bites she had received at the Pot. The professional way Ruth delivered her speech impressed Sally. She could ignore *the body* for a moment.

"It's so terrible about Rita," Ruth said, bowing her head. "Everyone holding up okay? Anyone need anything?"

"I could use a hug," Mae said, batting her long dark lashes. "But I'll trade you for it." From out of her huge purse she produced the sandwich.

Sally wanted to ask if Ruth knew anything about Rita's autopsy results, but Mae beat her to it, going straight to the point. "Well, what can you tell us about Rita's death?"

Ruth lowered her voice. "They still have to run a lot of tests and stuff to be absolutely sure, but it's probably going to come out that strangulation was the cause of death."

"Someone said there was something funny about the body. What does that mean."

Ruth shrugged. "Never heard that, but you know how the rumor mill grinds around here. I did hear someone say that it's funny that a boat dollie would die in a dinghy. Personally, I didn't think that was funny at all. But that's probably where the 'funny' quote came from."

Sally leaned closer. The doctor at the end of the room left when the women huddled together.

"What I'm telling you is not a secret or anything," Ruth assured them. Her eyes followed the doctor.

"Hey, come on, Ruth," Mae implored. "Sally thinks there might be some kind of nut running around who's de-cided to kill boat people for sport. We have to know what's going on. Our lives might be in danger."

Ruth looked at Sally, as though seeking confirmation of this boldfaced lie.

Sally nodded. This was no time to stop the flow of in-formation should Ruth be willing to divulge some inside knowledge. She would deal with Mae later.

"I couldn't tell you anything medical, you know that. But Rita did come to see me the other day. She wanted to use the copy machine at the nurses' station. I told her they had one at the library, but she said she couldn't use it because someone would see her."

"Do you know what she copied?" Mae clasped her hands together and pulled them tight against her chest, expectant, as though the world turned on Ruth's answer.

"It was a little red book, maybe a diary or a journal, I really don't know. But whatever it was, I saw her put the copy in a mailer that was already addressed. I couldn't, or rather didn't try to read the address on it."

Sally would have tried to read the address. If Rita seemed frightened, different rules should have applied. Reading the address was not the same as reading the diary. Ruth obviously had clearer moral directives than Sally.

"Oh well, shoot!" Mae picked up her bag and tugged on Sally's arm, just as Ruth's beeper went off. "Come to the Pot tonight, Ruth," Mae said. "Everyone's missed you."

"I will. See you around eight or a little after." She smoothed the skirt of her uniform. A buzzer attached to her uniform made a soft sound as it vibrated. "Sorry! I've got to respond to a page."

And I've got to get that little red book, Sally promised herself. And she had to speak with Elaine. If Mae was right, the girl had something on her mind or she wouldn't have joined them. Pete was going to hate this, but Sally intended to get very involved. She felt excited for the first time in ages. When Becky was alive the house often rang with the voices of young women. Sally had played confidant to a bevy of Becky's peers in their times of need. Perhaps this is what she had been missing, what she ached for. She relished being involved in the particulars of life, being touched by the emotions of others, being needed. Her mothering days had been abbreviated by cruel circumstances.

TEN

THE SUN BEAT down from straight overhead as Mae and Sally motored the dinghy back to Sere Dina. The wind abated and the water's surface looked slick and glassy. Sally peered into the clear, green depths. Giant clumps of coral rose off the harbor floor like surreal statues and schools of fluorescent fish moved beneath their long shadows in a silent pulsating rhythm. Feathery sea fan sentinels waved them on their way. She felt like Alice peering through the looking glass into another world; a world she could enter any time, though it too was not without its perils.

"What did you think of Ruth?" Mae asked over the hum of the little outboard.

"Well, I told you I would always be honest with you," Sally shouted at her. "So I've got to say that I have a very difficult time putting her in the category of *nunish*. Mostly from a physical viewpoint, of course. On the other hand, she seemed professional and sincere. I'm anxious to encounter her in a social situation."

Mae laughed, her smile bright. "You'll see," she said.

"Tell me, who was the young man with the puppy dog eyes? The one in the lounge we so rudely put to flight. He seemed to show more than a passing interest in Ruth."

They slapped across the wake of a boat and small bursts of spray arched above them. Mae raised her face to meet them, then flicked her tongue around her lips and licked off the cool salt residue, her expression a portrait in ecstasy.

"I don't think I could ever live on land again, Sally. I just couldn't," she said wistfully. "To wake up without the sound of water tickling the hull, no smell of fresh air from the sea, to miss the freedom of knowing you can raise your sails and fly away like a bird. That wouldn't be living." A hint of concern turned her look of raw joy into a frown. "Maybe I am a boat dollie!"

"Nonsense. For heaven's sake. Will you stop the dramatics and answer my question?"

Mae's heartwarming smile returned. "You remind me of my mother, you know that?" She quickly raised her hand to stave off Sally's next retort. "Okay, okay. The guy's name is Bill Winters, and he's a doctor. But she doesn't even know he exists. I know her, trust me."

"Sure," Sally said. "And pigs can fly." Then, like Mae, she turned her face into the spray.

Another boat approached them from behind. Sally recognized the driver as Joseph, the port official who visited their boat with the body of Rita in tow. He passed and nodded at them.

"Mae? Do you have the feeling there is something about Rita's murder that we know?"

"Something we know?" Mae sat up, giving Sally her full attention. "Like what? What could we know? I'm not hiding anything!" She cut the power on the outboard. "And you never met Rita, right? You mean something you saw? I didn't see anything."

"Let me put it another way. I get the feeling I've overheard a clue and it didn't register. Or I know something but can't pin it down. This has nothing to do with what I saw or didn't see that night. Something at the back of my brain desperately wants to surface." Sally slapped her knees with both hands in exasperation. "Perhaps I'm imagining it."

"What Ruth said about the red book maybe?" Mae bit her lip. She put the engine into neutral.

They drifted for a minute.

"Couldn't be," Sally said, "because I had the feeling before then. I can't quite grasp it." Sally tugged at one ear. "It's just that I would hate to have missed something obvious."

"Did you talk to anyone else at the Pot the other night? About Rita? Besides me, I mean?" Mae put her hands to her face and cradled it like a small child caught in the act.

Sally was amused by her antics. "What is it with you? The other night you thanked me for not considering you a suspect. And a minute ago you were afraid you were a boat dollie. Are you just generally paranoid or only when the moon is full?"

Mae stared at her, mouth agape, then to Sally's surprise, threw her arms around her. "You're better than my mom. You understand me!"

"No, I don't." Sally laughed. "But I know enough about people instinctively to say that you are not a killer. A boat dollie? Well…?"

Mae pulled away quickly. "I am not… Oh, you were kidding!" She smiled. "There I go again. Sorry."

"Come on, push that throttle back up." Sally laughed, feeling lighthearted for the first time in days. "We'll continue your counseling session another time." She faced the spray again.

After Mae dropped her off at Sere Dina, Sally watched her motor across the fifty or so feet which separated them. She could see Jeff on deck tightening a turnbuckle. Their little sloop looked inviting as it rocked gently at anchor. Its bright blue hull and cream-colored sail covers were a good combination. She was especially fond of the name of the vessel, *Dream On*. It was written in delicate script on the varnished transom of the thirty-foot craft.

"WAIT UNTIL YOU see the marina," Sally told Pete, as she spread mayonnaise on his sandwich. "They have this table from the land of the giants, and a unique way of dealing with food service. It boggles the mind. Tim is the manager; there's something odd about him and I can't quite put my finger one it, but he stands too close for one thing."

"Big mistake on his part." Pete whistled. "I know how you hate people in your space. It sounds as though you've already made yourself a member of the community. How was the hospital? Modern? Antiquated?"

"It was surprisingly well appointed." Sally put his sandwich on the small table, then sat beside him. Funny, she thought, how comforting it was when people knew the little things about you so well. Years of marriage did that, she supposed.

"But so are the hotels and some of the stores," she continued. "I would imagine that with the amount of money that passes through these islands they would have to maintain sophisticated facilities. Medical care would probably top the list of requirements for the wealthy."

"That's encouraging. But you know me, I'm used to primitive conditions. I was concerned for your sake. By the way, Jeff did come over to see me. Decided he needed to do a little maintenance on his own boat today. When they don't have a charter booked, he usually works on other boats for extra money."

Yes, she thought dreamily, I know you. Sally reluctantly brought up the subject of her subliminal clue. But like Mae, Pete could offer little more than a blank stare. It was something she would have to work on alone.

"Look, trying to keep you from becoming involved in

this mess is probably impossible," Pete said. "But I really wish you wouldn't, Sally. People are drawn to you, they can't help it. They tell you things they wouldn't tell their own mothers. And even you admit, this is not an average community. This is a slice of life far removed from the norm."

She opened her mouth to disagree.

"No." He raised his hand. "There are probably thirty-five people in this boating clique and chances are pretty good that one of them murdered Rita. We're not talking about a city of thousands where your poking around wouldn't be noticed. Be realistic."

"You make it sound as though I'd opened an official investigation. Everyone else is asking questions, too. I don't think they have a murder here on a daily basis. It would be unnatural if I wasn't as curious as everyone else."

"Just keep it surface level." Pete drummed his fingers on the table. "I mean it."

"Pete, you've got to stop trying to control me. It's the one thing you never seem to have grasped. I am my own person. Every time you came home you did the same damn thing. Maybe it's because you ruled when you were out on an assignment and your students jumped when you suggested something. Well, I'm not one of your students."

"Okay, okay, let me put it another way. I'll compromise. Please, keep it surface level?"

Sally sighed. "Deal."

Hell she could compromise. Talking to Elaine would be surface level. Was Elaine close enough to Rita to know if she kept a diary or ledger? Yes, she would definitely talk to Elaine soon.

ELEVEN

THE ATMOSPHERE AROUND the Pot had changed. The crowd seemed bigger and an intangible something electrified the air. Sally couldn't quite put her finger on it. It wasn't tension or fear. It was more like excitement or anticipation, as though something momentous were about to occur. The staccato beat of the steel band intruded from a distance. The players were seated in a circle near the water's edge. Only the vague outline of their angular bodies was visible in the fading light as they bent to their haunting music.

She recognized some of the regulars around the bar. Jake sat directly across from her, his handsome face pensive. Claudette passed a tray of exotic drinks over his shoulder, drinks sprouting plastic pineapples and palm trees. Jake's bright eyes flickered.

When Sally looked again, she saw that Jake had focused on Pete. "What's Sere Dina mean?" he asked above the din of surrounding voices.

Sally watched Pete study Jake in return. Would he tell Jake the truth? Usually Pete made up some ridiculous definition, mostly for fun. It wasn't the sort of word you could look up unless you happened to have a specialized dictionary.

"It's a Fijian chant, used for serious occasions, one of which is to ward off hurricanes."

The truth for a change. Surprise, surprise.

"I like that. Good name for a boat." Jake shook his

head affirmatively. "You used to be an anthropologist or something?"

"I'm on sabbatical."

"All right, then you're still an anthropologist," Jake announced with an air of finality. He took a long slow sip of the drink in his hand.

"You're right. And once you do something long enough it becomes part of who you are. Sometimes I find myself seeing people only in terms of a social study. Where do they stand in their particular social hierarchy? What ethnic forces influence their choices? Not a way to win friends, analyzing them like specimens." Pete smirked.

Jake shrugged. "We all judge each other. Maybe not as technically as you do, but it's natural. So, I take it you're not one to go on digs then, no wandering off to tombs at the ends of the Earth?"

"Right, archaeology is not my specialty. Was…am, an ethnologist. I study culture. The folkways and mores of a people, past or present. I prefer present. But yes, I do wander off to the ends of the Earth. Or at least I did."

"A social detective would you say? And why the *did*?"

Sally swallowed nervously, wondering how far Pete would go in explaining things. It was something he had promised, to talk about Becky, to say her name out loud. Sally had wanted to talk, to keep her with them always, not with pain, but with love.

"Sally's the detective, she's a writer. I'm just a stuffy old scientist of sorts. We had a daughter. She was killed in an accident and…I was at the ends of the Earth. This trip is our way of regrouping."

Sally ignored the remark on the subject of her proposed sleuthing. She didn't interrupt. A relationship between Jake and Pete was one she might want to encourage. She was relieved to hear Pete speak of Becky at last. If Pete made a friend here, he might want to stay on the island longer. A futile hope, no doubt, but it was the only one she had at the moment. Maybe they could work through their personal problems, after all. She felt a ray of hope light her heart.

Jake stared at Pete briefly, then at Sally. He winked at her. "Where did you find Sere Dina, Pete? I couldn't help but notice her. Great lines."

Pete let out a long sigh and plunged into general conversation with Jake.

Sally winked back at Jake, impressed by his intuitive sense in sounding Pete out, and particularly in knowing when to stop. Mentioning Becky had been a huge leap for Pete, and saying she was dead was a milestone.

Sally didn't see any sign of Mae or Jeff, but placed her purse on the adjacent bar stool to reserve it for Mae, just in case. Elaine and Lyle sat deep in conversation at one of the tables. Sally managed to catch Elaine's attention and waved to her. The girl rose as though to join her, a trace of desperation in her brief glance, but Lyle grabbed her wrist and drew her back to the chair.

Darn, Sally wanted to talk to the woman, find out what troubled her at the marina, and what troubled her now.

"Anyone heard any more about the tropical depression?" Jake asked. "I mean anything besides the usual overblown rumors?"

Everyone agreed this promised to be the year they got the big one. Each gave different reasons for thinking so. You could tell by the avocado crop, somebody's horoscope said so...

"The water's never cooled off enough," Lance contributed, "and the birds are acting funny."

"I saw a ring around the moon the other night," someone else added. "But I forgot, that's supposed to mean an earthquake, isn't it? In the tropics, right?"

Sally considered these reasons to be as valid as any she heard on the weather station. Predictions based on past hurricane patterns seemed blatantly absurd, when at the same time they warned of global warming, ozone holes, volcanic ash and various other conditions which were radically changing the environment.

Jake shook his head. "Claudette is the one to ask if you want local lore, although I've noticed nothing rattles her much. The last time the weather station said a hurricane was imminent, she kept the bar open all night, in case anyone got thirsty when the water went off." He laughed.

Mae and Jeff finally arrived with Ruth in tow. Sally took in Ruth's apparel. She wore drab brown slacks and shirt, baggy and unadorned. Again, she sported no make-up or jewelry. It was a commendable effort but a total waste of time because more than one eye turned in her direction when she walked by.

Ruth posted a notice from the hospital on the make-shift bulletin board. The message was simple. Contrary to popular opinion there was no major outbreak of any fever other than the usual range of flues brought in by the tourists. There was also a separate notice listing the symptoms of dengue. With the rumor dispelled, however, there was little or no interest in dengue anymore. No one bothered to read it.

The tempo of the music subtly increased and so did the consumption of alcohol. The boaters mingled with the tourists, most of whom were past or future customers on their charter boats. Some of the girls danced in the sand and encouraged others to join them. The crescendo of voices rose as competing conversations sought larger audiences.

Across the crowded bar Sally saw Tim, smiling at her through a sea of faces. There it was again, that hint of seductiveness. Was she wrong? So much for her astute impressions. He was two people, but wasn't everyone when it came to their baser urges? Everyone liked to flirt. Sally smiled back.

She glanced over at Elaine, worried because the woman still appeared distressed. The problem was Sally didn't know her well enough to interfere. Mae joined the dancers in the sand and Ruth disappeared. Someone put another drink in Sally's hand and the next thing she knew she found herself near the dancers on the sand. She glanced back at Elaine's table. Empty.

The pulse of the drums drew Sally like a magnet. She clapped her free hand against her thigh and swayed with the bystanders. Pete stood at her side. He smiled down at her, reached forward and took her glass. With a gentle shove to the small of her back, he pushed her into the midst of dancers.

Sally responded to the vibrations of the drums. This was the kind of dancing she loved, free spirited and bordering on the erotic. Those around her seemed only ghostly images. She was dancing alone and she was dancing for Pete. She knew he watched her every move. Sally used to dance for him alone, long ago, in another world.

The tempo picked up slightly and some of the dancers folded into lumps on the sand. The crowd gathered around the writhing performers and urged the musicians into an even faster beat. Sally closed her eyes and let herself become one with the music. She and Pete would make love when they got back to the boat. She knew it from the moment he had guided her onto the dance floor. She opened her eyes and searched for him, then saw him smile at her. *That* smile. He knew it too. Dancing was foreplay.

The band moved in close making the thunderous throb of their drums a thing felt as well as heard. Sally caught fleeting impressions of those in the crowd. Ruth trying to be forgotten in a corner, eyes downcast, so as not to see the conspicuous sexuality displayed before God and everybody. Did religion motivate Ruth, or fear of her own emotions? Immorality was one thing, but all sexual arousal was not immoral, though she doubted Ruth accepted such simplistic truths.

Jake remained at the bar, still pensive, but in position to see the dancers clearly. A short muscular man to his left was focused exclusively on Lisa. She rewarded him with an occasional kiss, blown from her palm. Her counterpart, Lance L'Amour, was nowhere to be seen.

Behind her and the other girls in the darkness, Sally saw a couple dancing by themselves. They seemed to be out of step with the music. Too much to drink, she thought. She could barely make them out in the dim glow of the bar's subdued light. They were too far away. Something in their movements didn't look right. That's when she realized the couple wasn't dancing. They were fighting.

The girl tried to pull away but the man restrained her. They could be screaming at the top of their lungs and no one would hear them over the hullabaloo from the Pot.

The music slowed and faded as the attention of those on the outside of the crowd turned toward the escalating altercation on the beach. The couple's angry voices could be heard now in the clear night air. The music slowed noticeably, then stopped altogether. The dancers melted away as though embarrassed.

"What in the hell were you thinking?" Lyle shouted at a trembling Elaine.

"I don't know what you mean," she sobbed. "Just leave me alone, I don't want to talk about it anymore! Oh please," she begged. "Everyone's watching us!"

"I don't give a damn if God is watching us!" he shouted

at the bystanders, who drew back in disorderly fashion. He shoved Elaine roughly, almost knocking her down. "Do you hear me?"

Whether she did or not didn't matter at that point. The shove had given her enough distance to escape his reach and she quickly wove her way through the onlookers before he could do anything about it.

"Damn it all," he hollered after her. "You'd better come back to the boat or I'll find you and drag you back!"

People drifted to the bar as though nothing happened. Elaine disappeared into the ladies' room followed closely by Mae and Ruth. Sally wanted very much to join them, but thought better of it.

The drum players mingled with the others, accepting drinks and praise for their efforts. One of the players looked familiar to Sally. She realized it was Joseph. A flowered shirt and straw hat had magically transformed his countenance. This was a happy man. Maybe it was his brother. He was in deep conversation with Claudette the bartender, and his attentiveness was decidedly intimate.

Elaine emerged from the bathroom in a huff a few minutes later, shaking her head. She left Ruth and Mae trailing in her wake. Surprisingly, she came directly over to Sally and climbed on the adjacent bar stool. She had freshened up. Jeff leaned past Sally to stare at Elaine. His expressive features ran the gamut of emotions from concern to confusion. Sally nudged him gently with her elbow to stop his gawking.

Jake was studiously ignoring a woman tourist who managed to lean into him as though by accident. She was heavyset, with bright yellow hair in the tight Brillo style often worn by older women. Vivid black mascara outlined somewhat deep-set eyes above overly rouged cheeks, a caricature of what may have once been an attractive girl. She proudly displayed a large shell she'd found while snorkeling. As she stretched out her arm, she managed to brush against Jake, again.

Jake stood and moved his stool a half foot or so to the right, then set it down heavily as a signal. He put his elbows on the bar and spoke to everyone in general. "Rita's parents are coming tomorrow to take her body home. Anybody willing to go with me to meet them?"

Mae immediately volunteered herself and Jeff.

"Good, I'll pick you up at the marina at noon."

"Jake and several others share a derelict car for occasional emergencies," Elaine confided to Sally as though they'd been in deep conversation or knew each other well.

Opportunity is knocking, Sally thought, Elaine wants to talk. On another level, Sally was trying to figure out how she could involve herself in this meeting of Rita's family. One thing at a time, she cautioned herself.

The mention of Rita, however, put a general damper on the social atmosphere. The evening was coming to a close. But the dowdy tourist somehow maneuvered closer to Jake once more, still waving her shell. The party wasn't over for her yet.

Jake gathered his features into an unpleasant scowl and turned to her, speaking in an even tone. "Excuse me, lady, would you mind moving downwind a bit. Your conch stinks."

A look of absolute horror crossed the woman's face. She opened her mouth to speak but nothing came out. The bright red of her lips met the rouge on her cheeks in an extraordinary blush as she gathered her purse and other belongings to make her escape. Ironically, she forgot the conch shell reposing on the bar directly in front of her. She fled into the night with the speed of a greyhound.

Sally tried making small talk with Elaine hoping for

an opening to the larger problem, but to no avail. She was close to giving up when Claudette came over. Her large bosoms jostled as she moved and her magnificent round face shone with concern. She took Elaine's small hand in her chubby black one. She patted the girl tenderly and almost reduced the girl to tears.

Now why didn't I think of that, Sally thought. One pat on the hand and Elaine's in touch, elementary psychology.

"You need help," Claudette crooned. "Don't you be like Rita now, girl. You talk to somebody. I got me five babies, I know trouble when I see it. And you got big trouble behind those pretty little eyes. You talk to this lady here," she pointed at Sally. "I bet she have lots of babies too. How many babies you got, lady?"

Sally was abashed. "Sorry, Claudette, I did have a daughter, but…she died."

Claudette was not easily deterred. "Ah…that is very sad, lady. But you going to be *Boat Mama* now. Good. Good. You see, girl," she said, turning back to Elaine. "Now you got a boat mama to talk to. Everything be fine!"

Sally couldn't believe her ears. This young girl was certainly not going to accept her as some sort of mother figure. She no doubt had a very fine mother of her own. It was her intention to explain this to Elaine and save her the embarrassment of declining, but the genuine relief in those sad eyes totally arrested any hope she had of resigning this field commission. She looked to Pete for a reprieve, but what she saw was the familiar smirk she knew so well. He had heard everything. It was one very big I told you so. And worst of all, she could envision him calling her Boat Mama for the rest of her life. She gave a sigh of resignation, and placed her arm on Elaine's shoulder, "if there's anything I can do to help, dear, you just let me know."

"Oh, thank you, Sally. Maybe we could talk or something one day this week. Okay?"

The innocent glow on Elaine's face reminded Sally of
her first confrontation with Mae. What was happening to
her all of a sudden? How had she gone from visiting tourist to Boat Mama in one short evening? Well, she would
certainly have ample opportunity to question Elaine now.
And she felt good inside. Maybe she'd found a way to se-
date the pain of Becky's loss. God how she missed the connection, the mothering thing. Maybe playing *boat mama*
would help her as well as Elaine.

The picture of Elaine and Lyle fighting on the beach
came to Sally's mind. "Are you afraid to go back to your
boat tonight?"

"No, not really. Lyle is angry, but he would never hurt
me."

"You could've fooled me," Sally insisted. "But perhaps
you should go back, before he becomes more upset. Or do
you want to talk right now? We could go to a table."

"You're right, I should go to the boat. I feel so much better now. Give me a day to calm things down. And really,
he won't hurt me." Elaine gave Sally a quick hug and left.

Pete and Sally yawned their excuses and headed for
the dinghy wall. "Now you see what I mean about people
telling you things they wouldn't tell their mothers." Pete
raised his face to the dark sky to push his point. "Hell,
now you've got one who thinks you are her mother." He
caressed her shoulder. "At least this involvement will keep
you busy in a nice safe way, Sally. Assuming it has nothing to do with Rita's murder, I approve."

"I'm happy that you're happy." She glanced up at him,
suppressing the satisfaction she felt at the way things had
turned out. Strange she hadn't encountered her stalker to-

night though. Could he be taking a more circumspect approach? Her attention to detail needed discipline.

An inky darkness surrounded them when they boarded Sere Dina and entered her cabin. Pete reached out and pulled Sally to him. His arms encircled her waist, then moved up her body slowly, gently. "Time to finish the dance," he whispered in her ear.

Yes, I need to pay a lot more attention to detail, Sally thought. She turned and wrapped her arms around Pete's neck and pressed her body tightly against his. Maybe this time would be different. She wanted it to be different. Her breath caught in her throat as Pete's lips brushed her throat. "You lead," she said.

TWELVE

SALLY ROSE EARLY the next morning. The crisp, fresh hours of dawn were hers. She carried a canvas deck chair forward and stretched out on it, her cocoa and toast by her side. The only thing missing was a newspaper, one of the few attributes of the other world they had left behind that she truly missed. Without it, contact with that world was severed. They weren't people who had left the mainstream because they hated it. They were taking some badly needed time out. Time to heal.

If the truth be known, she fit very easily into the role of boat person. A boat dollie? Doubtful. Even in her youth she had never sacrificed morality to passion. Of course the precepts of morality had changed in the last few decades, radically, thank heavens. Sally's list of moral tenets rarely had much in common with those of society. A circumstance which had caused her mother no end of alarm. Had she caused Becky alarm, too? She'd gone through this a zillion times. Were it not for the accident they would have made up the next day. They had been so close. Nor would Becky have married Dean, Sally knew. It was just one of those emotional stands taken by the young when faced with disapproval.

Were boat dollies bad girls or sinners? She would never make such a judgment. These girls were used and tossed around like chattel, then abandoned at their most vulnerable. Who were the sinners, the captains or the crew? And what the hell was she doing moralizing her morning away. She drank her cocoa and tried to put her mind on other things.

The egrets left the mangroves for their morning breakfast forage. The vendors leaked from the alleyways of the turquoise town, rattling their carts along the seawall. Yes, she could be a boat person. Every place they'd stopped on this trip had its own atmosphere, a separate culture, as Pete would point out. It was like visiting different planets.

She heard a noise behind her. Pete made stretching groans from the cockpit. "Well, I see Boat Mama is up early this morning. Does this mean Boat Mama wants to go sailing?"

"Damn, I knew this was going to happen," she muttered under her breath, but smiled anyway. Ignoring the remark seemed the wisest response for the moment. "I don't know about sailing, but I would like to explore the coastline in the dinghy for a few hours. If we could be back by noon, that is. I was thinking of joining Mae to meet Rita's family."

"You're really taking this boat mama stuff seriously, aren't you?" Pete asked with raised eyebrows. "What happened to not getting deeply involved?"

"Oh, come on. It has nothing to do with the murder. I want to know what makes a boat dollie tick."

Pete threw his hands in the air. "Okay, a dinghy ride it will be. But we're going to discuss this some more. You pack the brunch and I'll get the boat ready."

Sally went below. She put fresh bread, fruit and cheese into a basket and poured chilled wine into a thermos. What more could anyone want? She donned shorts and a T-shirt and grabbed her sunglasses and a wide-brimmed hat.

They drove the stout little dinghy near the shore for some time before leaving the last few houses of the village. Palm-lined beaches gave way to a rocky shoreline liberally

sprinkled with sea grape and mangrove. Several small but
deep harbors appeared. Pete and Sally investigated each of
them, with regard to using one as a haven in the event of a
hurricane. Sally knew every boat within a hundred miles
had done the same. These harbors would fill up quickly,
but they still had to check out every one because it was
not the sort of thing one did when a storm was imminent.
She noticed a few permanent moorings, staking out choice
anchorages. Sea grass bearded the buoys with authority.

They finally happened upon a larger bay; one with a
shallow entrance, but with deep water beyond. They had
to pull up their centerboard to enter. That would limit
boats with fixed keels. The entire shoreline was forested
with sturdy mangrove trees. There were miles of canals
running through the mangrove. While some of them were
wide enough for a large boat, they invariably narrowed
down to dinghy size, and even into tunnels. The ideal scenario would be to commandeer one of these canals as their
own, drive Sere Dina as far back in as possible, wedge her
tightly in place and then secure her to the gnarled, tough
roots and branches of the mangrove.

They explored one of the longer tunnels for some distance, finally exiting into a small clearing, almost a lake
within the bay. They secured the dinghy to a tree, then
waded along the shore, gathering small mangrove oysters that clung fiercely to the roots. Pete removed his shirt
and tied a knot in one end to use as a sack for their catch.

Sally moved without speaking, trying not to disturb
the creatures that called this place home. There were tall,
stately wading birds in abundance. Some shrieked at them
in angry tones and made stabbing motions with their long
pointed beaks. Fish darted between their feet, occasionally
nipping them as if to see if these strange interlopers were
edible. Tiny, almost invisible crabs magically material-

ized when Sally or Pete extended a hand toward a branch. Some stood their ground and waved tweezerlike claws in a threatening manner, but most scurried off the branches and dropped to safer haunts in the emerald green lagoon.

Sally and Pete returned to the dinghy and cast off, to drift in the morning sun. They ate the oysters and drank chilled white wine. Only the occasional drone of an airplane in the distance reminded Sally of the real world beyond the lagoon.

"I hate to ruin the moment with an argument," Pete said, "but we need to make some guidelines on how much prying you intend to do in Rita's regard."

Sally slapped her hand on the side of the dinghy. Nearby birds took flight in alarm. "Okay, Pete. Let's get this over with. First of all, let's discuss the *we* business. Why do *we* have to set guidelines for me? How about all the years I spent waiting and worrying while you went off to primitive hovels around the globe in search of answers to God knows what questions? *We* didn't make any decisions about you being exposed to exotic diseases. Or cannibals. Remember the cannibals, Pete? I have never forgotten the cannibals. I didn't sleep for weeks."

Pete looked skyward. "That was work, Sally. I'm an anthropologist. It was my job to go and study those cultures first hand."

"And I never said boo about it, did I? You took the risks and I did the worrying."

"I can see where this is going, so let me point out one thing. One big thing. You're a writer and maybe you see a story here, but we both agreed to take this time off, remember? And there is no analogy here. Solving Rita's murder is not your life's work!"

"Who said I wanted to solve Rita's murder? I want to get to know these women, the boat dollies and the others.

I don't know how to explain it but I think it might help me get over Becky. They're her age and they have problems. Learning about Rita may be part of that. So I'm no detective, but what if I do want to play one. Why not? Life doesn't have much meaning for me right now, maybe I need something to fight for. Rita was not just a boat dollie, she was a person. But back to the point. I went along with whatever you wanted to pursue. And it got a little dangerous at times, so why can't I do something a little dangerous for a change? And why won't you support me in the effort? I would think you would be interested in the boating subculture we've encountered, from an anthropological point of view. So…help me, don't fight me."

Pete's lips were tight. Sally's hands gripped her wine glass. Thunder rolled in the distance. Perspiration dripped from both their brows as they stared each other down.

"I want you safe, Sally," Pete finally said. "I'm sorry for all the times I made you worry. You never said anything, ever. I thought you liked it when I was away. I felt that Becky was your whole life. You were a saint."

She pulled back to look into his eyes. "I was not a saint! We both know that. After Becky died, I sulked. I drank too much. I thought you were happier when you were gone, that I had failed you as a wife like I'd failed as a mother. I was angry at both of us, for heaven's sake!"

"You're exaggerating. You were a wonderful mother and we belong together! I always felt left out with you *and* Becky. I know better now. I left myself out. And you've never drank too much in your life."

"You weren't there. I did too. I was lonely and miserable…and we're off the subject."

Pete looked away and exhaled. "I thought we had agreed," he sighed. "All right, you go play boat mama to the girls and I'll study the subculture as a group—for my book. But let's let the dead dollie paddle her way to paradise on her own."

Sally scrunched up her face to look as determined as possible, then blew the effect with a laugh. "Paddle her way to paradise?" she repeated after him. "You're sick, Pete." The tension evaporated.

"If," Sally continued, "I decide Rita's family—who I still intend to meet today—is sufficiently interested in seeking justice for their daughter, I'll stick to playing boat mama. If they're not, however, I'm going to ask questions until someone is interested. So, before we return to Sere Dina I want to stop and tell Mae that I would like to accompany her," Sally said. "I have the feeling Jeff would rather not go on this mission anyway. Mae volunteered him."

She saw the anger return to Pete's features. He always pursed his lips like a small child when he didn't get his way. Then inexplicably, the look passed. "I'll give your way a try," he said. He consulted his watch and announced it was time to get back.

Sally cringed when Pete pulled the starter on the outboard. The blast of noise and puff of smoke from the engine sent the nearby creatures into a tizzy. She hated having disturbed the peace of the little bay. It was no place for man-made noise, mechanical or emotional. She was grateful when the mangrove tunnel swallowed both.

WHAT HE OUGHT to do is blow up their frigging boat, Armando thought. Yeah, he'd enjoy that—boom, end of job. No more sitting in the sun all day or on the seawall all night. Of course that would be the end of some pretty easy money too. He scanned the horizon. No sign of their dinghy.

How could you scare somebody you couldn't get near. A good stab to the buttocks would have done it. Scared the shit out of the other girl. She wouldn't sit down for a while. Wonder who she blamed. Armando laughed. At least it was a mistake no one but he would ever know about.

He saw a dinghy coming into the harbor. He waited to see where it would go. It went to Sere Dina. Good. He needed a break to get something to eat and call the boss.

The boss said to make something happen. Hell, it wasn't his fault they were gone all morning. Tonight, maybe tonight he would get another chance at her. They liked to hang out at the Pot—and broads were forever running to the bathroom. Maybe this time he'd do more than lock her in.

THIRTEEN

THE COOL SHOWER water felt great against Sally's back. She had forgotten to ask Mae about joy-baths. Water wasn't a serious problem at the moment, since they usually managed to trap enough with their awning. Still, she had heard the expression in conversation and wanted it explained. She towel dried quickly, not wanting to be late meeting Rita's parents. She slipped on a pale flowered sundress and white sandals, then went topside to wait for Mae.

Old Jake waited near the dinghy wall as promised. He registered no surprise when Sally explained she would be substituting for Jeff.

The communal car he drove left room for improvement. "Hope you're not afraid of bugs," Jake said as he opened the back door for them.

"What kind of bugs," Sally whispered rhetorically. "And how many?" She and Mae exchanged tight little smiles.

The back windows of the car had ceased to close a long time ago and weather had etched a historical record on the interior. The head liner drooped like a hammock and flopped in the breeze as they traveled the long straight road—the only straight road on the island—to the airport. Sally sought a more comfortable position on the seat, but the cracked leather upholstery clawed her legs through her thin cotton dress. She watched in fascination as a prize-winning roach navigated the puckered dashboard. Then Jake's hand snaked out like a lightning bolt and snatched it from its path. He extended his arm very carefully out the window and set it free. Sally resisted the impulse to scratch the back of her neck.

She wasn't sure what she expected Rita's family to be like, especially since she had never known Rita. But she certainly never envisioned anything like the people who arrived.

They were tall, slender, beautiful people. Not a wrinkle in their clothing and every hair in place. Rita's father could have stepped out of a Wall Street ad and her mother and sister looked more like siblings than parent and child. Mae told her later that Rita had been stamped out with the same cookie-cutter as far as looks were concerned. From there on the differences were monumental.

The perfect mother spoke to her daughter. "I don't suppose, Cynthia, that Rita left any valuables behind."

Cynthia flashed a look of disgust in her mother's direction. "Really, Mother, Rita never took care of anything at home. Whatever made you think she might do so in her grubby boat world?" A sideways sneer took in Sally and Mae. "Even if she did have anything, it's probably long gone by now."

Sally was not at all sure what the woman meant by that statement, but she had a pretty good idea. She felt a seething anger. The highly suggestive remark set her on edge. And something else here that bothered her. Why no grief? No indignation? Did they know Rita had been murdered?

"Is that your car?" Rita's father asked, pointing to the respectable Lincoln parked next to Jake's junker.

"That's it," Jake said with a smirk.

For a minute Sally thought Jake misunderstood, then remembered his subtler nature. She might enjoy this journey after all.

"Thank God," Cynthia said. "The last time I visited her, Rita was driving the worst piece of trash I've ever seen. I wouldn't let my dog ride in the car she was using. Really, Mother. Thank goodness you'll be spared that!"

Sally watched Jake. He kept walking but he turned to look at Rita's family and his eyes changed, like Superman's when he wanted to burn something. He smiled but his mouth was a tight line. "I hope you're not afraid of bugs," he said to the trio.

"Bugs?" they replied in unison.

"Yeah, bugs. You know, the creepy crawly things. It's kinda hard to keep them out of the car with no windows and all. I sprayed a little this morning, but you never quite get them all. I did get the rat though, no problem."

He graciously held the door as they climbed in. They were red-faced and quiet. Cynthia cast an envious glance at the pristine Lincoln.

The drive to the morgue was pregnant with silence. The flapping head liner whipped with a vengeance, mussing the too, too perfect hairdos of the rear passengers.

Sally watched a small roach make its way up the back of Cynthia's dress as they climbed the courthouse steps.

"I suppose we should ask some questions, Mother, about unfinished business," Cynthia said, her face pinched as though there was a bad odor nearby. "Our reputation counts—even down here," she added, then glanced at the ramshackle wooden buildings adjacent to the courthouse. She took her mother's arm protectively.

"I must ask about the ring," Rita's mother said. "That ring's been in the family for generations. God knows why I entrusted it to Rita. Aunt Margaret considered it her favorite," she said, her voice breaking.

Emotion at last, Sally thought with disgust. The poor dear has lost her ring.

The entourage entered the building proper. At this juncture the little roach finally completed his arduous journey.

He hovered briefly on the back collar of Cynthia's Gucci dress, then dropped into the void. Sally watched, pleased with this exciting turn of events. First Cynthia gave a slight squirm, then a serious wiggle accompanied by a few audible squeaks. Moving right along, Sally thought. Then Cynthia suddenly let loose a full-bodied scream and made a beeline for the ladies' room, followed closely by her bewildered mother.

When they returned five minutes later, they had regained full composure. Rita's father finished the paperwork for the release of his daughter's body. Sally watched the process with growing indignation. He might have been signing a stock merger.

An officer gave them a bag of Rita's clothing. The women quickly searched and discarded the sack ceremoniously.

Joseph appeared from an office down the hall. He straightened his tie, nodded to the group, and shook hands with the father. "The young man who knew your daughter? You would like to speak with him?"

Cynthia and the mother cringed, as though he had offered them pornographic material. "I think not," Cynthia said, her mouth a taut line. "I think we're done here, officer." She turned her back on him and walked toward the entrance of the building, followed by her family.

None of them mentioned Rita's murder. None of them asked why or who had killed her. Rita no longer existed for them.

Outside the cold gloomy atmosphere of the courthouse they asked about taking a taxi back to the airport.

"The captain of the boat Rita sailed on promised to leave a few very personal belongings in his dock box, so why don't I take you there," Jake said. "I didn't say anything earlier because I thought it might be mentioned at the morgue."

"But why didn't you turn her things over to the authorities?" her father asked. He reached out and leaned on the car as he spoke, then quickly drew back and wiped his hand on his trousers.

Jake smirked. A frigid edge laced his words now. "A diary was mentioned and other things, things he thought you wouldn't want made public."

"Thank God, for that!" Rita's mother exclaimed.

"Really!" Cynthia agreed. "I can only imagine the kind of low-life episodes Rita detailed for posterity. Sick city. It's bad enough my friends know she was…murdered." She made a slight whimpering sound. "Oh, Mother. It was so embarrassing."

"I know, dear. I know." Her mother put one arm around Cynthia's shoulders. "We'll get through this, dear, don't worry."

Sally opened her mouth to say something, but thought better of it. She bowed her head. A heavy sadness overwhelmed her. This wasn't happening. These people couldn't be real. When she looked up, Jake stood only inches away from her, his eyes locked on hers. Sally sensed his understanding, without words, it was as though he looked into her soul and saw her pain. She fought back tears. Tears for Rita, tears for Becky, tears for all the boat dollies in the world. And, seeing the pain behind his own bright blue eyes—tears for Jake's lost love. Sally shook her head to regain a grip on her emotions, but she would never forget that brief foray into Jake's mystical envelope. The moment passed but the spiritual bonding was complete.

The group piled in the car once more to investigate the dock box. They drove in complete silence this time.

Several people watched the odd procession march down the dock. A few snickered as Cynthia caught her heels between the rough-hewn boards every few feet. Sally secretly wished she would fall and break a leg.

Jake indicated the dock box with a gesture and cautioned them to stand back. "Even more bugs on the dock than there are in the parking lot," he explained, then smiled evenly.

The family dutifully took several steps backward. Curious, Sally and Mae stayed where they were and watched as Jake lifted a small bag from one corner of the box. They also watched him remove a distinctive red book from the bag. He glanced at Sally and deliberately dropped it. It wedged silently between two sail bags. He slammed the box lid with a look of satisfaction on his chiseled features. It wasn't hard to figure out what changed Jake's mind in regard to giving her family the diary. And now she knew where it was.

Rita's mother snatched the bag, pawing through its contents like a vulture. Suddenly a look of exultation crossed her stone features. "The ring, it's here. I can't believe it."

Cynthia showed some genuine interest at last. "Is the diary there? I mean I know it's probably garr…baage, but I guess one of us should read it, after all." Retrieving the bag from her mother, she too searched the interior diligently. Finding nothing, she extended the bag toward Jake in a two-fingered grip. "Here," she offered, with an expression of disdain. "I'm sure some of Rita's boatie friends might want some of this…stuff."

Sally was sick of being with Rita's family. She looked at Mae and Jake.

Jake nodded and shook his thumb like a hitchhiker. "Are you ready, ladies?"

Rita's mother and sister looked up expectantly.

"Oh, not you two," Jake said sarcastically. "You're not ladies."

"I beg your pardon?" the father said.

"It's Rita's pardon you should be begging," Jake continued. "She was worth more than twenty of you people put together. Well, you've got the release for Rita's body. And you have her personal possessions. But we've got Rita's soul and you can't have that. The real Rita stays with us, folks!"

"What in the hell are you talking about?" Cynthia asked, in a superior tone. "Does this mean you're not driving us back to town? You can't leave us out here." She looked around at the bystanders as though they were aliens. Most wore cut-off jeans, no shirts and were barefoot. Their hair was shaggy and more than one of the men sported an earring.

"I wouldn't drive the three of you to a funeral," Jake said.

Sally hoped the irony wasn't lost on them.

JAKE DROPPED SALLY and Mae off at the seawall. It was time to meet his late afternoon charter.

"Could the parents of all boat dollies be so cold and calculating, Mae?" Sally asked as they walked along the dinghy wall.

"Weren't they unreal?" Mae agreed. "You know, I don't think either one of us said a single word to Rita's family throughout the episode. Personally, I was speechless." Mae leaned over the wall, gave a slight tug on the painter and tugged the dinghy toward them.

With a line, not her usual heavy chain, Sally noticed.

"I switched to the line with wire in it, like I got you to buy yesterday. I told Jeff that darn chain was too heavy for me to deal with every day. Geez! Now watch someone come along with wire cutters and it will be my fault when the dinghy's stolen."

Oh, oh. Would she be in trouble? Before she could ask, her attention alerted to another boat in the distance. It chugged slowly away from the seawall. She was startled to see the occupants were Tim, from the marina, and Lisa. She turned an inquiring look toward Mae. "Now what?"

"Lance and Lisa have a totally open relationship," Mae said. She raised her eyebrows.

Sally shrugged her shoulders. "You want to translate that for me, I suppose."

"Sure do," Mae said with an impish grin. "Lisa spends her day off screwing half the island."

"I see," Sally answered. "You certainly do enjoy exploding verbal bombs, don't you?" She laughed. "But never mind for now. What about Lance? How does he spend his free time?"

"He entertains hopeful dollies, and the occasional tourist, too."

"Fascinating," Sally said in awe. "But doesn't Lisa worry one of the hopefuls will get her position?"

"Nah, nobody but Lisa would put up with Lance's idea of a romantic relationship. The girls who do visit Lance aren't going anywhere, they just don't know it. As soon as Lance explains the ground rules they're gone in a flash, sometimes in a splash." Mae laughed heartily at her own pun. "Especially when he invites Lisa to join in the fun." She took a sideways peek at Sally.

Sally kept her expression noncommittal.

"Occasionally someone joins the game, but one of the rules is they don't get to stay on the boat." Mae let her eyebrows do the Tango.

Sally had to laugh, but she remained mute as she

watched Lisa and Tim's progress toward Lift Off's mooring. Behind the sleek racing hull she could see the larger silhouette of Lady Jane, the boat belonging to Lyle and Elaine. Or at least to Lyle, she corrected herself. The boat dollie world operated with a whole different set of rules, ones that left her mystified. The women became nothing short of…paid companions, to use the polite term.

Mae started the dinghy engine and backed the boat away from the wall.

"Let's drop in and see Elaine. Do you have time?" She still worried for the young woman's sake. The altercation she observed on the beach the night before wasn't actually violent, but the tone of Lyle's voice when he threatened to drag Elaine to the boat if she didn't return on her own, spoke of more than a simple disagreement. Why such high drama?

"Super idea," Mae called back over the hum of the outboard. She immediately turned the dinghy in the direction of the forty-three-foot ketch.

Lady Jane reminded Sally of a pirate ship, with her picturesque gaff rigging and large square ports in the stern. A high aft deck was encircled by a perfectly varnished taffrail and real wooden belaying pins nestled in beams mounted in the shrouds.

Mae carefully snugged their craft against the glossy black hull, then grasped a finger hold on the rubrail. "Ahoy there, anyone on board?" she called out in a loud voice.

Lyle's face appeared above the cockpit coaming, his expression pensive. He stared at them but did not speak.

"Permission to come aboard?" Mae requested in a more subdued tone.

"Sorry, not today, Elaine's not feeling well."

He did look sorry, Sally thought. "Can you ask her if there's anything we can get for her, or for you?"

Lyle's voice softened as he answered Sally. "We appreciate it, but no. I'll tell her you were here, Sally." He disappeared from view, leaving them no recourse but to depart.

Sally regretted not seeing Elaine. But the girl had asked for a day to calm things down. At least she would know Sally cared enough to visit. Where she failed with Elaine, however, she had succeeded with Jake. And Jake had the little red book.

There was something in Jake's personality that called out to Sally. Men who weren't afraid to show their emotions appealed to her. You could be friends with men like that. Men rarely made good friends with women. She hoped some of his attitude would rub off on Pete. She wearied of trying to rebuild their relationship on Becky's ashes. Would going on just prolong both their agonies? Sharing their grief hadn't worked when it was fresh, now the pain burned constantly. Would it never end? Were they destined to wound each other with their personal guilt for eternity? Their lovemaking had been intense last night, Sally recalled vividly, as though they were trying to prove something, as though they were making love for the last time. She needed someone to talk to. She glanced at Mae and shrugged. Someone mature. Playing boat mama *and* confidante were not mutually compatible roles.

FOURTEEN

When Sally returned to Sere Dina, she found Pete on deck making preparations for sail. "The dinghy trip this morning spurred my appetite for exploring," he explained. "Let's leave early tomorrow and take a short sail somewhere, to some empty atoll."

Sally read the excitement in his eyes. She caught the fever. Big decisions could always be put off.

"Do we need any supplies from shore?" he continued, a hopeful grin lighting up his face.

"I have everything I need." Sally smiled back. She patted the cabin top affectionately. "Old Tub here is ready to rock and roll. Let's do it."

"Sere Dina!" he insisted. "Sere Dina, not Old Tub!" He put his arms on Sally's shoulders for a moment, then raised her face to his, as though to read the answers to unspoken questions.

"It didn't go well with the family, did it?"

"They were worse than I imagined."

"I sat here and analyzed the situation while you were gone." He sighed while gently stroking her cheek. "Whatever else goes into the making of a boat dollie, it figures an unhappy home life is probably a given in the equation. Obsessive behavior fills a void and invariably the void has its roots in childhood."

Sally pulled away from Pete. "And that's just another way of saying her parents didn't exactly love her best." She smoothed her hair back from her forehead, sorry she couldn't smooth over the memory of Rita's family as easily. "Hell, they didn't even like her!"

"So I lose this round," Pete said in a whisper. He looked out past the harbor entrance.

"What?"

He didn't answer.

She glanced up at him, at the tall varnished mast at his back. Both signified strength to her. "Now you're worried, because of our discussion this morning, right?"

"No, no. I already figured out how your encounter with the family would go. I'll deal with it. Listen, I know we've screwed up our lives, my being gone and everything, but we did shower Becky with love. I think she knew that."

"I know," she said, and buried her face against his shoulder. "But I keep telling you. I didn't mind your being gone. It was what you were supposed to do. It was after Becky that it became difficult for me."

"Okay, okay. It's my guilt trip, let me wallow in it if I need to."

Sally kissed his cheek and smiled up at him. "Whatever, at least we're talking about it."

"And I've given some thought to something you said yesterday," Pete said, changing the subject. "Your feeling that you knew something about the murder. Let's go sailing and clear our minds, see what we can come up with together."

"Yes!" Sally said. She gave him a hug and went below to make preparations to sail. Every time she thought things were hopeless, Pete did something that rattled her, for the better.

PETE AND SALLY dropped anchor near a small island—one of many—about twenty miles down the chain. They combed the beach for the first few hours and Sally examined an abundance of treasures from the sea. Driftwood, dried sea fans of purple and pink, shells of every size and description. She took none of these prizes to the boat. They belonged to the island. Possession was for the insatiable.

The stretch of beach they chose was studded with giant boulders. Some perched atop others at precarious angles, frozen in motion. They walked faster beneath the shadows of these looming behemoths.

"Pete, look up there." Sally pointed. "There's something out of place in the landscape pattern. Let's investigate."

They worked their way up the steep sand hill for a closer look. At first Sally thought it might be a pile of flotsam left high and dry by a storm.

"It appears organized," Pete said. Heavy boards were stacked tepee fashion against a large crevice in one of the boulders, leaving a smoke hole in the top. A frayed piece of material served as a door flap.

"The sand is trampled by footprints here," Sally said. "I didn't see any on the beach."

"Check out that cluster of palm fronds." Pete pointed. "See, they've been tied together. Drag that contraption through the sand and it would obliterate tracks effectively. The owner of this shack is not some refugee awaiting rescue from a deserted atoll. He's more likely a hermit who wants fiercely to be alone. And ten to one, he's less than friendly."

Sally sensed movement to their right.

A stooped figure emerged from between two of the smaller rocks. He had long, shaggy, shoulder-length hair and his skin had the texture of an over-baked potato. The gnarled structure of his bony body reminded Sally of mangrove roots. The heavy sack on his back bent him almost double.

When he looked up, his shock was total. For a brief moment his eyes met theirs. His were pale green and they broadcast fear like a pulsating beacon. Emitting an animal-like cry, the creature dropped his bag and ran in a shuffling gait—head bowed all the way—for the security of his lean-to. Even standing where they were, Pete and Sally could hear his pathetic sobs.

"My God," Sally said, as they beat a hasty retreat. "Shouldn't we do something?"

"I think we have probably done enough already. We've found his very, very private sanctuary. At least we didn't violate it by entering. He is probably animal enough to know that, instinctively." Pete studied Sally for a moment. "And I know you well enough to know you have visions of rescuing this tragic creature. Forget it, my dear. There are no bars on this island and this fellow has gone to great lengths to remain unseen."

Sally frowned in disapproval. "Well, maybe we could give him something, bring little gifts from time to time? Not food or anything like that. Nothing to make him dependent. A hat, a jar to store things in, articles he can't get."

"I don't know," Pete said with a groan. "Anthropologically speaking, we should leave well enough alone."

"Don't start that stuff with me, Pete," Sally said. "This guy is not some primitive culture you have to protect. You promised we would spend the night at anchor here, so why don't we leave a small offering on the beach. We'll check it out in the morning. If he takes it, fine. If he doesn't, then we forget the whole idea."

"Okay, Boat Mama. Here we go again."

Sally laughed and squeezed Pete's arm.

Once back on board Sere Dina, Sally rummaged through storage compartments in search of something suitable to leave for the hermit. As seasoned travelers, they didn't carry much they didn't really need. Space was a luxury on sailboats. If an item wasn't useful it didn't stay aboard long. Sally always managed to fuzzy up the fine line between useful and useless.

"Ah hah!" she cried aloud with satisfaction as she came across a large magnifying glass in one of the drawers. Actually, it was indeed a useful item, but one she could replace. For some reason the magnifying glass inspired another thought. A mirror. An easy find. From a vanity in the head, she removed an old compact.

Sally felt she needed at least one more thing. Wasn't there a rule regarding doing things in threes or something like that? A search of the V-berth area produced an extra pair of Pete's sandals. She was about to put them with the other presents when Pete entered the cabin.

"Don't even think about it!" he threatened. "It took me weeks to break those in."

"Of course not, darling," she answered with a sly expression. "Besides, it would be silly. They might not fit him." She dropped them on the locker floor.

"Lucky me. I think I'll stay and watch this scavenger hunt if you don't mind." Pete sat on the small step leading to the main salon.

"Great. I'm out of ideas. Help me think of something. What would you want most if you were stranded on a desert island?" She cocked one eyebrow and waited for his response.

He made the shape of a woman in the air.

"Stupid question," she answered for him. "Try to be serious for once, Pete."

"I *was* serious. But I think this fellow might not be interested in the same things I am." He scratched his cheek. "How about a piece of rope? Everybody can always use rope."

"Perfect," Sally said. "Whenever we come here, we'll

bring him three things. Next time we'll have more time to think it out."

"Next time?" Pete gave her a thumbs-down sign.

The sun was just setting when they left their offerings on the strip of beach nearest the hermit's lean-to. There was no sign of him. Now that he knows we're here, Sally worried, we might not see him again. They returned to the boat.

"I'm putting the radio on to catch the weather report," Pete told Sally as the boarded the boat. "I want to see if that depression has been upgraded to a tropical storm. It's still pretty far away but it was holding a westward course. The local weather forecast didn't sound promising earlier. The clouds have been building most of the afternoon and it looks as though we might get some rain before morning. A little sprinkle wouldn't hurt us, but I know how you feel about rough seas."

Sally went below to work on dinner. She made cold pasta salad, fresh vegetable soup and as always, homemade bread. She carried a tray topside where Pete was pouring wine.

"I'm worried about Ruth's report," Pete said.

"About dengue fever?" Sally asked as she spread butter on her bread.

"No, the autopsy results. The *obvious* fact that strangulation was the cause of Rita's death. Remember, I said the killer might have tried to sever her spinal cord so she couldn't swim back to shore. I figured he wasn't sure the rope had done the trick."

Sally glanced up. "That's part of where I get mixed emotions. Where the story isn't right, a clue of some kind we've missed. Something to do with the rope or the knife, or even both." She stirred her soup, then took a spoonful to test for heat.

"The knife wounds were all on the back of her neck," Pete continued.

"Wait," Sally exclaimed. "That's it. That's what's wrong with the picture. He never did try to kill her with the knife. If he wanted to do that he would have just slit her throat—in the front." She put her spoon down and clapped her hands. "You're a genius! All we had to do was talk it out."

"Then why have the knife in the first place?" Pete asked.

"Mae gave me the answer to that one when we were talking the other night. She suggested someone killed Rita in an argument gone wrong. I thought the knife was just too handy, but she reminded me that boaters almost always carry knives because they never know when they will have to cut a line." She pointed to Pete's pocket knife that lay near the compass. "He wanted to remove the line from around her neck, so he cut it. And he made a mess of it because…well, because he must have been shaken up by what he had already done. Or," she looked up, "maybe because we arrived and panicked him."

"And maybe he never meant to kill her at all," Pete added, ignoring her last words. "Joseph suggested the rope was a line, or rather, the killer's dinghy painter, and that he might have been trying to get it back so he could tie his boat up when he got back to shore. So you could be right. In other words, the killer was in a separate boat."

"The answer is there somewhere. My *inkling* tells me so."

"Well, we have learned something else," Pete said. His features were shadowed in the half-light of approaching night. He scowled. "The murderer was, like I said in the first place, more than likely one of the boat crowd."

"Humph!" Sally said, knowing the way his mind worked. He probably had their next island all picked on the charts, convinced the murderer was one of the boat crowd. "Better eat your soup while it's hot," she said, and handed him a piece of bread. "By the way, not to change the subject or anything, but did you get a chance to call your sister?"

"Humph, back at you. The subject will come up again, Boat Mama! And yes, I did get hold of Marla." He sat back, his face reflecting an undercurrent of emotions. "She has some nebulous complaints, as usual, about health as always, but this time they concerned Barney. She didn't mention her own gamut of maladies for a change."

"That's scary. When Marla doesn't detail at least one physical complaint it's a miracle. But something wrong with Barney? Is this her idea or his?"

"Good question. She said he doesn't seem himself at all. I guess that makes it her diagnosis. Let's hope so, I can't imagine Marla taking care of Barney. That would be a switch."

Sally frowned and made a whistling noise with her lips. "Never going to happen," she predicted.

The sun sank slowly while Pete and Sally ate in silence, watching the fiery red underbelly of the clouds bleed into the horizon where it met the scarlet sea. High above, in the darker reaches of the night, flickers of lightning danced across the sky like whirling dervishes, with thunder for applause.

After dinner they laid on deck sipping brandy and listening to classical music. Pete went below and brought back some pillows. They listened to Placido Domingo and fell asleep to the gentle sound of the trade winds humming in the sailboat rigging.

In the wee hours of the morning the air turned to mist, followed by a torrential rain, driving them below. They had expected it, and had battened down in preparation.

Daybreak found them no worse for wear, and the weather outlook unchanged.

Sally emerged from the cockpit to greet the morning. She looked down the beach. Her cry of joy brought Pete on the run. The gifts on the sand were gone and she was beside herself with excitement. She hopped up and down on deck.

"Hold it," Pete warned. "You're getting carried away as usual. This doesn't mean the hermit wants to make friends. In fact, he might not have taken them at all. The wind and rain may have beat him to them."

"Don't be so negative," she said, her face aglow with satisfaction. "We're in touch! I know it. We'll stay clear of his section of island. Give him lots of space! Of course, he probably considers the whole island his."

After breakfast Pete said he wanted to give the little atoll a name.

"There you go again." Sally sighed. "You know it already has a perfectly good name on the chart." Pete tended to be compulsive about giving everybody and everything nicknames. She might as well join in the selection so they would end up with something reasonable.

After several atrocious suggestions by Pete, they agreed to name the island Eremites, a Greek word meaning desert dweller or religious hermit. It fit well enough because the island was desert-like and a hermit lived there. Sally doubted he was religious or even sane for that matter, but who cared? Pete went below and penciled the new name on their chart.

The wind picked up as another squall line moved in from the south. They decided to race before the storm, hoping to be back in the harbor before it caught up with them. Pete removed the engine from the dinghy and lashed it on deck and together they reefed the main, then Sally went forward to raise the anchor and they sailed off the hook.

FIFTEEN

THE DAY BLOSSOMED with promise, cool, crisp and blustery. Sea birds rode the currents of wind like roller coaster cars, only flapping their wings now and then to change direction. The surface remained choppy, but not uncomfortably so. The waves sent a fine spray of seawater over the deck as Sere Dina sliced through the closely spaced troughs.

The little squall caught up with them near the harbor entrance. Pete quickly lowered the sails and covered them while Sally started the diesel engine. They motored to their anchorage.

Then the rain came once more. It came in sheets and buckets, obliterating their view of the other boats in the harbor. Knowing the value of free water, Sally and Pete stripped off their clothes and bathed on deck.

Thirty minutes later the storm blew over leaving Sally unsure it had ever really occurred. The sun shone brightly and the wind wound down to a gentle breeze. She watched the steam rising from the sodden earth of the island, just as Mae described it.

The trip proved good for them. Pete refrained from giving her too much flak about investigating Rita's murder. Of course, the subject of the diary never came up, or things might have gone differently. She would have to tell him about it eventually, but why rile him unnecessarily when she might never even get her hands on the darn thing.

Sally glanced at the island and the surrounding boats, amazed how much at home she felt. Had Rita felt like this?

Damn! She would kill to get that diary. Well, maybe not kill, she thought with amusement. And why didn't Jake give it to the police? Someone murdered Rita. Surely evidence might be found in the pages of the little red book. And what a way to find out everything she wanted to know about boat dollies! Was this the book Ruth saw Rita copy at the hospital? The one she was afraid to copy elsewhere because someone watched her every move? It had to be. Sally needed the diary for a zillion reasons.

Joseph stopped by to inquire about their trip. "You need to clear customs, mon?"

"Thanks," Pete answered, "but we only visited an uninhabited island. Nothing for Sally to buy, I got lucky."

Joseph seemed considerably less remote than the last time they met him. Of course, the body of Rita might have been part of the reason for his cool attitude on their first encounter. He awarded them a pleasant grin when he departed.

Mae and Jeff came over late in the afternoon on their way to the Pot and Sally invited them on board for daiquiris and snacks.

"Sounds good to me." Mae immediately hoisted herself over the gunwale and Jeff followed after securing their little boat.

Mae plunged headfirst into harbor gossip. "No one has seen or heard from Lyle or Elaine. I swear, Sally, I don't think they've left the boat since you and I saw them yesterday." She settled herself into a comfortable position against the cockpit coaming and set her already sweating drink on the deck. "And Summerswind—the boat Rita crewed on—still hasn't returned to port!"

And this, Sally thought, was the girl she had judged to be so quiet. "Slow down or back up," she cautioned. "You make me feel we've been gone for a week and it's only been one day." She passed Mae a small plate of cheese and crackers. "But tell me more about Summerswind. Can this guy leave the area with a murder investigation going on?"

"I guess," Mae told her in a conspiratorial whisper. "Why? Do you think he did it? I mean, everybody saw him with that new girl most of the night. They were at the Pot until after midnight."

"Why would I think he did it, for heaven's sake? I don't have the foggiest idea who did it!" Sally sighed. "I assumed he might have to stay around for questioning. If she had any enemies, he would know who they were. Besides her wretched family," Sally added with a scowl. "Boy, wouldn't it be nice to pin it on the three of them!"

"I bet Don moves his charter boat to another island," Mae said. "People around here gossip too much. He did really care about Rita. Jake says he's hurting big time."

"Nooo…? Gossip? On this little island? I haven't heard a word of it," Sally said facetiously.

Mae giggled. "Don't be nasty, Sally. It's not gossip when I tell you something—you're like family. And you're a liar if you say you don't want to know all this stuff."

"You're right," Sally admitted. She looked aft, where Pete and Jeff sat on the stern discussing some problem related to the boomkin. "So…Jake is concerned for Don's state of mind. That's interesting."

Sally recalled her moment of silent communication with Jake. The way he handled the conversation when Pete mentioned Becky's death. She trusted Jake's intuitive sense, but Don's behavior on the evening of Rita's death was less than commendable. Jeff said he spent the evening with another girl. Jake knew them all better than she did though. Shouldn't she trust his judgment?

"How can Jake feel sorry for Don?" Sally asked. "Let's face it, if Don hadn't driven Rita off by flirting with the other girl she might not be dead. We still don't know if someone planned to murder Rita, or things went wrong somehow and she was just a hapless victim."

"You answered the main question. Why Jake would feel sorry for Don. Don has to feel somewhat responsible because he drove her off that night, right? Besides Jake cared for Rita and Don a lot. He respected their sailing ability for one thing and he probably spent more time with them than anyone. They were the best in the harbor. Rita and Don fought on a regular basis. Shoot, I doubt they loved each other anyway. But they were a good team and I think underneath it all, good friends. Big deal, they fought as usual. Only this time they didn't get to make up." Mae ate the lemon slice off her drink and stared at Sally with an expectant expression.

"Just for drill," Sally stirred her drink, "let's pretend that Don did murder Rita."

Mae came to attention with a perceptible shiver. "All ri...ght, Sally Sleuth! I'm with you."

"You ninny! Be serious for a minute. If Don had some reason to kill Rita—and I won't suggest one since I didn't know either of them—but pretend he did, the smart thing for him to do would be to establish an alibi, a very believable alibi. You say they fought regularly. Why mess with an established pattern? Why not use it instead. Get Rita drunk, flirt with another girl, get in a fight, then have everyone witness Rita's departure."

Mae fluttered her long eyelashes, her face a puzzle as she listened to Sally's scenario. "Motive," she said after a moment. "We need a motive. He could have dumped her any time he wanted. Why set up anything. Happens all the time in the boating scene. It sure wasn't for money or love. Rita was short on both."

"You never really know what goes on in other people's

lives," Sally said. "Perhaps she knew some horrible secret about him and he was afraid she would tell. Was she much of a talker when it came to other people?"

"No, not really, I mean not much of a talker, but yes she knew a lot about everybody. And I think she did use it for her own self-interest." Mae drained her drink. "Rita's been around though, if you know what I mean. And not just with the boating crowd. She could write a book on this island."

"She did write a book. Remember what Ruth said? I really would like to get my hands on that little volume. It has to be the same one we saw Jake drop back into the dock box when Rita's family came for her things." Sally frowned in remembrance. She rose to make them another drink.

"I asked Jake if I could see it," Mae admitted as she followed Sally below to the galley.

"You're kidding," Sally turned to her. "What did he say? And when did you ask him?"

"He didn't say anything. Just gave me one of those looks he reserves for tourists. It was embarrassing. Oh well, I tried. I crewed on his boat yesterday after you left, because Jeff is still working on our electrical problems. Which reminds me, Jake asked if you would like to go along tomorrow. Not to work, just to see what chartering is like. He thinks you're special, mumbled something about Claudette being a genius to appoint you as boat mama."

Sally felt flattered by Jake's vote of confidence. To go along on one of his charters seemed a heaven-sent opportunity. It would give her a first-hand look at the realm of boat dollies. And she could use the occasion to quiz Jake; perhaps even talk him into letting her take a peek at Rita's diary.

"Sounds like fun." She handed Mae a fresh drink. "Now I need to convince Pete that I didn't invite myself. He feels

I stick my nose in dangerous territory every time I ask around about Rita."

As though on cue, Pete and Jeff arrived for the cheese and crackers. They met in the close confines of the main salon.

Sally studied Jeff. He looked particularly wholesome today. That was a worrisome thought. She'd been in the islands too long when Jeff struck her as normal.

Jeff smiled his brightest for her as though aware of her approval.

"There's something I want to ask you, Mae," Sally stated, changing the subject for the benefit of the fellows. "What is a joy-bath? I've heard you use the term."

"That's easy. Let's go topside and I'll tell you how it got started."

They went forward and sat on the cabin top.

"You know how not having enough water can be a real problem on boats in some parts of the world?" Mae asked. "And how we all try to take a bath with hardly a teacup of fresh water, which is not always pleasant? The best thing to do is bathe in salt water and save the teacup to rinse with. The only problem is that it's almost impossible to work up a lather in salt water. It doesn't bubble up, suds or whatever. Then somebody discovered that Joy dish soap does, and...the Joy bath was born."

"But I've seen soap in the marine stores that promises to work in salt water," Sally interrupted.

"Sure they make them now, especially for salt water. But have you checked the prices on those bottles?"

"And you say that Joy is the only one that works in salt water, outside of the ones in the marine stores, that is?"

"No, in fact it turns out that a lot of liquid dish soaps work pretty well, but the term 'Joy bath' stuck." Mae smiled. "I think it's because it so perfectly describes the activity. I remember one time when Jeff and I had been out for about four days. We were low on water and miserably salt encrusted. As soon as we dropped anchor I climbed into the dinghy with a bucket and filled it with salt water. I let the sun warm it for about thirty minutes and then I took my bottle of Joy and had the most wonderful bubble bath of my life."

Jeff's expression when he came up the companionway implied their time was up. Sally wondered why he talked at all when he could say so much without words. They agreed to meet later at the Pot.

Pete and Sally went to dinner at a restaurant Jeff suggested earlier. It served seafood the way the locals preferred it, spicy! They ordered grouper, marinated in an exquisite red sauce, then broiled to perfection. Sally washed hers down with a rum punch, but Pete stuck to beer. She recognized several boaters among the customers.

They arrived at the Pot after nine and the crowd was already pretty well oiled. They squeezed in next to Mae and Jeff. Sally once again found herself facing Jake across the bar. She watched Jake's gaze wander up and down the group with a decidedly bored expression.

The noise level made it hard to carry on a conversation. Someone at the far end of the bar tried to get a singalong going. Impossible. Sally saw Jake shake his head. A small smile played at the corners of his mouth. He raised his hand in the air with a flourish.

"Excuse me. "Excuse me, please!" Jake waved his arm to get their attention. Some of the noise died down as more and more of the group turned to the commotion. "I need to ask a question here."

The bar became quiet. "I need to know something," he said, his arm still held high. "How many men in this room have been circumcised? Please, raise your hands."

There was dead silence at the bar now. People from the tables gathered around. The men looked at each other for guidance.

"Come on now," Jake insisted. "This is not a difficult question, is it? We're all adults here. I'll repeat the question for you. How many men here have been circumcised?"

One hand at the end of the bar crept sheepishly into the air. Then another. Jake started counting aloud. "Three, four, okay there's five." No more hands appeared. "Five of you, huh?" Jake chuckled. "Well I'll be damned!" With a satisfied smirk he sat down.

One of the hand raisers muttered under his breath. "Son of a bitch. We've been had!"

The man next to him nudged him. "Hey, man, that's far out. Cool. I didn't know you were circumcised."

"Remind me never to answer any of Jake's questions right away," Sally said to Mae.

Mae repeated her suggestion that Sally go out on Jake's boat the following day. When Pete didn't react negatively to the idea, Sally jumped on it. But she begged off the early morning charter, opting for the late one. She planned to track down Elaine.

During a lull in conversation, Claudette drew Sally aside for a private drilling. "How Elaine be, Boat Mama?"

"I'm working on the problem," Sally assured her.

"You hear about that Rita girl? You know she be murdered?" Claudette asked. She leaned close to Sally's ear.

"I've heard the rumors, murder by strangulation, right?"

"No rumor, Boat Mama. Somebody strangle that girl, for sure. Somebody real mean. You got to do something before another boat girl die."

"Why me?" Sally asked in alarm.

Claudette looked at her incredulously. "Because you

the boat mama now, girls going to talk to you. You tell me, I tell Joseph."

Before Sally could reply to this outrageous suggestion, Claudette was called back to her duties at the bar. Sally decided she would keep this subtly official request to herself.

SIXTEEN

GAINING AN AUDIENCE with Elaine the next day turned out to be easier than Sally expected. While she enjoyed her usual morning cocoa on deck, Sally saw Lyle leave Lady Jane in the dinghy, alone. She quickly went below, threw on some clothes and told Pete she would be back. He more or less snored an acknowledgment.

Getting Elaine's attention once she tucked alongside the Lady Jane proved more difficult. After a few loud shouts, she knocked on the hull in the vicinity of what she imagined should be the aft cabin. Elaine at last appeared at the rail. She looked pale and tired.

"Are you all right?" Sally asked. "I hope I didn't wake you," she continued, without waiting for an answer. "Mae and I came over the other day but Lyle said you weren't feeling well." She certainly didn't look well now.

"I think it's just a flu or something." She didn't meet Sally's eyes when she spoke." Sorry it took me so long," she apologized. "Come aboard. I'll make some coffee."

Sally climbed to the deck and waited in the cockpit while Elaine made the coffee. Permission to come aboard was one thing, and permission to go below, another. Many small boats were just one large area inside, so going below was like walking into the bedroom.

Elaine brought two coffees on deck and they made small talk.

Sally studied her. It was time for the direct approach. It worked for Claudette, why not for her? "My dear," Sally said, placing her hand over Elaine's. "You and I both know why I'm here. The other night you said you needed to talk. If you've changed your mind or the situation has resolved itself, just say so. On the other hand, I'm here to listen... and help if I can. You don't really have the flu, do you?"

Again, the tactic worked magically. Suddenly Elaine was reduced to a sobbing heap. "What am I going to do? I'm pregnant!"

Sally sighed. "Elaine, being pregnant is not the end of the world, you know that. I won't bring up the subject of marriage or anything, but I have to assume Lyle is less than happy about the situation."

"So am I. What are we going to do? Marriage has nothing to do with it. I mean I guess we'll probably marry, but it's not important. How are we going to live? No one wants to charter a boat with a pregnant woman on it, much less a baby."

"Okay, okay. So, is this what you and Lyle argued about? Is adoption a consideration? Surely you've discussed options. Can either of you do something besides the charter business?"

"I guess one of us will have to, because we would never abort or put our baby up for adoption." She sobbed again. "That's what we fought about. He thinks I've done something to lose the baby."

Sally stroked Elaine's hair gently, soothing her as she would a small child, as she wished she could have soothed Becky. "Obviously, you did not. Now what made him think so? Did you sound him out on the idea? Something certainly set him off. When did your disagreements start?"

Elaine sat up straight, wiping her face on her sleeve. "Last week. I went shopping. I was gone most of the day, longer than I usually am. I started having some weird pains, so I took my time, trying not to exert myself. I've been so tired lately anyway. I had a terrible time getting back to the boat. When I got on board, I passed out. I woke up and Lyle was standing over me, asking me what the hell I had done. He said I was bleeding. I looked down at my dress. It was true. I was scared to death. There was blood everywhere. I went in and cleaned up. It had stopped. It hasn't happened again. He thinks I went to one of those places and did something to lose the baby!"

"Let's talk about the pregnancy for just a minute. Exactly how pregnant are you?"

"Three or four months, I think. I've never been regular so I can't be sure."

"You can't be, but a doctor can certainly give you a pretty good estimate. Please…Please tell me you have seen one, haven't you?" Sally was afraid of the answer.

The sound of Lyle's outboard made Elaine jump up without answering.

She wiped her face on her sleeve again. "Let's talk about something else. Lyle is a very private person. That's why I couldn't talk to the other girls. There are no secrets in the harbor. He said I could talk to you, but…."

"Fine, I understand. Answer my question though, have you seen a doctor?"

"No, I don't need to. I know I'm pregnant. I took one of those tests you give yourself."

"Oh, great, just great." Sally flinched, horrified by her own words. The same last words she said to Becky.

Would they never stop echoing through her life. Becky was gone. Never forgotten, but gone. She would not leave Elaine with those same words. "Elaine, I think you should go to a doctor, and I think you should do it right now. Let me take you. Please."

"I'll get Lyle to take me tomorrow."

"I think you should go right now!" Sally insisted.

SEVENTEEN

THERE WERE TWENTY people waiting on the pier when Sally and Mae arrived. Jake wouldn't allow anyone to board his charter boat until they got there, because he didn't, as Mae explained, "want those sneaky tourists prowling around down below by themselves."

Jake's boat was named Fidelity. She was forty-six feet in length overall, had a full keel and a beam that made her roomy, though rolly at sea. "It's not the sort of boat I imagined Jake would own," Sally told Mae.

"You're right," Mae agreed. "This boat is strictly business for Jake. Have you seen the gorgeous green sloop anchored near the marina? That's Jake's true love. One of these days he swears he's going to sail away on her, to someplace where the tourists don't shine, as he puts it."

Sally and Mae helped the customers board and explained how to work the handles on the heads so as not to sink the boat. Mae cautioned her they would still have to check them from time to time.

"Isn't it nice the way Jake takes the time to talk to the children?" Sally observed. "He even smiles at them."

Mae's expression froze. "He's really a jewel, right? Why don't you move up close and see what he's saying to the little darlings?"

Sally drifted along the deck in Jake's direction just as a family boarded with a chubby young boy in tow. "Go along, folks," Jake encouraged the parents, "and I'll be explaining a few nautical facts to the lad here." He patted the boy's head affectionately. Sally could see the flash of appreciation on the faces of the parents. A real sea captain was going to give their little Johnny special instruction.

What Sally had taken for a smile from a distance, she could see close at hand, was Jake talking through clenched teeth. He took the boy firmly by the arm and led him aside. "Son," he said, pointing skyward. "You see the pole there? Well, that's the mainmast. Can you remember that?"

"Of course," the boy answered in a sarcastic whine. "Everybody knows that. Can I climb it?"

"Nope." This time the smile was sincere. "I've electrified it!" Jake stared down at the child and increased the pressure on his arm.

"That's stupid, you can't do...." The words died in his throat when he looked up into Jake's stony features. A glimmer of doubt crossed the boy's cherubic, spoiled features.

Jake pointed to where the boy's parents leaned contentedly against the rail. They waved and smiled to their son and his new friend, the captain. "That part of the boat is called forward," Jake continued. He turned around. "Back there, where I sit, that's called aft. If you misbehave on this trip, or even set foot on the aft deck, you're going to be shark bait. Do you want me to explain to you what shark bait is?"

A hint of intelligence flickered in the boy's deep-set, brown eyes. "Ah... No, I think I get it."

"I think I get it, *Captain*!" Jake corrected. "Wave at Mommy."

"I think I get it, Captain," the boy repeated, waving dutifully at Mommy.

"Good lad. Now run along. I believe we'll both enjoy ourselves on this voyage."

Sally gleefully revealed the highlights of this conversation to Mae while they made sandwiches for the tourists. Like most charter boat captains, Jake deposited his charges on a small island where they could picnic or snorkel along the shore.

"Jake handles each kid differently." Mae laughed. "He uses the instruction with the mast, or another elementary item, to sound them out, to see if they smart off or not. Sometimes he's actually nice to them, he even let one hold the wheel yesterday. I could hardly believe it! He's the same way with kids as he is with grown-ups I guess. He either likes them or he doesn't, no middle ground."

The sail to the island was accomplished without incident. Soon, most of the passengers strolled the beach or paddled along the edge of the reef with Mae for a guide. Sally offered to assist but Jake suggested she stay aboard with the few remaining tourists.

"You want the truth, Sally?" Mae had told with a sly grin. "It's time for Jake's nap. Jake is not about to play host. You're in charge." She giggled.

The steam rose off the deck in the late afternoon sun, but Sally didn't envy Mae's duty on the beach, it might be worse there. She felt relieved two hours later when Jake came on deck to signal a return to the boat.

Once underway, the breeze made life comfortable again. For a while it looked as though they would be able to maintain a beam reach all the way to the harbor. Mae and Sally joined Jake in the aft cockpit and concocted rum punches for the customers.

Everything seemed fine until Sally noticed Jake glance behind him more often than she thought normal. When the passengers stared aft too, she and Mae turned to see what captured their attention.

Mae stifled a small gasp. A huge boat bore down on their stern—only yards away.

"Keep the panic to yourselves!" Jake ordered quietly. "The passengers think this is all in a day's sail. He's been back there for about ten minutes, but he's just playing with us. Don't worry." Jake grinned.

Don't worry? Sally thought. Easy to say, but it looked for all the world as though the other boat might soon ram them. Sally braced herself against the coaming.

"I'm going to pull off a bit now and see if he'll pass us." Jake steered slightly to starboard, but the other boat held her course in Fidelity's path.

"Mae?" Sally turned and spoke softly. "What the hell is going on?"

"That's Don in our wake, on Summerswind, you know, the boat Rita was on? And I don't know what he's up to any more than you do."

"Hold tight!" Jake warned under his breath. The sleek little yawl behind them made its move, closing in on their port side. For a few heart-stopping moments the people on Fidelity could have alighted on the other deck without missing a step. Then the other vessel took their wind and Fidelity's sails fluttered briefly and they dropped back. Without warning, Summerswind cut sharply to starboard, only inches short of their bow.

The tourists cheered and waved.

"Damn," Jake exclaimed for Sally and Mae's ears. "The morons are encouraging him."

Sure enough, the other boat came about once more.

"Is he crazy, or what?" Sally demanded.

"Well, he's probably drunk, but I don't believe he's crazy," Jake said. "Let's just hope he's as good a sailor as I think he is. Don's got a few problems to work out of his system, that's all. Hot damn! If I had Verity out here, I'd give him a run for his money." His face lit up at the thought. "Here he comes again!" Jake clenched his teeth into a smile and the tourists cheered.

"Verity is the name of Jake's other boat," Mae told Sally. "Do you think he cared that much about Rita?" she asked Jake with a frown. "Do you think he loved her?"

"Hah!" Jake snorted. "About as much as Lance loves Lisa! No, I don't think this is about love, ladies. I think it's about life. Don's a pretty regular guy. He's working off a heavy case of guilt and he's working it off the only way he knows how. He's probably been charging reefs and rocks for the past few days. Another sailboat makes a more worthy opponent. Son of a bitch!" Jake muttered, as Summerswind came-about directly in Fidelity's path.

Jake pulled the wheel to starboard just in time. Again the two boats almost kissed. "I hate this damned walrus of a boat!" Jake swore, slapping Fidelity's hull as he watched the other boat slice through the water with grace.

These maneuvers continued for a full thirty minutes, till Don finally tired of the game. Sally felt weak from the tension of so many close calls. Jake, on the other hand, seemed invigorated by the encounter. The tourists gave Don an enthusiastic goodbye, waving wildly when he raised his hand in a salute to Jake.

Sally needed a drink. She made herself a second rum punch and settled back in the cockpit while Mae went below to check on things.

"Saw your boat over at the Lady Jane this morning," Jake said in a low voice. "Visiting Elaine were you?"

Evidently, Sally speculated, Elaine was right when she suggested everyone in the harbor knew each other's business.

"Yes," she replied, carefully, remembering her own caution about answering Jake's questions too quickly.

"Those two seem to be having some problems," Jake continued. "Nice young couple like that, it's a shame."

"Really." Sally was on the defensive now. Jake was the last person in the world she would suspect to be nosey. He had to be up to something.

"They haven't been doing much chartering lately. This is the peak season. You've got to work every day just to keep afloat. Little pun there." He raised his eyebrows and smiled. "Wonder what the problem is?"

"I'll say this for you," Sally responded. "Your humor is better honed than your subtlety."

"Okay. Point well taken. Now, are you going to tell me what the hell their problem is or not?" Jake countered.

"Or not!" Sally retorted a bit too loudly. Several tourists glanced at them. She frowned at Jake.

Jake's eyes glinted with satisfaction.

"Is this a test?" Sally asked, not sure what Jake was up to.

Jake laughed at her. "It was," he said. He reached into a compartment in the hull. "Here. This is for you. Since you obviously intend to take this boat mama thing seriously. This might give you some insight into what these girls are really like from a slightly more subjective angle."

Sally recognized Rita's small red book. Her heart raced with excitement. Rita's diary!

She looked up at Jake, trying to read his expression. "Have you read it?" she asked.

He sneered at her. "Is this a test?"

It was Sally's turn to laugh.

"Destroy it when you're finished reading it, or do what you like with it. You care more about Rita than the vipers she called family, and you never even knew her. I trust you'll put the information to good use."

Their eyes met. There it was again, that contact. She hadn't imagined it. She nodded in agreement.

"Wait a minute!" Sally worried, coming to her senses. "Rita was murdered. Shouldn't the authorities have this? There might be something incriminating in here." She held the book in the air.

"Put the damn book down," Jake yelled in a harsh whisper. "No one is going to know you have it unless you tell them. I made a copy of it and gave it to Joseph, day one." He bared his teeth when he spoke. "Do you take me for a dolt?"

"But shouldn't they have the original? I mean…."

"Confound it, woman! There are no buts. They have a copy I told you, and a copy is just words. Rita *touched* this one. It's the one you need." Jake stared stonily out to sea.

Sally went below properly chastened, careful not to let anyone see her when she placed the valuable little diary in her purse. Not even Mae. She knew that whatever Rita had written in those pages might be the insight she sought to help unravel the mystery of the boat dollie milieu. Revelations concerning Rita's murderer, she dared not contemplate. Sally felt she was the recipient of a great treasure. With strong resolve, she promised herself not to open the first page until she was back on Sere Dina. But, she would tell Pete. Even he might be interested in the inner thoughts of a boat dollie.

EIGHTEEN

SALLY AND PETE listened to the weather report during dinner. It wasn't too promising, although the tropical storm had been downgraded to a depression. Unfortunately, it still churned in their direction. At least they wouldn't have to seek safe harbor, Sere Dina could ride this one out at anchor.

Pete and Jeff managed to sort out the electrical problem on Jeff's boat. It came down to a short, but it had taken them all day to find it.

"Jeff and Mae have a weekend charter coming up," Pete told Sally. "I found out a few other interesting facts that I know will fascinate Boat Mama, too." He whistled as he passed Sally on his way topside.

Sally grabbed her cocoa and followed. "Like what? Don't toy with me."

"How about the fact that Jeff and Mae own the boat together?" He studied her for a reaction.

"Together, as in man and wife?" Sally asked. "Now that I think of it, I never asked Mae if they were married or not. What else?" She could tell by his expression he held something back.

"Don't know about the man and wife part, just that they own the boat together. No mortgage either, it's theirs free and clear. Doesn't mean much I guess. On the other hand it speaks of some small security for at least one of Boat Mama's charges."

This information did comfort Sally, because it meant

there wouldn't be any dollies bumping Mae off a boat that was half hers. It meant other things, too, things she couldn't quite put her finger on—good things for Mae.

She told Pete the events of her day on Fidelity in great detail.

"I would have loved to have seen Don cutting-up out there. Especially if he's as good as Jake claims. Darn, I never get to have any fun," he teased.

"Fun? Right. I was scared spitless!"

Pete was surprisingly disinterested in her attainment of the diary. The difference, Sally thought, between men and women, lies therein. It required great willpower for her not to attack the diary during dinner. And it was almost ten o'clock before she finally got a chance to open the book, because she could swear Pete deliberately stalled her with after-dinner conversation.

Sally crawled into the V-berth and turned on her reading light. The first entry in the book was simply dated by month.

March

I've decided to leave. There's nothing here for me. There never was! I'm not giving notice either. I've saved enough money to last a while, so color me gone. I hate my stupid job. It's time to start over again. I saw a beautiful, beautiful boat today. It was named Odds Are and it was from Port Charlotte. That is so weird. It was like a sign or something. That's exactly where I am planning to go anyway. It would be so cool if I ended up on Odds Are. I called home today. Mother was too busy with her bridge group to talk to me. I hope she's not mad at me. Sometimes I feel so lonely. I wonder if anyone will

miss me when I leave here. I can't believe I've been
here almost a year. I don't think I'll even say goodbye to anybody. I'll just disappear. Let them wonder
what happened to me. I hate this place.

Sally felt like a peeping Doug, but not enough to stop
her from reading. Rita's handwriting was so small and
tight it was hard to read even with glasses. Every inch of
every page was full, right up to the last entry. Sally read
quickly. An entry in 1989 saddened her.

April 1989

What the hell's wrong with me anyway? I can't believe the mess I've made of things. Why am I so stupid? I almost landed the perfect boat. But no, I get
drunk and make an ass of myself. It's no wonder nobody likes me. I am dumb, dumb, dumb! Mother was
right. Why couldn't I have turned out like Cynthia?
I don't know if I'll be able to keep my job much longer, not without screwing that fat pig of a manager
anyway. I'd rather starve. He practically drools on
me every time he passes my counter. Help! I talked
to Evelyn yesterday and she said they were hiring
at that new restaurant on the water. Shit, I hope she
hasn't heard about last night. With my luck, the
whole world has heard. One good thing I guess. I
sure enjoyed the look on that woman's face just before I threw her in the pool. Mother and Daddy have
one of those new tape things on their phone. Maybe
it's not working. I've been leaving messages for a
week. I'll try again tomorrow. I wish I were dead.

Rita, Rita, Sally thought. Why were you so hard on

yourself? Sally bet anything Rita's wretched parents received every one of those messages, and probably bought the machine so they could screen out her calls. Sally read the entry again. Who was the manager Rita mentioned? Could it be Tim? Where was Tim before he came here? Sally propped herself up on her pillow.

Sally read for an hour, randomly. One hour of her life and years of Rita's. Several really nasty characters were described who were worthy of a second look. Could one of them be Rita's murderer? One recent entry intrigued Sally. It described a confrontation with someone, probably someone at the Pot. Unfortunately, no name was mentioned.

August

Dealt with the creep again. We almost got in a fight. I think he would have slapped me if we weren't in public. He's useful at times but sometimes he's a little scary. I've thought about telling Evelyn the truth about him, but on the other hand why give away all my secrets. At least he's not after me lately, not since he focused on Ruth. Of course, everyone's focused on Ruth. Was I ever that innocent? When I was ten maybe. Worked my butt off today on the bottom of the boat. We always manage to haul-out in ninety degree weather. I am so tan I could pass for one of the natives. I'll probably end up looking like a piece of old leather before I'm thirty. Hope I can sleep tonight. I'm burnt up and worn out and I've got the frigging cramps again.

Was everyone after Ruth? Apparently so, there was no real clue there. Or was there? Sally turned to the final entry in Rita's book, an innocuous one, detailing a slow day-charter on Summerswind. It could have even been written the day before she died, but there was no way of telling. Rita only recorded dates by months and years, not days. Sally put the book aside, then reached up to turn out the light. Her hand brushed Pete's gun. The muzzle had been bumped and now faced her head. She cringed, then gently turned the gun around with a sigh. Rita's revelations left her feeling lonely and insecure. She slid down and nestled against Pete.

She conjured up the picture of Rita's body in the dinghy once more, the body that was now a real person to her. A sad woman whose self-esteem had been wrung from her at an early age, then generously poured over her sister Cynthia. Sally squeezed her eyes tight to keep from crying.

What made someone murder Rita? Joseph had a copy of the diary and he hadn't arrested anyone. Still, reading it brought the woman to life for Sally. She almost wished Becky had kept one, but then thought better of the idea. Preferable to remember all the good moments unblemished by the inner thoughts of those you loved the most. One wound inflicted by Sally and recorded by Becky might be more than she could bear.

Her last thoughts before falling asleep were not about Rita, however, they were about Elaine. Rita deserved justice and Sally was determined to find it for her, however long it took. But Elaine was alive and needed her help, now. She consoled herself with the fact that Elaine had sworn to see a doctor. The problems she described might mean many more things than being pregnant. Sally was no doctor, but she had clearly seen the girl was in pain when she visited.

NINETEEN

ARMANDO ACHED ALL over. Damp and tired. Here he sat on a fish-encrusted seawall in the middle of the night. Definitely not his kind of assignment. How in the name of Jesus, Mary and Joseph was he supposed to follow people who lived on a sailboat? Armando hated to do water things. And why in the devil did he have to sit here day after day and watch these people run around in a rubber dinghy?

He'd hoped when they'd sailed out of the harbor they would keep on going. Or that he would be free until he got a call that they returned. But no, sailboat people were different he was told. They sometimes arrived in the middle of the night, or the middle of a storm even. Idiots! So he sat there for two days and sure enough they returned in a raging squall.

He took a long pull from his hip flask. It scorched his throat and heated his guts. Good stuff. He flashed his pen light briefly around the area where he sat, checking for roaches. The frigging things were everywhere at night. Worse yet were the rats. Some of those suckers were the size of cats. Hell, he couldn't tell one from the other half the time. Except when the stupid cats started hollering, fighting over fish remains or mating half the frigging night!

Armando startled at the sound of an approaching vehicle. Lights appeared at the end of the alleyway. He quickly moved behind one of the dry-docked boats that peppered the area. He waited—and watched.

A jeep pulled up to the seawall with its lights on to illuminate the boats. A man got out, went to the back of the jeep and removed a small outboard engine. He carried it to one of the dinghies, then returned and turned off the headlights.

Armando recognized Joseph. Where could he be going this time of the night?

SALLY DREAMED THAT someone knocked at the door. She woke up to tapping on the side of the hull. She nudged Pete. "There's someone outside."

"What the hell?" Pete turned on the overhead light.

A soft voice called from outside. "Boat Mama, Boat Mama, you got to come!"

"Now what?" Pete said aloud. "Sounds like it's a job for...*Boat Mama.*" He swung his feet over the side of the bed and grabbed a pair of shorts. "I'll go find out what the problem is."

Sally pulled the pillow over her face to block out the light.

Pete was back in less than a minute. "It's that customs fellow, Joseph. Bad news I'm afraid. It's Elaine, she's in the hospital. He says they don't expect her to live. She's asked for you. He wants to take you to the hospital."

"I'll go, of course. How terrible! Damn it all. I can't believe this. I've let her down. I should have dragged her to the hospital when I had the chance."

Pete wrapped his arms around her. "Stop it! You are not responsible for everything." He tipped her chin up. "Do you want me to take you instead?"

"No, there's no reason for you to sit in a hospital waiting. And you're right, I need to get a grip. Blame serves no useful purpose." She straightened. "Leave the radio on and I'll reach you through the marine operator."

He frowned. "I know this is important to you. But what if I want to be there for you? Isn't that what this trip is all about? My not being there when Becky died? Not being there when you needed me afterwards?"

Sally reached up and took his face in her hands. "It was once, but not anymore. It's my dependence on you when you weren't there that I'm dealing with now. For us to be whole together, we have to be whole alone too, secure in ourselves so we can give of ourselves, not just take from each other."

Pete hugged her tightly, then held her at arm's length. "I'm working on it. I'll go tell Joseph you're coming."

Sally threw on some clothes and grabbed her purse.

"How did you become involved in this, Joseph?" Sally inquired as they rode the dinghy to shore.

Joseph patted the side of his boat proudly. "Because I have this, my boat."

The jeep he drove to the hospital reminded her of Jake's car. Sally was glad it was dark. If crawly things scurried underfoot, she couldn't see them.

Sally followed the signs to the intensive care unit, where she found Lyle perched on the edge of a chair, head bowed, with a large Styrofoam cup in front of him. Hot steam rose from it. Sally looked around for the source of this treasure. She could certainly use a hot cup of coffee right now. It was two-thirty in the morning.

Sally squeezed Lyle's shoulder lightly and he jumped, almost spilling his coffee. He sprang to his feet and extended a hand to her. "Sally, thank you for coming."

"Don't be so formal." She reached past his extended hand and put her arms around him. She could feel him tremble.

"Where did you get that coffee?" she asked, taking the

seat next to him. "I need a kick start to wake me up. You can fill me in on the situation while we walk."

"Let me get it," he insisted. "What do you take in it?"

"Cream."

"It's just around the corner. I'll be right back."

Sally stared at the door beside her, labeled ICU. Just then, Doctor Winters exited—the doctor who had shown such an interest in Ruth. She resisted an impulse to stop him and ask what was going on. She would find out soon enough.

Lyle returned with the coffee. "She's been really sick for a couple of days now. You're probably aware of that. I don't know what all she told you the other day. Damn, I treated her so badly this last week. It will be my fault if she dies."

"I know you thought she had done something to abort the pregnancy."

Lyle looked up at her with a pained expression. "I feel horrible about everything. It's hard to explain."

"Come on, give it a try, Lyle." She looked at the door. "What's going on in there? Joseph said she might die. Did she lose the baby? What went wrong?"

Lyle shuddered and stared at the floor. "It was a tubal pregnancy. It must have ruptured into her abdomen a few days ago. They've given her blood. There's a lot of infection and all, which is why they're telling me she might not make it." He buried his face in his hands. "She woke up a few times but she won't talk to me."

"I'm sorry, Lyle," she consoled him. "But don't lose heart. I think what doctors do is tell you the worst that can happen, to prepare you I guess, in case it does. She's still alive in there, right? And she made it through the operation. Have you contacted her family?"

"I asked her tonight. She said she has no family. Thinking back on it, she never did mention a family. Listen, you're not going to like this, but there have been other girls on my boat, okay? I never asked about their pasts. And mine was none of their business. They're boat dollies, for Christ's sake. They come and go like the weather. You may interpret that as shallow, but some of the women are damned callous, too. I know a couple who would abandon you with a two-week charter coming up, because a nicer boat came along that day."

"Is that how you see Elaine, as a boat dollie?"

Lyle turned his deeply tanned face toward Sally. He reminded her of Pete when he was younger. "She came to the Lady Jane from another boat. What can I say? Somewhere along the line I began to care about her. I managed to shut down the feeling several times, because I knew she could disappear the way she came. Then, when she became pregnant, everything changed. I let myself care, a lot. And you know the rest. I figured she tried to get rid of the baby and I almost hated her."

"Sounds like love to me. Love hate, love hate. The old yoyo syndrome. How about her? Does she say she loves you?" Sally put her hand on his shoulder.

"I don't know. It's something we never discussed. It's like the background stuff. There are things we never talked about."

"Good grief!" Sally exclaimed. She wound her fingers through her pony tail.

"I know," he said. "It's a mess, isn't it? I wish the doctor would come out."

"He did, while you were getting the coffee."

Lyle jumped up and dashed to the nurses' station. "Could you tell me where the doctor went, please? I want to talk to him."

Doctor Winters came down the hall straightening his collar as they spoke. "I'm right here, Lyle."

He nodded to Sally when Lyle introduced them. "I'm glad you were able to come." He doesn't remember me, Sally thought. Because he never saw me, just Ruth.

"I assume Lyle has informed you the prognosis isn't favorable at this time. Elaine is very weak. Elaine has been asking for you, but she probably shouldn't have any visitors until tomorrow."

"I would like to see her now," Sally said. Doctors did not put her at a disadvantage anymore. Not since Becky's brief stay in the hospital. Now she was careful never to let her requests sound like favors when she spoke to doctors. If Elaine wanted to see her, Sally would make it happen.

Doctor Winters shrugged and took her arm. "Let's go."

Sally hated the dismal, sterile atmosphere of hospitals and the intensive care unit was by far the worst. Many people never came out of this room alive, she knew. Becky never woke up in just such a room. Thank God this island had a medical facility that was fairly modern. Some did not. Money made the difference. Machines blinked and gurgled as she passed betubed patients on either side. There were four patients in the room. Elaine's curtained-off area was the last on the right.

Sally could hardly believe the shadow of Elaine that occupied the bed in front of her. She looked as though someone had pierced her already tiny body with a pin and deflated it. Blood and various other life-giving elixirs dribbled into her emaciated body. Sally hadn't fully accepted the suggestion that Elaine might die. Now, she gave the prognosis credence.

Doctor Winters touched Elaine's hand gently. Her eyelids fluttered briefly. He checked her pulse and made several notations on her chart, then smiled at her. "There's someone here to see you." He stepped back to make room for Sally.

The intense eyes that stared back at Sally were not those of a dying woman. It was as though Elaine's soul reached out to clutch her. The strength from within was palpable. Sally let out a sigh of relief. It would not be like it was with Becky. Becky had left her body long before the tubes stopped their relentless drip.

"Hello, dear," Sally said with renewed confidence. Elaine tried to raise her hand. Sally patted it. "Just relax for a bit. I'm going to sit with you for a while. As soon as you gather a little strength, we'll talk." She glanced at the doorway where Lyle stood with a forlorn expression. Sally gave him a thumbs-up signal and a smile. He smiled back and went outside to give the women some time together.

Sally waited, listening to Elaine's breathing. It was an hour before she opened her eyes again. Then, her voice was quiet but strong, another reassuring sign. "I'm so glad you came. Thank you."

Sally took her hand again. "I'm angry at myself for not dragging you to a doctor when I visited Lady Jane. I only left because you promised to see one yourself. I knew when I drove away from Lady Jane that something was seriously wrong."

"I sort of did too. After you left I got to thinking, what if I wasn't pregnant at all? I could have a huge tumor or cancer or heaven knows what. I might have died."

"Well, you almost did do that."

"I did?"

"Take a look around. This isn't exactly the out-patient clinic, you know. You're in intensive care. You've lost a lot of blood and you're still not out of danger. Is there someone you would like me to call?"

"No, there's no one really. Is Lyle still here?" Elaine lowered her eyes.

"Yes, he's very concerned. He feels extremely guilty about all this. Lyle loves you, Elaine."

"I thought so, until a few days ago." She turned her head away from Sally. "It doesn't matter anymore. He'll have a new boat girl before I'm even out of the hospital." She turned to Sally. There were tears in her eyes. "He should have believed me, you know. If he loved me he would have." She started to cry. "What makes you think he loves me?"

"So it doesn't matter, huh?" Sally shook her head and smiled. "I spent some time out in the hall talking to him. I recognize the truth when I hear it. Lyle's tried not to love you for a long time. He figured you would disappear on him—until the baby entered the picture and made it safe for him to love you. Then he thought you tried to get rid of it. He saw that as proof you wanted to be free to leave. I believe he was more afraid of losing you than the baby. And he's afraid you might die. He's mortified. He thinks you hate him for the way he treated you this week. Lyle's world has pretty much collapsed."

Elaine hung on Sally's every word. The knowledge of Lyle's feelings for her would probably do more for Elaine's recovery than all the bottles hanging over her bed, Sally decided. She hoped the girl wasn't too doped-up to remember the important parts.

"You're a good boat mama, Sally," Elaine said through her tears.

Sally reached out and touched Elaine's forehead, then sighed. *I was a good real mother too, I was.* "Why don't I go find the cafeteria while you rest?" Sally said. "I need a hot cup of something other than coffee. I'll send Lyle in. And speaking as your personal boat mama, it's time you two did some serious talking. You certainly can't solve all your problems tonight, or even tomorrow, but how about the basic *I love you* words for starters?"

"I'll think about it. I wish it were that easy. He should have believed me, Sally," she said, "he should have!" She closed her eyes and turned away.

Sally watched the sun rise over the harbor from the window of the waiting area. The hospital sat high on a hill overlooking the pastel buildings of the town below. The morning light brightened each house like the stroke of an artist's brush as it rose above the blue green sea. A soft breeze stirred the palms along the seawall. She looked beyond the harbor entrance, at the distant islands, her thoughts touching on the plight of the hermit. She would shop for things to bring him on their next trip.

"Sally?" A voice inquired from across the room. Ruth stood at the nurses' station. "I just came on duty. What are you doing here? Has something happened to your husband?" She consulted the list of new patients on the counter.

"No, it's Elaine. Ruptured tubal pregnancy. You know, I don't even know her last name!"

Ruth shook her head and wrung her hands. "I knew something was wrong with Elaine! I should have dragged it out of her. She'd seemed desperate to confide in someone lately."

"She did confide in someone, me," Sally said. "Unfortunately I let something get in the way of insisting she go to a doctor immediately." She turned from Ruth and stuck her head inside the door to Elaine's room. Lyle sat in the chair beside Elaine.

"I see that Doctor Winters is taking care of her," Ruth said when Sally turned around. "That's terrific." Ruth studied the records again. "Elaine could use some gentleness right now."

"Do you know Doctor Winters well?" Sally asked.

"Me?" She shrugged her shoulders. "I don't really know him at all. He seems pleasant enough. I've had lunch with him in the cafeteria. Nothing more. Why do you ask?"

"Just wanted your personal opinion." Sally wondered what went on inside Ruth's head. Didn't she know the man obsessed over her?

Sally walked to the window and stared at the entrance to the hospital. A man in a black shirt and pants lounged against a palm. The fisherman? Lack of sleep on her part, more likely, paranoia comes easily to the weary. Probably some expectant father on a cigarette break.

TWENTY

SALLY LEFT THE hospital at seven-thirty in the morning and went to the marina to call Pete on the radio. And, it crossed her mind there was that lovely supply of food they maintained. Hospital food on the island was the same as institutional food anywhere. Unpalatable.

"How's the patient?" Pete sounded wide awake.

"Improving a little. But I'm tired. I'm going to do a little shopping before I return to the boat though," she told him. "Let's meet at the seawall around ten."

Sally was famished. Bacon and eggs were calling her name. And juice. She needed juice!

Tim materialized from the woodwork, following his nose to the sizzling aroma emanating from the kitchen area. "You wouldn't want to help a poor bachelor by cooking a little extra bacon would you?"

Sally gave him a warm smile. He looked so pathetic. "Sure, why not. I suppose an egg or two and an order of toast wouldn't be rejected either?"

"Well, now that you mention it."

Sally marveled over the table again as she set their plates down. She looked under it and across it, admiring its strength. Several people wandered in and out. When Jeff arrived and stared at her in disbelief, it finally occurred to her that breakfast with Tim suggested things. She stifled a laugh.

"What is it?" Tim asked.

"Nothing serious. Haven't you noticed? Several people

have looked at us. Jeff is the one who gave it away. Whatever Jeff thinks is written all over his face. He's absolutely amazing, really. I presume our having breakfast together is suggestive. You must have quite a reputation!"

"Is that a compliment or should I be insulted by your smirk?" There was that enigmatic expression again. Tim definitely had bedroom eyes.

"Don't be silly," she said. "Nothing is a secret on this island. Half the harbor knows I've been out most of the night." The glimmer of hope on Tim's face made her laugh aloud. He was probably hoping for another Lisa. And what about Ruth? Had Tim, like everyone else, ever focused on Ruth? Could he be the one Rita called the creep? A moot question, one she would worry about later. She enjoyed Tim's confusion and was not about to reveal the innocent nature of her late-night trip to shore. He would find out soon enough anyway.

Tim shrugged. "That tropical depression should be hitting us this weekend sometime," he said, changing the subject. "Shouldn't cause any problems for the boat people. You might want to lay in some extra food supplies though. Kind of hard to get anything dry to the boat when we get a few days of downpour. By the way," he said, "they're having a predepression party at the Pot tonight, in case you're interested."

"I get the feeling people here don't have to look very hard for a reason to party."

"You got that right! You're about to see what happens when we get an almost hurricane." He shook his head.

"I hope an almost hurricane is all I ever see," Sally said, as she picked at her plate. "Tim, what can you tell me about Rita? I'm trying to put together a mental picture of her."

He frowned. "Are you asking me to gossip? You don't seem the type."

"I certainly wouldn't like to think of myself as a gossip. For some reason, Claudette has appointed me to sort out the problems of every boat girl on the island. Understanding Rita seemed a good place to start."

Tim's eyes bored into hers. His mouth curled at the corners. He leaned close to her. Too close. "Rita's dead," he said. "I fail to see how you're going to solve any of her problems."

Sally drew back and sighed. "No kidding! But don't you see, understanding Rita will help me to understand the others. People will talk to me about Rita precisely because she is dead. What she did with her life can no longer be affected by what they say. I need to know the real Rita, through your eyes for starters, if you'll let me."

Tim stretched his shoulders and contemplated the ceiling. "Let's go to my office," he suggested when others approached the table. "Really give everyone something to talk about," he chuckled, "'cause I never close my door, but I will today."

The office was small but comfortable. Tim settled in a heavy swivel rocker, his feet propped on his desk. Sally chose an overstuffed chair, happier with some distance between them.

"Rita," Tim began, "was the perfect boat dollie. You know what a boat dollie is, correct?"

"Certainly," Sally said. She did, after all, have a basic idea of what one was. Tim was unlikely to confide in her if he felt they weren't speaking the same language.

"Well then, you know how they are, undependable as hell. Most of them are transients. Here today and gone tomorrow. I hire them all the time. Rita worked here between boats once. The difference between Rita and the rest was that she made no bones about what she was. Told me the first day she wanted a job till she found a boat. She

was a good worker though, everything she did, she did
her best. Like she was trying to prove something, know
what I mean?"

Sally nodded absently, remembering details from Rita's diary. Rita, wishing she had turned out as well as her
sister. Rita, hating herself. Rita, wishing she was dead.

"It's been a few years since Rita came to the island,
but I just remembered something. I'm sure this is the first
place she came looking for work. Most of them come here.
What better way to find another boat than a marine store.
Anyway, what was strange—no, scary really—was that
she had bruises all over her, like she had been beaten or
something. I guess that's why I hired her right off. I felt
sorry for her."

Sally sat forward in her chair. "And somebody murdered her the other night. My God, Tim, did you find out
who beat her up? What you're telling me might be important to the authorities."

"What I'm telling you was too long ago to have anything to do with what happened to her this week."

Sally didn't agree but sensed the conversation would
end if she put him on the defensive. "Did you ever find
out what happened to her?"

"I questioned her on the subject after I got to know her,
but she wouldn't tell me, the truth, I mean. Made up some
story about having been mugged. I could tell she was lying.
She seemed scared for a time. Asked me a hundred times
if anybody had been asking about her." Tim eyed Sally.
"You lying to me, too?"

"Lying about what?"

"Well, first you tell me you want to know the real Rita,
so you can understand boat girls. And the next thing I
know we're discussing murder suspects."

Sally understood his discomfort. She hadn't planned for

their conversation to take this unusual turn. "We did become a little sidetracked," she admitted. "I saw her body when Joseph towed it in. I wanted to know about Rita before I heard her death was not an accident. Before Claudette appointed me to my dubious position as boat mama. But I wouldn't blame you if you didn't believe me."

He studied her for a minute. "Claudette has her finger on most everything that goes on. What did she tell you about Rita?"

Sally shrugged. "Now that you've brought it up, I'm annoyed to report she didn't tell me squat. Told me to ask around. Help the other girls…and report to her."

Tim tipped back in his chair, shook his head and laughed. "She's something, that Claudette. Anyway, there's not much more I can tell you about Rita, except that I liked her. Everyone did. She wasn't real close to anyone. Well… Don I guess, on Summerswind. And then again, maybe not. Sorry. I guess that's it for now, unless you have some more questions." He opened a drawer, pulled out some papers and dropped them on his desk.

Sally took the hint. She got up to leave. "Another time maybe, after I fill in some of the blanks."

Jeff was still at the table so Sally joined him. She still had plenty of time to shop.

"Sally," Jeff said, "I have an idea for you. Actually it's Mae's idea, because you're interested in Rita and all." He reached over and patted her on the arm as though congratulating a star pupil. His expression was one of concern. "Evelyn, that's who you need to see. She used to work here once. Another dollie. They were pretty tight for a while. Roomed together. I almost forgot about her." He nodded and smiled.

Sally searched her memory. The name Evelyn had been in the diary several times. But nothing clued her that the woman was local. "I've met most of the boat girls. I don't remember meeting anyone named Evelyn." Tim hadn't mentioned her either. Strange.

"That's because she's not a boat dollie anymore. Wasn't a real good one anyway. Had a problem with seasickness. Married a local boy. They live up in the hills somewhere. He won't let her have nothing to do with boat people now."

"Thanks, Jeff, I'll look into that." Sally was pleased. The visit to the marina proved fruitful. She sat back and listened to the conversation around her.

It seemed no one was particularly concerned about the weather system other than regarding it as a nuisance. A reassuring development. Tim launched into one of his stories. Sally didn't stay to listen, but was intrigued when it began with an AA meeting he'd attended. Perhaps Mae was right, his stories *were* always a put-down of himself.

Sally went to several shops to find the things she wanted for the hermit. She found a small bucket for him and a plastic jar with a lid. At a secondhand store she picked out a long-sleeved flannel shirt in a desert camouflage pattern. She also bought a magnifying glass for herself, to replace the one they had given him.

ARMANDO ENJOYED THE morning. At least the woman left the boat anyway. It sure as hell beat sitting on the stinking seawall. He called the boss after Sally stayed in the hospital for hours. Armando enjoyed the phone call too, got to wake the bastard up. He pulled out his little notebook and wrote down the name of the shop Sally entered. This could get boring though. The woman was shopping. The only interesting thing that happened was when she and the marina guy closed themselves in his office. The boss would be interested in that little piece of information.

Yeah, he might get a few more dollars out of this job if she did more of that kind of visiting. Armando wondered what the guy did with her in there.

TWENTY-ONE

SALLY WAITED NEAR the seawall. She leaned against a tree and yawned.

"Old Boat Mama looks all done in this morning," Pete teased.

"Old? Since when did I become *old* Boat Mama? You ever call me that again and I won't speak to you for a week."

"A week, huh?" Pete looked pleased. "I'll take it under advisement. Could it be that we're a little irritable this morning?"

"Hah!" Sally said loudly. "Incidentally, I had breakfast with Tim, the marina manager. Actually, I made him breakfast. The guy with the bedroom eyes, you remember?" She climbed into the dinghy and sat down demurely.

"Great. And I had breakfast with Lisa," Pete lied. He used an oar to push away from the wall.

Sally feigned an attempt to push him overboard.

"I'm joking, I'm joking!" he said.

Pete dropped her at Sere Dina to catch up on her sleep and informed her he was going to town to buy boat parts.

Sally couldn't believe it was almost five o'clock when Mae's knock on the side of the boat woke her.

"I heard about Elaine," Mae said, climbing aboard a few minutes later. "Is she going to be okay?"

"They said she might move out of intensive care tomorrow if she keeps improving," Sally told her. "And yes," she squeezed Mae's arm, "I think she'll bounce back quickly. She might appear frail, but there's a fighter inside that tiny body."

"Thank goodness," Mae exclaimed. "I'll go by and see her on the way to the Pot tonight. Are you and Pete going to the party?"

"If we're there, we're there, that's all I can say at this point. I have to visit Elaine again, too. And I haven't discussed plans with Pete. In fact I don't even know where he is."

Mae pointed in an upward direction. Sally looked up. There sat Pete, halfway up the mast in a boatswain's chair.

He waved a varnish brush. "I was trying to do the quietest job I could, so I wouldn't wake you," he called down. "Let's do go to the Pot tonight, Sally. I have a feeling we're going to be stuck on board for a while with this storm coming."

"The captain has spoken," Sally shrugged.

ELAINE SIPPED SOMETHING from a straw. "I feel so weak, even drinking a glass of milk exhausts me." She reached for Sally's hand.

"You probably shouldn't have visitors," Sally said, "but I wanted to see how you were doing." She sat on the edge of the bed and tucked Elaine's covers against her sides. "At least your color has returned."

A heavyset nurse marched in and took root at the foot of the bed. Her lips were a thin tight line. She made a few scribbles on Elaine's chart, then her eyes darted back and forth from Sally to Pete and she snorted like a bull ready to charge.

"We were just leaving," Pete said. "Weren't we?" He nudged Sally.

"I'll be back tomorrow." Sally planted a quick kiss on Elaine's forehead and gave the nurse a small wave. "No matter what."

THE BOATERS WERE at the Pot in force and the party was in full swing. A few tourists hung around the outskirts but they were not encouraged by the regulars and eventually drifted away. "Looks like a locals only party to me," Sally said.

Pete chuckled. "I see Doug Wilson is getting his usual warm welcome."

Everyone moved away or squirmed at his approach, but Doug remained oblivious to any subtleties suggesting disfavor of his presence. Good, bad or otherwise, he was as much a part of the island as they were. In fact, Sally thought, Doug seemed a happy man tonight. The coming storm made for hot, muggy weather, which in turn made for scantily clad women, just the way Doug liked them.

Claudette ousted one of the boat captains off a stool when Sally arrived at the bar. "Make room for Boat Mama!" she bellowed.

"How that little girl be?" she asked Sally with a worried scowl.

"Elaine will snap back like a bowstring, I feel it in my bones. So, not to worry," Sally said, leaving out the finer details.

"You're a good boat mama, Sally girl." Claudette grinned from ear to ear, then nodded. It was difficult to determine Claudette's age. She wore her jet black hair in a tight bun on top of her head. A ring graced every finger of both hands. Two sets of gold hoop earrings decorated either side of her broad, cheerful face. An inner strength emanated from behind her regal, black features. If something needed to be done, Claudette would see to it, whether it was her business or not. Sally felt a kinship with this strong woman and was glad she was not her enemy, certain that same strength could wield some powerful weapons.

Sally glanced at the familiar faces around the bar. Someone was missing. No, not someone, she thought, something. The steel band wasn't there. It wasn't down the beach either.

"The fellows be playing a house tonight," Claudette said, as though reading Sally's mind. "They come later. Rather be here tonight, for the party, you better believe it."

Lisa pushed up to the bar to order a drink. She *almost* had a bikini on. Claudette served her solemnly. When Lisa wiggled away, admirers cleared a path for her.

"One of these days, going to be big trouble with that one," Claudette nodded sagely. "You watch, Boat Mama. You watch."

"Are you suggesting I should play boat mama to Lisa, too? I'll be real honest with you, Claudette. I think little Lisa goes in more for boat daddies." Sally smiled slyly.

Claudette's body shook with laughter. "That be true, Boat Mama." She howled, holding her ample stomach with both hands. "That *dooo*...be true!"

Conversation drowned out the music once more. Sally ordered another rum punch and tuned in on the things being said around her.

"I PUT THIS ad in the paper for someone to work at the marina," Tim was saying. "We've got food there and all, so I included in the ad that applicants should bring health certificates. Only it didn't come out that way. It read, Africans please bring health certificates. I've had three official visits today!"

"Any of them Africans?" Jake asked sardonically.

"Very funny, Jake. I hope they get it right tomorrow."

"Remember when women wore those three-inch spike heels?" Jake asked. "They were always breaking ankles by getting them stuck in drains and subway vents in the big cities. I saw this article in the paper back then, it said: Women Wearing Spike Heels are a Pubic Menace. Don't you love it when they get it right?"

No one ever bested Jake, Sally concluded.

Doug scampered along behind Lisa like a dog in heat. The other women were safe from his sleazy advances for a while. Sally wondered if the list of Lisa's sexual conquests with everyone on the island included Doug.

Mae tapped Sally sharply on the back. "Are we having fun yet?" she asked. "Come with me a minute, there's someone I want you to meet." Mae led her across the sand to several of the group who had broken off from the main crowd. "You'll really like this gal. She's the only older boat dollie I've ever known."

"You have my attention. I didn't know there were any. Lead me to her."

TWENTY-TWO

SEVERAL PEOPLE LOLLED in a circle on the sand, a few faces aglow in the harsh aura of a lantern. One of the group read poetry, aloud. The woman was probably forty-five, with dark curly hair, which would be salt and pepper in daylight. Sally guessed she would stand tall. The selection in progress was one Sally recognized. It was Kipling's "A Song in Storm." The woman read eloquently and her audience honored her with their rapt attention. Mae told her the woman's name was Debra. Sally settled herself on the sand, content to enjoy the magically transported moment. Then the music of distant drums came drifting on the wind as the poem ended. The ambience was lost. But the steel band was inbound. She smiled at the thought.

Sally watched the real party commence in earnest, and with it the outer edge of a small squall. A fresh breeze swept along the beach. The long awaited relief from the humidity of the past few days arrived and kissed the island like a cool gust of autumn. Empty paper cups, left unattended, blew off tables and tumbled across the sand. Sally and Mae chased them down. The palm thatched roof of the Pot flapped in the breeze and rained down a summer of trapped sand on those seeking shelter under its eaves. The heartier of the group covered their drinks with their hands and spat sand through their teeth. Then as quickly as it began, the wind abated. It would be back.

Sally sat down next to Debra. The woman's designation as an older boat dollie made an encounter irresistible.

"The boat I'm currently crewing on is bound for the Mediterranean," Debra told her. "I'm not terribly excited about the vessel. Its destination is the important thing."

"How do you know you'll like the Med?" Sally asked. "I mean what if you get there and you don't like the place or the boat?"

Debra grinned. Her well-tanned face contained the smile lines of a woman not concerned with vanity. "Easy, I've been there before. And I can tell you there is nothing more beautiful than the Adriatic along the coast of Yugoslavia. Or the Greek Islands. But don't get me started, I can go on and on, Sally." Her face shone with the pleasure of remembrance.

"Yes, I'm sure it's beautiful," Sally agreed. "And your confidence impresses me, but what if things don't work out on the boat? Aren't languages a problem? Surely there are other obstacles as well—if you become sick or get hurt. Pete and I may go there when we leave the Caribbean."

"Having a husband certainly might make it less complicated. On the other hand, I had one of those once. As for languages, I speak several. I have medical insurance and the Med is not another planet. They do have doctors and hospitals there. Many places I've been have better medical facilities than ours. And certainly better than most of the island hospitals I've visited in these waters, except for this one. Are you wondering what became of my husband?" Debra asked without pausing, as though the question followed naturally.

"Yes and no," Sally replied honestly. "I'm curious because you brought it up, but I don't want to pry."

"You'll find the boat world is full of people who will tell you anything you want to know about themselves and a lot you don't. I've often wondered why. Perhaps it's such an insecure environment at times, physically and emotion-

ally, that telling-all is therapeutic. Mind you, there are the
recluses too. Personally, I figure they are either running
from the law or they're the nut cases." She looked at Sally
and laughed. "Don't worry, I'm not going to unload on you
philosophically. You really want to know what made me
become a boat dollie, don't you?"

Sally was startled. Debra talked about personal subjects
as though she were exchanging recipes.

"Don't look so stunned," Debra chuckled. "*Boat dollie* is not a dirty term to me. In a funny way, I sometimes
think of myself as the boat dollies' revenge. But, that's
another story."

"Okay, since you aren't offended, what did happen to
your husband?" There was a story here and Sally wasn't
about to stifle the source. She propped her feet on the bar
rail, crossed her arms in front of her and gave Debra her
full attention.

Debra put her fist to her mouth in concentration.
"Where do I start?" she said aloud. "I was brought up
well, education-wise and all. I won't bore you with that.
Anyway, after a storybook romance I married the perfect
man. He became an executive with an important nation-
wide company. We had two wonderful children. In all, I
had twenty-six years of bliss. Everyone's heard stories like
mine a million times. You know what's coming. My husband ran off with his twenty-five-year-old secretary. Was
I shocked? Hell yes! I was devastated. Who wouldn't be?

"One of the main things that bothered me was coming
to grips with my own stupidity. I should have seen it coming. I never had an opportunity to fight back. Seriously, to
have fought and lost would have been living. This was like
sudden death! But I wasn't sure which one of us had died,
him or me." Debra smiled and shook her head.

"I finally decided it was him! For me, he had died. It

was about that time I knew for certain, because my brain finally cleared, he would be back. Once the bloom came off the rose, the thorns on the bimbo would start to prick and I decided not to be there waiting with open arms. My children were grown and on their own. Besides, they were already delivering little lectures concerning their dad, explaining to *me* how I should forgive him, about middle-age crisis!

"I went charging down to the travel agency as fast as my little Jaguar would take me. I threw in the Jaguar to make a point. It was an anniversary present from you know who, six months before he '*died.*' Was I dumb, or what? I sold the guilt-mobile on my way home from the travel agency." Debra paused for a thirsty gulp of her exotic drink.

"So where did you go?"

"Everywhere. I bought a three-month Eurorail pass and I had myself a marvelous time."

"Well, you've told me this much," Sally encouraged. "Are you going to tell me how you became a...boat dollie?"

"Sure, why not? I was down on the south coast of Portugal, in a place you must go to, by the way. It's called the Algarve, a glorious place. My whole life changed the day I stopped for lunch at a restaurant overlooking the water and the boats. I made a small comment to the waitress about a gorgeous sailboat at the dock. The man at the next table turned around and said thank you. And to make a long story short, I went sailing that afternoon. A month later I was sailing the Mediterranean with him.

"I stayed on that boat for five years, until it came here. I wanted to stay here for a year or two and then return to Europe. The owner wanted to go to the Pacific. I left and found another boat, several boats, actually. Now I've found one that's going where I want. Not much of a story, is it?"

"There is a lot missing from the story, that's all. You

were on a boat with someone for five years, so leaving couldn't have been quite that easy."

They ordered fresh drinks. Sally watched the people around them casually. Lisa still led Doug around by the nose. The real surprise was Lance. He was wrapped tightly around a native girl Sally had never seen at the Pot. Their gyrations left little to the imagination. It was a mating dance, plain and simple. No music necessary. Sally caught Mae's eye and raised her eyebrows as if to say, will you look at that? Perhaps Lisa's tenure was not as secure as Mae imagined. Sally brought her attention back to Debra.

"It wasn't easy, you're right. But it wasn't as hard as it should have been. I didn't start out caring and I meant to keep it that way. Once you've suffered first-degree divorce burn they can never get to you the same way again. The loss of innocence is irreversible. The next time and the time after that become so much easier."

"That's sad," Sally lamented.

"Not really. The way I see it, it's healthy. What would you have me do, be devastated on a regular basis?"

"No, I would like for you to have fallen madly in love again and lived happily ever after. And that sounds so immature I can't believe I said it. But somewhere deep inside all of us I suspect the happily-ever-after dream is universal." Sally made a face and laughed. "All right, so I'm a romantic."

"Unfortunately, I am too." Debra sighed. "But I could never trust enough again to let it happen. Such is life."

"We're getting maudlin, aren't we? Sorry. So…why do you call yourself the boat dollies' revenge?"

"This is the fun part." Debra brightened. "I guess you're entitled to hear it all since you've reminded me that I'm human. I owe you for that. I'm usually so busy always trying to indulge myself in outside stimuli that I forget there are still some embers burning inside this body. I only travel on a boat because it suits me. I don't need to be on the look-out for a better deal. It's difficult to explain."

"How do you survive? Money, clothes, the essentials?"

"I'm wealthy," Debra answered candidly, under her breath. "Now there's one item I shouldn't have told you. I'll have to trust you won't pass that story around."

"You have my word. I'm not sure I understand your reasoning though. Why don't you just buy a boat and hire your own crew?"

"I gave it some thought when I first became enchanted with the lifestyle. Then I saw a similar situation. It was an old lady with a gigolo, but she didn't know what he was. He made jokes about her behind her back. No thank you. No, no, nooo…. Getting back to the boat dollies' revenge, however, I'll give you one shining example that pretty much says it all.

"I answered an ad for a position as cook on a boat mak-ing a trip down to South America. It was a passable boat, a thirty-seven foot yawl. She was older and needed more loving care than she was being given, but I'm a fixer-upper at heart." Debra paused and stared at Sally.

"It's rather common knowledge," she continued, "that crewing means screwing in the boat dollie world."

"I'm not from Oz, Debra, and you're overstating the obvious," Sally countered.

"Exactly my point," she said. "Well, this captain felt it *was* necessary to mention the obvious. That screwing would be one of my duties. Only he used a different word."

"He said screwing would be one of your duties?"

"Close enough. I was actually embarrassed for both of us. After that I just said, sure, sure and okay as he showed me around the boat. I told him I would think it over and let him know. I walked down the dock so angry I could feel my blood pressure going sky high. There was a little cafe nearby so I wandered over to it and ordered myself a drink to calm down. Then I came up with an idea for a way to fix the bastard. I ordered another drink, a double. "About thirty minutes later I walked down the dock and knocked on the side of his boat. He invited me on board once more, and as soon as I was inside I started to take off my clothes. He was stunned and asked me what I was doing. I told him I was concluding the interview, that I wanted to inspect his equipment and his performance. I assured him I was not about to sail on his boat if he was lousy in bed. Honestly, Sally, I can still see him now. There is no way he could get it up."

"Boat dollies' revenge is right! I'm speechless, Debra."

"Yeah, but I'm going to ruin the story for you."

"What did you do?"

"I went sailing with him for a couple of months."

"Why, for heaven's sake? After that dreadful approach!" Sally snatched at Debra's shoulder, pretending to retrieve something.

"What are you doing?"

"I'm removing your boat dollie medal."

"Let me finish, Sally. It turns out, his wife had just left him and this was his first time at hiring a boat girl. He had this fantasy about being a macho sailor. He told me later that he had asked advice from a guy on another boat on how to hire a boat girl. Some joke, right? I'm telling you this guy was really very shy and unworldly. Until I gave him three months of boat dollie training for our side. Someone should thank me…and I want my medal back," she said petulantly.

"You win," Sally relented. She reached over and replaced the make-believe medal.

Debra waved to someone across the crowd. "Got to run,

I've enjoyed talking to you. I'm afraid I'm not much of a party person, I usually turn in early."

ARMANDO WASN'T WORKING, hc was having fun for a change. Following Sally paid unusual dividends, she hung out with attractive young women. The Pot was not the sort of place he usually frequented. The dives on the poorer side of the island were more his style. Maybe he could pick up one of these girls. Hell, they were half dressed and acted pretty damn available. Then he saw the boss and received a look that scared him. He downed his drink. He would come back another time, when this job was finished.

TWENTY-THREE

THE EVENING WAS young and the booze flowed like water. Lance and the island girl still danced, entwined like a pretzel. Sally stood near Lisa and Doug. Lisa's face as she watched the couple on the dance floor changed, like Jekyll to Hyde.

"Come on, baby," Doug begged. "Let's walk down the beach a little, just you and me." His pudgy hand moved up and down her back, lower each time.

Lisa, now totally distracted by the dancers, was no longer amused with Doug. She pushed his arm off roughly.

"Hey, what's the matter, baby? You want me to buy you another drink?" he groveled.

Lisa bestowed a malevolent glance on him. "What I want you to do, Doug," she replied in a tone that dripped venom, "is to kiss-off!" She grimaced and blew through her lips as though ridding herself of a bad taste.

Evidently, Sally concluded, there was someone who knew how to handle Doug's advances. He slunk off into the crowd. The bystanders snickered.

Claudette came over to Sally. "I told you, Boat Mama, be big trouble tonight."

"You know," Sally suggested. "They say that when a storm is coming the pressure change does strange things to people. Maybe it's true."

Claudette crossed herself.

Claudette's gesture triggered a thought. Where was Ruth tonight? Sally scanned the crowd and finally located her sitting at a table with Mae. She picked up her drink and headed their way.

"Welcome," Mae said warmly and continued a conversation, to which Sally only half listened because Lisa's antics begged attention. She emerged from the crowd and moved past the tables to the dance floor, passing behind Mae's chair. A wave of electricity passed with her. Lisa carried a fresh drink. Fuel for the fire, Sally thought. This could get exciting. Mae and Ruth exchanged glances.

"Oh no!" Ruth said, alarmed. "I noticed Lisa earlier. She's already all coked up and Lisa doesn't handle alcohol well either. Where is she going?"

"Lance is dancing with a new girl," Sally explained. "I would assume from light observation that an extreme case of jealousy is about to be resolved."

"Jealousy?" Mae asked. She sat up straighter in the cane chair. "Not Lisa, Sally. If Lance brought that girl to the boat, the three of them would have a fine old time. No, this girl must represent a threat to Lisa's position on Lady Jane. Lance never brings other girls to the Pot. It's more than jealousy you see in Lisa's eyes, it's murder!"

In a blur of motion, Lisa closed the distance between herself and the couple on the dance floor. Her arm snaked out like a lightning bolt and she grabbed the back of the woman's one-piece dress. She ripped it from her body, then threw her fresh drink in the black woman's face when she spun around.

The startled woman recoiled briefly, her nakedness revealed to the crowd, but she made no attempt to cover her body. Instead, with a fiercely proud expression, she raised her head to glare at Lisa. The drink dripped from her chin and an orange slice slid down one breast.

A hush came over the customers of the Pot.

Sally held her breath as the women faced each other

like fighters waiting for the bell. Lisa radiated fury, but the other woman stood her ground like a statue and her noble features gave no hint of what transpired behind her dark eyes. A slight shift in Lisa's posture caused the first move, but it was not by either of the young women.

Lance suddenly stepped between them, facing Lisa.

The black woman quickly seized the opportunity, bent to pick up her dress and disappeared into the night. Lisa stared into Lance's cold eyes, her body still tensed for action.

"Asshole!" she shouted in Lance's face. "You frigging asshole." Lisa too took flight.

"Boo," one of the customers at the bar yelled. "What kind of fight do you call that? It never even got started."

"Get off the dance floor, asshole," another yelled at Lance. "You ruined the whole show! We never have any fun around here."

Lance, stone faced as a Greek god, smiled and bowed, his blond hair settling perfectly into place as he straightened. Someone bought him a drink.

The music of the drums resumed and the party picked up its own rhythm. Sally left Mae and Ruth to their discussion of first aid and returned to the bar and Pete.

"I really love these family places, don't you, sweetheart?" Pete said in an unusually loud voice. "Where close friends meet to toast each other's success. Teary-eyed farewells brimming with sentiment. Makes your heart...."

His words were cut short when a cherry was thrown at him by a patron from the opposite side of the circular bar. Pete picked up the cherry by its stem and continued. "Makes your heart sing when you experience the generous sharing of their meager staples."

"I think that pretty well sums it up, dear," Sally said, as another cherry came their way. "Please, Pete," she begged, sotto voce. "This crowd is dying to bury us in fruit salad, you know that." A shower of lemon slices and cherries rained down on them. Sally put her arms up and groaned. "Perhaps we should retreat."

"Insulting suggestion, my dear. The crew of Sere Dina will never retreat!" Pete bobbed his head to try and catch a newly launched cherry.

"Excuse me! I would like to buy my pal Don here a drink," Jake announced, interrupting the onslaught of fruit. He maneuvered Don into position at the bar.

The crowd quieted out of respect for Jake and the captain of Summerswind.

"What the hell are you all staring at?" Jake demanded. He used his forearm to sweep slippery debris from his area of the bar, then looked at the crowd. "Drink, you damn fools, drink!"

Sally followed this advice gratefully. She took a healthy swig of her drink and plucked a lemon slice from her hair. There was nothing she would like more than to start a conversation with Don, but she knew this was not the moment.

Claudette and Joseph exchanged looks across the bar, and Sally was not surprised to see Joseph saunter in the direction of the telephone. Someone in authority would want to speak with Don, too. Probably not tonight, she guessed. But she bet he would not go unwatched until they did.

Back aboard Sere Dina, Sally checked the galley for the third time to make sure everything was secure for the rough weather, while Pete rigged a canvas over the V-berth hatch, so they could take advantage of the increase in fresh air without the rain. She opened Rita's diary to a page that mentioned the boat called Odds Are.

January

I am so excited. I knew it was going to happen, I had this absolutely wild dream about it. I almost decided to quit and go home last week.

I'm going to crew on Odds Are! It was my turn at the diesel pump, and it was fate. The boat pulled right in as I came on duty. Judy was livid, I could tell, but that's what she gets for goofing off. Anyway, Paul asked me if I would like to go sailing after work. Just like that. The boat is so perfect, I could just scream. Paul seems really nice. At least he's not one of those guys that swear at you all the time, I hope. We screwed of course. He's pretty good in that department. I can handle it. I got the boat! I got the boat! Yahoo! We leave next week for the Keys. Goodbye Port Charlotte. I liked it here.

Sally closed the book. Rather a graphic selection. But at least it was a cheerful one for a change. With the book still in her hands, she nodded off to sleep.

TWENTY-FOUR

THE USUAL HEAVY rains came in the wee hours of the morning. Sally slept fitfully, dreaming about the hermit, boat dollies and storms. Her cast of characters was all wrong. She tossed and turned in frustration. The hermit had Jake's face. The body in the dinghy drifted on the tide and she tried to rescue it. The hermit helped her tow it to shore and they rowed for hours before they were able to drag it up the beach. Lightning struck everywhere as Sally secured the dinghy to a tree so it wouldn't be lost again.

She stared at the bundle draped across the seat. Rita would be safe now. Unable to resist, she lifted the corner of the tarp. The wide-eyed face that stared back at her was not Rita's. It was Elaine's. Sally tried to scream but nothing would come out. She couldn't move because her feet wouldn't answer the call. The face stared and stared and the water in the bottom of the dinghy turned to blood.

Sally woke up, her face drenched with perspiration. She went to the head and splashed cold water on herself. Careful not to wake Pete, she grabbed a jacket from the hanging locker and went topside to get some air.

Rain came down in sheets and the wind was gusty and cool. The water catcher stretched over the cockpit provided cover from the deluge. The storm raked the mountainside with giant fingernails of rain. All the cisterns on the island would greedily gulp down this long awaited blessing. The lack of water was the one great flaw in the perfection of the islands. There wasn't any. If they didn't trap it and save it, they didn't have it.

What did the hermit do for water? She recalled the rocky configuration of the small atoll. There were probably plenty of places where the water collected naturally. He would have to get it while it was fresh and store it somewhere, otherwise it would turn rancid. She could picture him now. He would glory in this unexpected downpour and fill his storehouse of containers with life-saving water. He might not know either, whether this was an evening's rain or the leading edge of a hurricane. He must have a special place earmarked for protection from a violent storm. He would never survive in the lean-to. The special place would have to be a cave.

She relived her dream. Why did the hermit have Jake's face? And why did the body have Elaine's? Probably because Jake struck her as a very lonely man and because Elaine had had a close brush with death.

Sally would visit Elaine in the morning, storm or no storm. She looked at the choppy waters of the harbor. It would be a wet ride to shore. Reluctantly, she went below and prayed for a few hours of dreamless sleep.

Morning found the weather unchanged. Sally made a huge breakfast of bacon, pancakes and fruit.

"Why is it," Pete asked, "that on a day when we are least likely to get any exercise, we seem to eat the most? I plan to do nothing but catch up on my reading for the next two days."

"The only reason I can think of is that there's not much else to do. But you're right, I probably would have made a scrumptious lunch too. Lucky for you I don't plan to be here for lunch. I want to go visit Elaine again. Terrible dreams haunted me last night and she played a major role in one of them."

"I noticed you thrashed in your sleep quite a bit." Pete looked out the porthole of the main salon. "It's pretty nasty weather out there, you'll be soaked before you get to shore." The village was only a vague outline in the distance.

"I know. I keep telling myself it will slack off in a minute, but my forecasting is dependably wrong."

The ride proved worse than predicted and the walk up the hill left her feeling lonely. Only an idiot would be out on a day like this, Sally thought. Her sneakers squished with every step. A zipped waterproof bag containing dry clothes, shoes and a towel hung from her shoulder. She took cover for a minute under a store awning, mostly to catch her breath from the climb up the hill. She glanced back the way she had come. Another fool braved the rain. Like her, he ducked into a store front, too. Poor guy. She watched as he stuck his head out and glanced in her direction. Was he waiting for her to vacate the shelter of the awning? She stepped out into the rain once more.

ARMANDO SWORE. Damn, the woman had seen him, looked right at him. Would she remember him from the Pot last night? He noticed a mirror in the store window, set in the open lid of a large jewelry box. He bent to it. Shit, his own mother wouldn't recognize him. He looked as though he'd just been fished out of the drink. Good. He wouldn't tell the boss she'd made him, because she really hadn't. Why get his ass in trouble for nothing?

MUCH TO SALLY'S relief, Elaine was out of intensive care. The dream had left her with an ominous feeling, one she was glad to have dispelled, and the smile with which Elaine greeted her made the trip through the storm worth it all.

"Could I be in the wrong room?" Sally joked. "You

don't even look like the same woman. You look wonderful!" Sally gave her a hug.

"Oh, Sally, I'm not the same, everything's changed."

"You've patched things up with Lyle?"

"Only this morning. He sat here with me all night again. Every time I woke up, there he was. Neither of us talked or anything. It was terrible!"

"This is your idea of good news? That's not exactly what I hoped would happen."

"No, no. I'm not finished. I finally decided to take your advice. I remembered all the things you said about Lyle, and how either way he figured I would never care about him anymore. So I tried what you said, I just looked at him and told him I loved him. Well, he started to cry and so did I. And then we talked for a while. Finally the subject of the baby came up and we both cried again. We wanted it so much but we didn't know how to talk about it." Elaine sniffled, about to cry once more.

"Sounds like there was more water in here than there is outside."

Elaine giggled. "Yeah, you're right about that. So, guess what else happened?"

"I can't think of anything that would be better than what you've just told me." Sally raised her hands in the air as though to invoke the heavens.

"We want to get married." Elaine grinned. "And we plan to have a baby as soon as I'm well enough."

"Wait a minute! What about the story you told me? No one wants to charter with a pregnant woman on board, not to mention a baby."

"We talked about that, too. I won't show right away, of course, and when I do we'll have to hire someone to take my place during the day. And we'll only do day cruises until the baby is older. Other people work and have someone take care of their children during the day." Elaine delivered this little speech with some authority.

"It's amazing, isn't it?" Sally nodded, incredulous. "How the mountains become mole hills when you communicate. I am truly flabbergasted. When is the big day?"

"I don't know yet. We'll make that decision as soon as I get out of here."

"What can I do to help? I realize you didn't want to call your family before, but this is different. Surely you'll want to share this with someone."

"No, Sally. There really isn't anyone! I was raised in foster homes all my life and the last one I was in was awful. They were very poor people who took in children to make a living."

Sally said nothing. She ached for Elaine. Life was not fair. Pictures of Becky flashed through her mind.

"Don't look at me so funny, they really did. Sometimes there were six or seven of us."

"When you say it was awful, you could be covering a lot of territory. Were you mistreated?"

"No, they didn't mistreat me. They didn't beat me or abuse me if that's what you mean. I'm not sure they even knew I was there. If I wrote to them, I'm certain they would have to check their records to figure out which one I was."

"It's none of my business," Sally said, "but where were your real parents during all this?" Sally could not imagine parents letting their child be raised by others. She had always resisted having a babysitter for Becky.

"They were killed in a car accident when I was four."

"And you had no other relatives?" Sally straightened Elaine's blanket. Her need to mother this girl was stronger than ever. She placed her hand over Elaine's.

"Not as far as I know." Elaine looked down at Sally's

hand and squeezed it. "You see, they were immigrants, and they'd left Germany just before I was born. I hardly spoke any English, which made me a poor adoption candidate. I wasn't a baby, and I was foreign."

"I'm sorry, Elaine. I can't imagine what it would have been like to grow up without a family."

"Don't feel sorry for me. It wasn't that bad. The stories I heard from some of the girls I met at different homes were scary. I realize now how lucky I was. No one ever hurt me, and one or two families were so nice to me I hated to leave."

"Did you ask to stay?"

"I should have. Maybe they let me go because they thought I would be happier somewhere else. I never said anything. It's like with Lyle, I never let him know I wanted to stay either."

"Well, now that you've opened up, try to stay that way."

"I'll work on it. Anyway, I don't have any family coming to the wedding," she said with a smile, "but I would like my personal boat mama to be there."

"Try and keep me away." Sally hugged her.

"Say hello to everyone for me," Elaine pleaded. "And tell everyone at the Pot they're invited to the wedding."

"Careful now, they can be a wild crowd."

"I know, but they're our crowd and I want everyone there."

"Right. And speaking of everyone," she said. "Do you know a boat girl, or a used-to-be boat girl named Evelyn?"

"No, but I've heard Ruth mention her. I think she visits her sometimes. You should ask Ruth."

"I will, I definitely will."

TWENTY-FIVE

"THREE DAYS OF rain makes me feel like a caged animal," Sally complained. "The sun is finally shining, Pete, Let's hoist our sails and head for Eremites."

"You're just anxious to deliver you newly acquired gifts to the hermit. But it would be interesting to explore the interior of the island this time. We'll hike to the top and have lunch."

The hike to the top of Eremites was tougher than Sally anticipated since the large boulders scattered up the trail didn't provide very convenient handholds.

"I thought this island was perfectly flat, like a table," Sally said. "Now I realize it is a very high table!" On the rim, she saw the foundations of an old building and they chose that as their site for lunch.

On closer inspection they decided the building was an old lighthouse. Other than the thick, slab foundation, only a few feet of wall remained on two sides which was why she had not seen it from the water. Sere Dina, on the other hand, was quite visible from the floor of the structure. It was like a picture postcard and Sally was entranced by the view of their sleek sailboat in the small lagoon. The blue green water and golden sand made her wish she could capture the scene forever. Pete produced their small camera from his pack.

"You're so smart!" she exclaimed. "Why didn't I think of that? Never mind," she said, "that was too easy an opening." Something caught Sally's attention out of the corner of her eye. She saw movement below, about halfway down the side of the cliff. Where Pete and Sally had climbed was a pretty steep slope, but this was a rugged cliff face. It could possibly be scaled, if you were a mountain goat.

Sally had packed them a picnic lunch of cold turkey sandwiches on crusty French bread, assorted pickled vegetables, chips, and as always, chilled white wine.

"Pete!" Sally sprang up. "Do you see anything? I think there's someone down there watching us."

"It's probably just an animal of some kind. Don't worry about it." He took another picture of Sere Dina.

"There," she insisted, "by those big rocks. I'm telling you I saw something. Maybe it's the hermit."

"Well, if it's anybody, it's him."

"But what if it is somebody else?"

"Then our guy is not a hermit. Elementary, my dear. Two guys on one island disqualify him according to the hermit rule book."

"I give up." She sighed, and sat on the low wall. "Let's eat, I'm tired of lugging this stuff around." Twice during lunch Sally had the eerie feeling that they were being observed. And not by an animal.

"Who do you suppose murdered Rita?" Sally said between bites. "After reading her diary I have to say there is nothing in there that points to anyone. Anyone specific that is. But I have a few suspects in mind. Tell me what you think. There's Don, first of all. If he wanted to get rid of Rita, from what I've learned about the boat dollie lifestyle, all he would have to do is deposit her things on shore and wave goodbye."

"True enough," Pete agreed. "So even if she pitched a fit, there would be no real reason to kill her."

"How about the girl who was supposedly a threat to her position. What do we know about her?" Sally asked.

"Jeff told me the other day when I helped him on his boat that she was just passing through in search of a boat and fled after the news of Rita's death."

"Can't say I blame her," Sally shuddered. "She probably thought she drove the poor girl to her death! Write her off as a suspect, then. I still want to know why Rita arrived here beaten up, as Tim put it."

"And I have to agree with what Tim told you. It was too long ago to figure in her death." Pete poured wine. "We're not even close, yet. I think it all revolves around drugs. We know she used them, right? And she used them regularly, according to local gossip. *There's* the contact we don't know about. Who supplied Rita? If you're looking for the type of person capable of murder, it's the criminal element that seems most likely."

Sally picked up her glass and cradled it in her hands. "I haven't read any serious mention of drugs in her diary. Well, let me rephrase that. She mentioned getting some good stuff a few times, but nothing about drug dealers or anything. The police would have picked up on that."

Pete put his glass down at the mention of police. The plastic click on stone echoed in the stillness. He stood, then paced in front of Sally. "I still feel you should put Rita's story to rest and let the authorities handle it. It's one thing to be interested in her for curiosity's sake, but a murder investigation may be a little out of your league. I'm getting tired of pointing out that it can be very dangerous if there is a criminal connection, like drug dealers. We've already had this argument, but I have to keep throwing up caution flags."

"I understand," Sally said. "I've considered mob connections. Strangely enough, it first occurred to me when I talked to Tim. He's probably as innocent as a lamb, but you never know. Seriously, he's only been here four years.

He's in a perfect position to supply drugs to all the boaters right along with their boat gear. The story he told me about Rita's bruises and all could be a great cover story. I haven't forgotten seeing him on his way to Lisa's boat that morning. Even that might not have been the sexual assignation Mae suggested. And I know Lisa is a drug user, too. And what about Tim for other reasons?" She related the nebulous entries from Rita's diary. "Is Tim the manager she didn't want to sleep with years ago?" Sally rested her head on her knees.

"Listen to me, will you?" she continued. "The next thing you know I'll be accusing Jake, or God forbid, Mae! I sound crazy." She opened a bag of chips and dumped them onto a paper plate.

"Exactly," Pete agreed. "That's why I feel you should stay out of this mess." He took a handful of the chips.

"I'm sure you're right," Sally said without conviction. She packed the empty paper containers into their pack. "Time to explore." She wanted to stop the direction of their conversation before it escalated into another argument.

The top of the island held a zillion surprises. Although it seemed to be all the same, heavy brush and cactuses galore, the landscape was not as flat as it appeared, and was in fact, pitted like the lunar surface. Sally walked carefully after she stumbled across the first hole. "The whole island is probably honeycombed with caves," she told Pete.

"Right, and since we're ill equipped for cave exploring, we'd best do little more than glance past the dark entrances. Now we know where the hermit gets his water. There are storm shelters aplenty. After the last three days of steady rain, water must be caught in pockets everywhere."

Sally noticed the tracks of what appeared to be wild boar and goat. Life might not be as tough as she estimated on this remote atoll. Iguanas were in abundance. They sunned themselves on outcroppings of rock everywhere. Although iguana might taste better, Sally would rather eat goat. How did one catch iguanas? They resembled dragons, not lizards.

She left her gifts for the hermit in the same spot on the beach. It was then she noticed that the lean-to against the rocks was gone. "Pete, did he move because of our last visit?"

"Probably. Come on, don't be discouraged. He's not your problem. If this guy wanted to make friends he wouldn't be here in the first place."

Sally had never meant to cause the recluse undo hardship. They returned to the dinghy in silence. Something was on the seat. It was a small package wrapped in palm leaves. "This must be a present from the hermit!" Sally exclaimed. She hurriedly unwrapped the package the minute they were on board Sere Dina. There was a large shark's tooth suspended from twine, a spray of tiny dried flowers bound with the same type of twine and a silver cufflink.

Pete selected the cufflink for inspection. "Sally!" Pete said. "There's an inscription on it. It reads, To Archibald, and it's signed, love M. So, our hermit now has a name. We'll call him Archie. I don't see him as the formal type, do you?"

"Come on, Peter, don't start, okay? He probably found that thing on the beach or something. We don't know that his name is Archibald at all." Sally smiled inwardly. She'd forgotten how much she enjoyed Pete's foolishness, his boyish enthusiasm.

"It is now. I like it, too. It lends our friend an air of sophistication. Archibald, who owns an island named Eremites."

After dinner, Sally reread another entry from Rita's diary.

July

> We have the worst couple on board. She is a rat-
> faced shrew and he is such a wimp he deserves her.
> She has not stopped complaining since we left the
> dock. The potato salad was too salty. Her bunk is
> too hard. It's too hot outside. What the hell can I do
> about the weather? Two more days. Thank goodness
> I got some good stuff before we left. I could never
> have put up with these people otherwise. I'm getting
> a little nervous about Judy. She always manages to be
> on the dock when we come off a charter. This busi-
> ness of coming to see me because we're such good
> friends is a crock. I've told Paul what a bitch she
> was to work with, but he thinks she is sooo…sweet.
> I gave Mother the number for the marine operator.
> I cannot believe Cynthia got married without let-
> ting me know. Mother said it was a small wedding,
> but it looked like half of Boston was there from the
> pictures. They were probably worried I would lose
> my job if I went.

Rita's first out-and-out mention of drugs. She alluded
to them in other entries, but this time the message was
clear to Sally.

She heard Pete call to her from the salon.

"It's another storm," he said in answer to her quizzical
expression. "Off the coast of Africa. They say it looks like
a pretty big system and expect it to be a tropical storm by
tomorrow. We could experience our first hurricane in the
not too distant future."

"Damn," Sally swore. "I hate that. Can you imagine
what a full blown hurricane could do to these islands?
This constant line of small squalls is wearing me out as it

is. I guess it's a good thing we found a good place to tie up, just in case."

"Forget the islands. They will survive very nicely. Even the sturdy buildings above the harbor will hold up. A lot of lesser structures could go, that's for sure. And don't fret about our friend Archie, he has a labyrinth of caves to ensure his safety. No, Sere Dina is our problem, and I'm not convinced someone won't have already staked out the harbor we found. Let's go back in the morning and check out that hurricane hole. We should have a backup, too."

"You're making me nervous." Sally dropped into the nearest chair and pulled her feet up. She wrapped her arms around her knees.

"Sorry," Pete said, "I just think we should be prepared. We'll head out at first light."

TWENTY-SIX

ANOTHER VESSEL OCCUPIED their usual anchorage and Sally felt strangely resentful of its presence. Sere Dina didn't own the spot or anything, it was just that Sally was used to having Mae and Jeff for neighbors and a stranger resided between them now. But who knows, they might be wonderful people. Wrong, she decided an hour later. Her first hint that the new residents were less than perfect came when she heard the stream of obscenities that periodically emanated from their cockpit. "Stupid bitch," a voice rang out across the water. "Can't she ever do nothing frigging right? I have to do every damned thing twice around here."

The woman gave no response to these rants; didn't even flinch when his voice rose. Tough woman, Sally decided. Most boaters used a greater than average share of four letter words, Sally knew, so the rude expletives added nothing titillating to her seagoing vocabulary. The viciousness with which the words were delivered however, disturbed Sally.

The couple was older, much older. He was mostly bald, with a fringe of shoulder-length gray hair and a full shaggy beard. A dingy white tank top didn't quite cover his double paunch. The recipient of the obscenities was a short stout woman, who was also gray and untidy. If she responded to the verbal abuse, it must have been in a whisper, because Sally never heard her utter a peep. Very tough, indeed. Or scared. Sally hoped for tough.

"Pete?" Sally hollered. "How about a dinghy ride? We can look for a backup hurricane hole. And maybe the vulgar language from our new neighbors will settle down while we're gone!" She said the last loudly enough for the neighbors to hear.

When they returned, however, they saw that Mae and Jeff had moved their boat. Pete and Sally quickly followed suit. The message was clear.

Mae arrived at Sere Dina late in the afternoon, full of news. "Elaine and Lyle plan to get married. She gets out of the hospital tomorrow."

Sally answered her from the galley. "Old news, Mae." She emerged with two exotic drinks and handed one to Mae.

"Don, on Summerswind, is back in the harbor and is on the lookout for a new boat girl," Mae reported.

"Maybe Lisa ought to look into that opening," Sally said. "Things weren't looking too hot for her at the Pot the other night!"

"Boy, have things changed in that situation!" Mae arched her eyebrows. "The gorgeous black girl moved onto Lift Off last night."

"Oh dear. Poor Lisa. Well, I'm sure she can find plenty of people to put her up until she finds another boat." Tim came to mind.

"No, no, wait till you hear this! Lance, Lisa and the new girl—her name is Julia, by the way—are all lovey-dovey now. The girls held hands like sisters at the Pot last night." Mae flashed Sally a smile.

"You're kidding," Sally said, exasperated. "Well, you told me Lisa rather enjoyed the threesomes."

"I'll tell you what I think it really is. Lisa knows that nobody else would let her have the sexual freedom that Lance does. They're two of a kind. She will outlast this new girl. You watch. And if she doesn't, maybe the three of them will live happily ever after!"

Sally raised her hands, as though to ward off an odi-ous presence. "Does anyone in this world ever discuss so-cial diseases? I mean, honestly. What are they thinking?"

"You know the old story. Diseases only happen to other people. And speaking of diseases, Ruth said they actually are seeing a few cases of dengue fever all of a sudden." Mae scratched an imaginary itch.

"Thank you for the warning. I'll be sure and spray my-self with repellent before I go to shore. Do you want to go with me in the morning? I thought I would stop at the hos-pital and say hello to Elaine and I need to go to the marina store. We could have lunch there."

"Sounds great," Mae answered. "Are you going to the Pot tonight?" She shifted her position in the cockpit to get out of the sun.

"No, I'm tired from running around in the dinghy. To-morrow night we will go and catch up on everything."

Mae scrunched up her face. "Did you hear that couple on the boat next to us this morning?"

"Yes, I couldn't help it."

"God, they repulsed me! Why is it there is always one boat around like that? You should have heard them when they pulled in. It was just awful. He screamed at that poor old lady so much I wanted to shoot him. And you could see the more he yelled, the more incompetent she became. They live on a boat for crying out loud. The idiot has to know how sound carries over water."

"I'm with you. We encountered the same type of be-havior at several of the marinas on our way down here. It always amazes me that anyone would put up with such treatment. They've probably been at it so long they aren't aware how offensive it is."

"I'll bet they don't stay long," Mae sighed. "And I hope

they don't find the Pot. We've got enough weirdos hanging out there already." She checked her watch. "I must run."

SALLY WAS CURLED up in her berth with Rita's diary before ten o'clock. She carefully turned the pages to review unusual passages. Rita managed to stay on Odds Are for a little more than two years before moving to a boat named Sea Heir. Where did people come up with these names? On the other hand, some people came up with names like Sere Dina. She smiled and turned back a page.

Sept.

> Paul and I have taken the week off. We found another neat island today. It is so cool. The reef is pretty bad though. There is only one spot you can cross over and not rake the hull. We took the dinghy through the mangrove tunnels to a gorgeous lagoon. We caught two lobsters and had them for lunch. I felt like a tourist. Two more days and it's back to the grind. Five guys are coming next week. They want to do a lot of diving. Had a lot of fun with the little kids on the last trip.

Sally liked Paul. It's too bad Rita hadn't stayed on Odds Are longer. Paul's influence was healthy. Rita wrote happy entries when she was with him. It provided insight into the lighter side of Rita. She was a warm and sensitive human being. How had she turned out to be nice with such cold fish for parents? Would a few years in the harsh reality of the boating world improve her sister, Cynthia? Doubtful, Sally thought, she was entirely too self-focused. She closed Rita's little book. There was nothing so far to point to her murderer. Nothing obvious, or the police would have arrested someone, anyway.

Sally rose early and gathered the few things she needed—a tote sack, the film from the camera and her purse. The brightly colored carts carrying fruit and vegetables parked haphazardly along the seawall and their owners opened huge, rainbow striped umbrellas. Heavily accented voices rang out like music in the cool morning air. Joseph passed them on the way to his boat. He nodded and smiled at Sally and Mae.

At the hospital, Elaine looked like a shadow of her former self, but her spirits soared.

"Where's Lyle?" Sally asked.

"Can you believe it?" Elaine replied. "He's gone to get the marriage license."

"You're joking," Mae said. "You are in no condition to get married. I mean, you won't exactly be ready for the honeymoon for a while."

"Get real, Mae. We know that. We just want to be married, that's all. Real romance involves belonging to each other."

"Well," Mae laughed, "no one will ever doubt your sincerity on the 'in sickness and in health' part. And I'll shut up because I think that was very nice, what you just said about romance." She glanced out the window.

"So when is the wedding?" Sally asked.

"Today is Tuesday," Ruth said. "You'll need a dress."

"Will I be strong enough by Friday?"

"Would that stop you?" Sally asked.

"No, you're right. Then Friday it is. Can you come over to the Lady Jane tomorrow, Sally, so we can make plans?"

It was an opportunity Sally wouldn't miss. She was fulfilling a role now. An important one. All the pent-up emotions of the last year were slipping away. "Of course. Call me on the radio when you get up."

Mae and Sally dropped the film off at a one hour processing place. Then Sally mulled over purchases for the hermit. She decided on a dipper and a funnel. The third gift would have to present itself, she was out of ideas, her mind too busy with the excitement of Elaine's wedding and the coming storm.

They headed for the marina.

"I've never seen so many people here," Mae said as they gathered supplies from the marina kitchen.

"It's the storm," Sally said. "Everyone wants information. Last I heard, it borders on hurricane status now."

"Yeah," Tim stood behind her. "Has its own name— Brody."

Sally turned around and took a step away. "Let's hope it turns north soon." She followed Mae to the table.

Tim affixed a little red tack to the large tracking chart on the wall, then wrote the latest coordinates on the chalkboard. No one voiced the opinion that it might just disappear like the last one.

Sally divided a huge sandwich and gave half to Mae. The smell of hamburgers and bacon dredged up long forgotten memories. When she closed her eyes, she was seated in her high school cafeteria. Pete was seated across for her. He was a to-die-for hunk.

Mae nudged her gently. "Earth to Sally, Earth to Sally."

"What? What do you need, wretched alien?"

"See that guy in the corner, immortal time traveler? Well, I think he participated in our last space leap. I could swear I just saw him in the hallway of the hospital!"

Sally examined the appointed corner. Several men occupied the area. "Any special one? I don't recognize anyone."

"The short guy. Looks kind of Latino, maybe even local. Could be a mix."

Sally stared at the shortest man. He had his back to them as he angled toward the door. "You really think he followed us here?" She recalled Pete's constant warnings about the dangers of getting involved in Rita's murder case. But she hadn't done a whole lot of digging into anything. She had managed to get her hands on the diary. Surely no one knew that. Sally wished he would turn around. He could be the fisherman.

"Now that I think about it," Mae announced in a breathy whisper. "I could swear he was a passenger on Jake's boat the other day." She pressed her hands to her cheeks. "I'm sure of it, because I recall thinking he didn't fit in. He looked like one of the goons from the resort."

Sally pushed her sandwich aside. She tried to catch a better look at the man. If he had been on Jake's boat, he could indeed have seen her wave the diary in the air. She would never recognize the fisherman, anyway.

"What goons? What resort?" Sally asked. "I haven't seen anything I would call a resort. You mean one of the hotels?"

"No. It's private, or rather very exclusive. It's on the other side of the island."

"We've explored the other side of the island. We've gone there in the dinghy to hunt for a hurricane hole. I didn't see any high-rises or anything."

"Not surprising," Mae told her. "It's not that kind of resort. It's more like a time share for millionaires. Bungalows and villas. That sort of thing. And all the amenities to go with it, shops, bars, even a casino. Everyone says it's mafia owned. Jeff says that's why we have a modern hospital. Sure there's a big tourist industry here—but not that big."

The underworld element of drug trafficking. Pete's

words rang in Sally's ears. No, it was too far-fetched. Mae exaggerated everything. Sally would not be spooked by rumors. Just because there was a private resort on the island didn't mean it had to be mafia connected. And even if it was, it didn't have to be connected to Rita's murder. But the modern hospital had amazed Sally, since the population didn't warrant such a sophisticated facility. Most of the islands they visited were lucky to have air conditioned clinics. A resort for drug related millionaires might account for the difference.

She watched the Latino depart, but didn't see his face. Should she run after him and confront him? Making a scene would certainly throw him for a loop. But would it provoke him to desperate action?

"I'm sure it's just your imagination, Mae. All this talk about Rita's murder is making you more paranoid than usual."

Mae shrugged her shoulders. "I don't know, Sally. I think it's the same guy." She picked at her sandwich, opened it and put a pickle slice on it.

Sally hoped Mae was wrong about the guy. Could it have been the fisherman?

A familiar voice caught their attention. Sally and Mae exchanged puzzled glances and turned in unison to see Ruth and Doctor Winters approaching a table.

"Don't kid yourself, Sally," Mae said. She shook a finger at her.

"Why, what could I possibly say? There is no doubt in my mind that it's mere coincidence that brings those two together."

"I'm telling you," Mae insisted, "Ruth's passions don't include men. Religion and her work are the only interests in her life. Honestly! I know her."

Sally leaned across the space between them with a

serious expression and spoke in a confidential tone." I'm beginning to wonder whose idea it truly is that Ruth should have been a nun, yours or hers."

Mae's dark lashes hooded her eyes and a frown of concentration pinched her forehead. "Is it really me?" she asked aloud. "Is it me who wants to see her as nunish? Or do I see her that way because it's the only side she has ever shown me?" She stared at Sally. "Be fair, Sally. Maybe I'm the naive one!"

"Damn," Sally said. "Remind me not to play psychologist with you again. Besides, I feel as though I'm orchestrating a soap opera. 'Will sweet, innocent and sensual nurse Ruth, find romance with the strong, silent and noble Doctor Winters? Tune in next week this time and find out if the embers of their secret passion will at last be fanned into flames!'"

Mae giggled.

Tim tapped Mae on the shoulder. "Jeff just called. Said one of those instant charters came up and could you come to the boat right away."

Mae leapt up as though on springs. "Super! We sure need the business. It's going to be slow going for a while if we do get a storm. Sorry, Sally," she said and gathered her things hurriedly. "You understand!"

"Of course. Get out of here."

ARMANDO WAS FURIOUS with himself. The young girl had looked right at him. She had seen him before and it registered. As much as he hated the idea, he would have to tell the boss. The first thing to do though was change clothes so Sally couldn't make him, too. A hat would help too. He might still get away with tailing her for the rest of the day.

TWENTY-SEVEN

SALLY FINISHED HER sandwich, absorbed in the effort. She was taken by surprise when Ruth asked to join her. Doctor Winters had departed, to handle his rounds, she presumed.

"I take it you must be off work this afternoon." Sally looked at her watch. It was one-thirty. She motioned for Ruth to sit.

"Actually, I was supposed to be off at eleven, I only stayed to see Elaine check out. Then Doctor Winters wanted to talk to me about another case, so I guess I was still working. And please," she added, "don't think I'm complaining. I'm not. I really love my work. Sometimes I go to the hospital when I have nothing else to do. I enjoy my profession."

"I believe you." Sally held up her hand. "It's wonderful that you're so dedicated. I thought however, that lunch with Doctor Winters might have been a date."

"Heavens no," Ruth replied, blushing. "Doctor Winters would never be interested in me."

Sally couldn't believe her ears. The whole island was interested. Sally wanted to shake some sense into the girl.

"Listen," Ruth said, "I have a car. I know you don't, and I plan to visit the other side of the island today. I thought perhaps you might want to join me. You've never seen it, right? It's really different. Nothing like here at all."

Sally pushed her plate away and wiped her mouth with a napkin. The suggestion more than piqued her interest. This jaunt might provide the perfect opportunity to unravel the

enigma of Ruth. And Mae had mentioned that Doug operated a restaurant in the resort, another peculiar fact worth
investigation. He hardly seemed personable enough to be
successful in a business that required at least a minimum
of social graces. Last but not least, Sally might get a chance
to meet the ex-dollie named Evelyn, who lived over there.

"Sounds like a great idea to me." Pete's objection to
this expedition might be volatile, but she would handle
that problem when she came to it.

Ruth's car, as she called it, was really a cross between a
jeep and a golf cart. It was open all around with a fringed
top. The seats, the fringe and what little there was of the
vehicle's body, were indigo blue. Adorable described it
best.

The ride over the mountain made Sally nervous. She
tried to become one with the seat as they negotiated a few
hairpin turns. Ruth pulled over at the rest area near the
summit so they could appreciate the spectacular view of
the island spread out below them. On one side Sally saw
the little village, the marina and the boats anchored in the
crescent-shaped harbor. She looked beyond to the horizon
where dark, craggy atolls dotted the blue green sea like
jacks tossed by a giant.

"Look," Ruth pointed, diverting Sally's attention to the
other side of the island. "That's where we're headed."

Sally gasped. The base of the mountain ended abruptly
at a flat, verdant plain that stretched for several miles to
where the island met the sea. She could discern patterns
suggesting plantations. Another village lay below. A village of single level structures painted bright colors. They
were unnaturally close together. And farther away, on the
coast, she spied the resort. The low buildings, all uniform
in size and structure, were cream colored and topped with
terra cotta tiles.

"Do you mean to tell me this has been here all the time and I didn't know it? Good grief! Why don't the tourists come here? It looks like the Garden of Eden!"

Ruth smiled and shook her head in agreement. Her long hair swirled gently, then settled like fine strands of silk across her shoulders. "It's unbelievable, isn't it? But the tourists aren't interested in what's down there. And they may be right, it might appeal to the horticulturist, ornithologist or some other ologist, but making a living down there is tough."

"But it's so green!" Sally said. "Wait a minute though, aren't there tourists in the resort?"

"Yes and no," Ruth replied. "Those are little villas in the resort and the whole place is self-sufficient. The boaters get quite a few charters from the operation and they love it because the tips are outrageous. Other than that, the people in the villas rarely mingle with the locals. Nor do they socialize with the common tourist herd. Their tastes transcend the mundane."

"How nice for them," Sally said. "And how fortunate for us. There's nothing more obnoxious than people who think they're too good for the rest of the world."

"Perhaps I was unfair," Ruth said. "I think with fame and fortune, comes paranoia. Movie stars and politicians and even mafioso vacation in that villa. They often deal with stalkers and fanatics, so the fear factor may motivate their behavior."

"I guess," Sally conceded. She waved her hand in a downward sweep as though to wipe the villas from an imaginary canvas. "It's not important. Who lives in the turquoise village?" she asked. "It looks so perfectly jumbled together, like dominos deliberately leaned against one another, ready to fall." She turned around once more to take in the beauty. "Maybe Tim is right, and this is paradise."

"It's not paradise, Sally. But it is the essence of the island's soul. It's where all the people live who make the tourists—*be happy*."

Sally laughed. "Well, I'm no tourist." She grabbed Ruth by the arm. "I want to get down there and have a look around."

At the base of the mountain, they traveled along what passed for a two-lane highway. It had a line dividing it and it was paved. Sally hoped they wouldn't encounter anyone from the opposite direction as the lanes were the width of bicycle paths. Ruth suddenly pressed the brakes and turned right onto a dirt track that meandered through the palms. Sally could see a clearing ahead. Children were everywhere, along with chickens, piglets and half-starved dogs. This incongruous entourage assaulted their little vehicle before it fully stopped. They climbed over the hood, back and sides like bees on a honeycomb. Sally carefully disentangled herself from the seething mass of bodies and stood clear to watch the proceedings.

Ruth produced a bag of candy from the jeepster. "Here, here!" she said laughing as she tossed some to gain space.

From within the large house situated on spindly pilings, a voice thundered in unintelligible patois. Whatever this voice proclaimed, it was obviously a threat. The children receded from Ruth like a tide in full ebb.

Ruth smiled brightly as the owner of the voice emerged from the shadowy doorway of the building. There, to Sally's amazement, stood a larger version of Claudette. When she moved forward to embrace Ruth, Sally expected the ground to tremble.

"This is my friend, Lorna," Ruth said. She hugged the woman.

"It's a pleasure to…." Sally's words were cut off by Lorna's embrace.

"Lorna is the mother, aunt, sister or cousin to these children," Ruth said. She unearthed a second bag of goodies from the back of the jeep and gave it to Lorna.

"Come," Lorna said and waved the two women into the house and taking another bag from Ruth. "We put this good stuff away now."

Sally and Ruth helped put the articles on a high shelf, out of reach of the children. There were soaps of every kind, shampoos, detergent and even dog soap. Next came cough syrup, Band-Aids and aspirin. Lorna was the recipient of a mobile medicine cabinet. Last but not least were several large cans of insect repellent. Sally didn't have to understand patois to know what that conversation was about. She heard the word dengue several times.

"Lordy!" Sally exclaimed as they flew up the dirt road toward the highway thirty minutes later. "How does she handle that brood all by herself? Where is everyone else?"

"*I tell you, mon, they be making the tourists have easy life,*" Ruth said imitating the local dialect. "Seriously, Sally, where did you think all the people lived that work in the shops and the hotels? Look back at the mountain now."

Sally did as she was told. The back side of the mountain was terraced with stone houses. They lacked the size and splendor of those on the other side, but they appeared sturdy.

"Okay," Sally acquiesced. "I'm a believer, now what?"

Ruth laughed. "Now we go shopping where no tourist would ever dare to go."

"You know, you're a different person on this side of the island, Ruth. You seem more alive, adventurous. I guess I really mean less inhibited. Why is that?"

Ruth stared straight ahead and her hands gripped the wheel tightly. "Oh no, I hate this road."

Sally brought her eyes to the road reluctantly and her

worst fears were confirmed. A huge overstuffed truck bore down on them. There was nothing to do but leave the road. The monster truck blew his horn, but Ruth held her ground, intent on reaching a small clearing only yards away. Sally closed her eyes tightly and cringed when the car swerved roughly. She could smell and taste the acrid breeze created by the passing truck loaded with smoldering sugarcane. She breathed a sigh of relief when the truck careened down the road behind them.

Ruth continued as though there had been no break in their conversation. "No one expects anything of me over here. I don't have to fit in, or say or do the right thing socially."

Sally watched her for a moment. "Is that a problem for you on the other side?"

"Well, not for me really, but for other people. When I go to the Pot and everyone's dancing, I don't particularly want to dance, but nobody believes that. It's a problem for them. I don't fit in. You see, I find it harder to be accepted there. The girls need me though. So I go."

Sally nodded. Ruth was a nurse on and off duty. She would see to the needs of the boating community like she did her patients. The boaters were lucky to have her around. For Sally, she represented something else. Perhaps a friend she could confide in that didn't need her, a friend like Debra. She hoped she would see more of Debra. She turned to Ruth. "There is one more question I would like to ask you. If it's too personal, just say so. Did you ever want to be a nun?"

"If the answer to your question was yes, it would be terribly personal. If I had felt that particular call and resisted, I would be emotionally torn in two. My mother, however, would have thanked all the saints in heaven if I had become a nun, a cloistered nun." Ruth smiled broadly at Sally. "I think I mentioned that to Mae one time. Mae tends to add high drama to other people's lives, with the best of intentions, of course."

"Of course!" Sally agreed with a laugh. "I said one more thing, but I've thought of another since we're speaking on a different level on this side of the island. I think Doctor Winters is very interested in you."

Ruth glanced at her and blushed. "That would be nice. I'll make it a point to notice, thank you." Ruth slowed and pulled into a parking area. "And here we are."

In front of them spread the turquoise village. Sally was on target about it being close knit.

"It's a city of stalls, and food booths, bars and fruit stands and...just anything you can think of," Ruth said, "all connected by little alleyways and paths. You can get your shoes fixed, your hair curled. You can even buy love potions or all-purpose snake oil if you're so inclined. You're going to love it!" She locked her arm through Sally's.

She led Sally through the alleyways, finally stopping at a shop that specialized in hair ornaments. The square footage of the stall probably measured less than twelve feet. The young woman behind the counter of colorful bows, smiled a greeting to Ruth as they approached. She wore a brightly flowered dress and her hair sported a plethora of ribbons and barrettes. Advertising pays, Sally decided. She noticed something else about the woman. Her left arm was bandaged from shoulder to elbow, so she wasn't surprised when Ruth produced a fresh dressing and ointment from her purse. She should have guessed the real reason for this excursion. Nurse Ruth goes shopping? Hah! Not likely, but Sally was touched by Ruth's caring ministrations.

Sally bought a three-tiered basket to hang in the galley while Ruth visited with numerous friends. Sally insisted on a break when they found themselves on a street of food vendors and drink stands. She spied a corner stand with outside tables and chairs and made a beeline for it. "Either we stop and get something to drink or I'm leaving you, Ruth!" Sally insisted.

"Best punch on da whole island," the proprietor of the stall proclaimed as he set down their glasses. He placed a small bowl of fried banana chips in the center of their table.

Sally sipped gratefully on the libation and stretched her legs in front of her on the hard packed dirt.

"Sally?" Ruth whispered to her. "Look behind you a minute, very casually. Isn't that Doug Wilson down the alleyway? Take a quick look, but for heaven's sake, don't let him see you!"

Ruth moved her chair back about a foot, so that she could no longer be seen from Doug's vantage point and Sally turned as inconspicuously as possible, trying to copy Ruth's maneuver by moving her chair at the same time. The result was disastrous. Her chair caught the corner of the building jarring her abruptly. This caused her to lurch forward, slightly off balance. Sally's cursory glimpse of Doug was not only unfocused, it was upside down, with her rear in the air.

"Did he see you?" Ruth choked back a giggle.

"Well, let's just say that if he did, I would like to believe he wouldn't recognize me from that angle!" She snickered. "I wonder what he's up to. Does he buy stuff for his restaurant here? Fruit, vegetables, that sort of thing?"

"I doubt it. Besides he's the type who would send someone else to do the shopping. Let's look through the cracks in the back of the stall and see what happens."

"Ruth! You amaze me more every minute. Hell, it sounds like a terrific idea to me. Let's go."

They quickly approached the juice vendor's stall and asked if they could hide in the back of it for a minute.

The man looked incredulous for a second, then narrowed his eyes and nodded, as if to say, he never knew what to expect from *Americanos*.

They crept to the back of the stall and peered through the cracks in the wall.

DOUG LEANED AGAINST a door frame. His eyes scoured the alleyway in both directions. It was a different Doug than the one Sally had seen at the Pot. This was a stern-faced, alert Doug Wilson. Gone was the slack-jawed wimp from the Pot. Another man appeared at the end of the alley. Doug nodded to him and ducked into the darkened doorway. The other man scrutinized the area, too, then followed. The women drew back instinctively as he examined their end of the passageway.

He was Latino, his dark hair was slicked straight back and he was too well dressed for the local marketplace. In his hand he carried a package. Sally compared him to the man Mae claimed had followed them. The clothes were different, and the clothes were all she'd really seen. She studied him. He was quite good looking, surely she would have remembered him if he had been on Jake's boat, unless he made it a point to be inconspicuous. Not a pleasant thought. She was not too great in the sleuthing department. Then she remembered that the suggestion about the guy in the marina was entirely Mae's. She looked at the man once more. Could he be the fisherman from the boat. That would be too much of a coincidence for her to swallow. Surely not? Just because he was Latino, didn't make him her watcher. Besides, he was much stockier than the other man. The island was filled with dark-haired men. She wished he wore black like the fisherman, maybe then she could be sure. She berated herself. He was not the fisherman.

He stepped into the same doorway as Doug.

Sally and Ruth waited, five minutes, then ten. They could see the vendor was becoming very unhappy. They reluctantly returned to their table and sat there for a few minutes, chins on fists.

"Does Doug have a twin?" Sally worried her ponytail idly. "It's just a thought."

"Pfft! Not your brightest one, Sally. No, he doesn't have a twin." She laughed. "Maybe he's selling black market goods?" Ruth suggested. "It's tough to run a business in this part of the world, everything is so expensive."

"Phooey," Sally exclaimed. "That's not your brightest idea either. He's really up to something no good and we both know it. I say it's drugs. But let's just say that you're right and it's black market goods of some kind. Then he's still not the Doug Wilson we think we know."

"I don't know," Ruth sighed. "Maybe it really wasn't Doug we just saw. It just doesn't make sense to me." She leaned to one side and took a quick look around the corner. "Come on, hurry. The door is opening in the alley."

The women returned to the crack in the back of the stall. The vendor raised his hands in the air resignedly.

Doug came out first, adjusting his shirt around his shoulders. The Latino was right behind him. He mumbled something. Doug's reply was clear.

He grabbed the Latino by the front of his shirt and slammed him against the wall. "Listen, you piece of shit, don't tell me how well it went, you screwed up! Ten people saw us out there. It's a damn good thing I got more guys than you to depend on. You mess up again and you're a dead man." Doug glanced from side to side. "We stand out like sore thumbs in this hole. No more pickups here. *Comprende, hombre?*" Doug kneed him in the crotch and released his hold on him. The Latino hunched over and vomited. Doug walked quickly down the alley. Then he turned back and walked past the Latino without another glance. He headed their way.

The women looked at each other in panic. If Doug turned the corner, and he was certain to, there was no way he could miss them. There was nothing left to do but duck under the counter.

The shop owner opened a carton of paper cups and eyed the women with a curious expression, muttering to himself all the while. Sally knew their behavior transcended the normal, even for crazy Americans. He stared at them, but only for a moment, because a patron demanded his immediate attention.

The vendor could surely see they were hiding from this customer. Sally prayed he wouldn't give them away. Please get rid of him, she prayed. Then throw us out, give us hell, who cares. Just make Doug disappear.

She peered up. The vendor's fingers curled tightly around the razor he used to open packages and his gaze rose to meet the man in front of him.

Sally tensed for his decision.

The vendor placed the razor within reach on a shelf behind him and smiled stiffly at the sour-faced man.

"Give me a beer! Any kind, it doesn't matter!" Doug insisted in a harsh voice. A voice quite alien to the whine he used at the Pot.

"Sure, mon, sure. I have da best cold beer on da island."

"Yeah, I'll bet you do." Doug's voice changed. The anger abated as he slid back into his role of innocuous nobody.

Sally held her breath while Doug drank his beer. The tight confines beneath the counter cramped her muscles, but even worse was the smell of the dirt floor. Chicken feathers and food scraps had long been swept under the shop's handy counters, accumulating into fetid piles in the corners. Sally and Ruth pulled the necklines of their shirts above their noses to keep from sneezing.

As unpleasant as the experience was, they refused to leave their hiding place until they were certain Doug departed.

The shop keeper sorted his supplies and swore incoherently until his customer left.

When they did leave, the first thing they noticed was Ruth's large flowered bag on the table. Sally's tiered basket sat on the ground next to her chair.

"I'll burn the bag," Ruth suggested. "I rarely carry it anywhere but here."

"It's a thought," Sally agreed. "I don't know about you but I'm ready to go home. I've had enough adrenaline rush for one day. Besides, I need to get back to Sere Dina."

"I'm ready too, but I did want to stop at one other place. It will only take a minute. And it might prove interesting. The woman is an old friend, named Evelyn. I need to tell her about Rita. She probably knows, but still…."

Sally felt her excitement rising. "Someone else mentioned her to me. Would she mind answering a few questions about Rita, do you think? I don't want to upset her."

"Evelyn is a good soul and a tough one. She'll handle it."

Evelyn's house was small, nestled on the side of the mountain. She had a freckled face and perfect teeth. Braided red hair gave her a youthful look, but the lines in her face told another story.

Sally's brain slipped into overdrive before they entered the house. She turned to glance up and down the street to see if they were being followed.

She saw nothing to alarm her at first glance, but when she looked to her left she saw a car glide smoothly to a halt down the road. Sally could not determine if the driver was male or female. One peculiar fact did register, however. The driver did not get out of the car, an unusual decision in the tropics. One arm protruded out the driver's window, so the air-conditioning wasn't on. Sitting in a hot car was suspicious.

Sally followed Ruth and Evelyn. The house was cooler inside than Sally expected. The thick outside walls were painted white, unlike the neighboring, pastel structures. Pictures of sailboats graced the interior walls. Shells and driftwood peppered the tabletops. Small reminders of another life, the boat dollie life, Sally surmised.

"Please sit," Evelyn invited, nervously glancing out the window. "I've heard about Rita," she announced. "I tried to talk her out of the boating life, you know that, Ruth!"

"I know you did," Ruth consoled. She patted the girl reassuringly. "Listen, I hate to do this to you," Ruth continued after Evelyn finally sat down, "but it's important, I wouldn't ask you otherwise. Sally wants to ask you a few questions."

Evelyn glanced at Sally and lowered her eyes.

"You can trust her," Ruth assured Evelyn.

"All right." Evelyn gnawed on her knuckles. She stared at Sally. "I don't live on the other side anymore, you know, but I do know everything that goes on. Julio tells me. He understands that it's important to me. You're the one Claudette calls Boat Mama, aren't you?"

Sally nodded, thinking how unselfish it was of Julio to keep Evelyn informed of her old world.

"I can't become involved in anything to do with the boat world, though. I have a whole new life now, and I don't want to mess it up."

"We won't involve you, I promise. In fact, let's not even talk about you for a minute. Let's talk about Rita."

"Is it true what they're saying?" Evelyn asked with a shudder. "That someone murdered Rita?"

"Apparently," Ruth said, "someone strangled her and dumped her body in the sea."

Evelyn looked ill. "What do you want to know?"

"Can you think of any reason someone would murder Rita?" Sally asked. "Would it have anything to do with drugs? It's no secret Rita used them. How much did she use them, is what I'm asking."

"Everybody knows this place is crawling with drugs. All you have to do is mention the need and before you know it someone will approach you. Besides, Rita wasn't into drugs as much as you think. Two drinks and she was snockered. Like me." She put her head down and pointed at Ruth accusingly. "Come on, Ruth. We've been through this before. You're a nurse. You know as well as I do that most abusers use multiple substances. Rita's drug of *choice* was booze. She might smoke a little pot now and then, and even take the occasional snort of the hard stuff. But if you think she was killed in a drug deal, I think you're way off base!"

"Let me be more specific then," Sally interjected. "In fact, let's forget the drugs for a moment. Did Rita have much to do with Doug?"

Evelyn made a face at the mention of Doug's name. "I wouldn't think so, but I know Rita had something on him. But hell, Rita had something on most everyone. I've never understood how she knew so much, but she made it her business to find out stuff about people. You know what I mean?"

Sally and Ruth exchanged glances.

"Not really." Ruth looked pained. "Are you suggesting blackmail?"

"Do you know what that something was?" Sally asked, before Evelyn could reply. "The something she had on Doug?"

"Let me think a minutc." Evclyn twisted her long braids in contemplation. "It seems so long ago now."

"She and Rita were very close friends," Ruth explained to Sally as they waited.

"We were drinking buddies, first and foremost, and yes, we did ultimately become friends." Evelyn corrected. "Before I got myself in too deep with booze and drugs." She twisted her braids again.

"Anything you can remember," Sally coached.

"She used to tease Doug real bad. She knew him from somewhere before I think. I hate to say this but it's like I said, Rita liked to have things on people. I guess she had been pushed around a lot. She told me once that I needed to find out stuff too, so people wouldn't push me around, to protect myself. Which reminds me, I know she kept a diary if that's any help."

Sally felt herself flush, guilty of suppressing inside knowledge. "Someone told me Rita was pretty badly beaten up when she first arrived here. Would you have any idea what happened to her?"

"Yes, I do know what happened in that case. She told me she left a boat down-island. Said the guy was a real sicko. Got his kicks with a whip, handcuffs, that kind of stuff. I know she was afraid of him. When you run into weirdos in the boating world, you have a real problem. Especially if you're traveling. No neighbors to report anything. And you're usually in a foreign place, too, which adds to the danger. Who are you going to report them to? And who's going to believe you anyway. Boat girls? No way. The best thing to do is jump ship, which is what she did. After a while, I think she forgot about him though. She went off

on another boat and had a great time for several years, or
so she said. You think the sicko could have killed her? I
forgot about him. Damn!"

"Probably too long ago to mean anything," Ruth sighed,
echoing Tim and Pete's words.

She checked her watch. "Well, we'd better head back.
If you think of anything worth mentioning, especially if
you remember what information she had on Doug, you
call me okay?"

"Wait. Why the interest in Doug? I wish I could remember, but I can't see how it could be important. I remember her saying she had him by the *cajones*." She flinched.
"Sorry, those were Rita's words, not mine. She knew things
about everybody though, so you ought to be looking at
lots of people."

Sally studied Evelyn with renewed interest. "What
things? Give us an example. Dangerous information? Life-
threatening information?"

"Certainly a lot of what she told me was rumor, but she
often hinted at knowing secret things. Gossip, you know,"
Evelyn said. "Things like Mae and Jeff being cousins. And
that Claudette and Joseph are lovers, but they're both married, stuff like that."

Sally tried not to show her displeasure at hearing such
news regarding either couple. Ruth ignored the input, leaving Sally on her own.

"Rita was always saying that if she wanted, she could
blackmail some people on this island. Tim from the marina was one of them, and Doug of course. I don't think
she would have. It gave her a sense of power, that's all.
There's not a whole lot of security in the boating world.
Everyone needs an edge. Anyway she used to talk about
the resort, too. Made jokes, said she could probably get a
suite there if she wanted." Evelyn's eyes focused on her

lap. "There was something, I'm trying to remember, but I'm not sure she actually told me the details, except the gossip stuff, and that's really no help, is it?"

"It's all right," Ruth said. She placed her arm around Evelyn's shoulders as they walked to the door.

"Rita saved my life, you know?" Evelyn confided to Sally in the doorway. "I mean it. If she hadn't helped me tough it out, I would be dead. We were going to straighten up our act, together." Her features scrunched up as though she were in serious pain. "Rita had too many problems. I tried to help her. She had nowhere to go. She couldn't leave the boating lifestyle."

"You would have made it on your own!" Ruth insisted.

"No, I would not have!" She shook off Ruth's embrace." Well, bye now and thanks for coming." She turned and touched Sally's sleeve. "Find out who killed her, Boat Mama. Make them pay."

TWENTY-EIGHT

SALLY WATCHED FOR activity in the car's rearview mirror as they made their way across the island's hump. She debated whether or not to tell Ruth her suspicions concerning the car near Evelyn's house. But it was not Ruth the car followed, so why worry her? Ruth carried too many people's burdens already.

They traveled up the side of the mountain. "What an interesting side trip. I feel I've gotten to know you, Ruth." Sally cradled her head back on the car seat. "You're quite the Nightingale at heart. I feel privileged to have been invited along to watch you work. Not many people give so much of themselves."

Ruth pulled over to the side of the road. She studied Sally. "It's my turn for a question. There's a sadness that hangs over you. You laugh easily, but I sense a restraint. I'm almost afraid to ask what's wrong, afraid I'll intrude."

Sally sat up straight. "You're very perceptive, which does not surprise me. There's a selflessness about you that sees to the root of other people's wounds. I lost my daughter, Ruth. When I say lost, I mean she died. Somewhere, sometime while the grieving took place, I almost lost my husband, too. That's the problem. He wants me back, wants things to be the way they were. I'm not sure I can do that. Somehow, seeing Rita's body the other day brought me out of myself. Finding out about Rita and being with the other girls has given me a reason to go on. Becky was the age of most of the boat girls here. They're not taking her place, of course. I'm still trying to find out who I am and what I want. I feel guilty about getting over Becky."

"I don't have a husband or a child, but I know what it is to want to be your own person. I like to believe that I am. The role I play in life I picked for myself. So many people must fight for their identity once they have a family. But I believe in marriage wholeheartedly, Sally. I'm Catholic enough to hope people will never divorce, but I see where it is better sometimes."

Sally lowered her eyes. "You seem so young," Sally said, "to be so wise. Pete said something that's bothering me these last few days, something I'd never considered. He said that Becky and I had shut him out. I'm thinking that might be true. My relationship with my mother was a cold one and I was determined to make Becky's experience different. In the process, I may have shelved Pete. I've always accused him of wanting to be away from us. Am I the one who has it all wrong?"

"Whoa! You blame yourself too much. You have a handle on the problem, the guilt, probably for both of you. Try just letting it go, Becky would want you to." Ruth drummed her fingers on the wheel. "Elaine told me the advice you gave her, about just saying I love you. You might want to try the recipe yourself, see if it rings true." She reached out and squeezed Sally's shoulder, then pulled back onto the road.

"Yeah, right, I'm some boat mama, all right!" Sally laughed and threw her hands in the air. "I do feel better talking about Becky, Ruth. Remembering her puts the agony behind me. And analyzing my situation with Pete. What I'm trying to say is thanks for asking—and listening. Helping girls Becky's age with problems satisfies the mothering instinct in me, but the consolation of another woman's friendship on an equal level helps even more.

"But enough of the personal divulgences for a minute." Sally felt the need to withdraw. She would mull her questions and Ruth's suggestions later when her mind was clearer. "Let's get back to Evelyn's remark, that Rita needed to have something to use on people. I found the idea surprising."

"Me too," Ruth thumped the wheel with one hand. "I certainly would like to see Rita's diary."

"Jake said the authorities have a copy of it," Sally said. She was not ready to admit she also possessed a copy. "I'm sure if there were anything in it pointing to Rita's death, they would have already arrested someone," she assured Ruth, as she had assured herself several times in the last few days.

"I suppose you're right, we'd have heard something," Ruth admitted, glancing at Sally briefly. "And what are we going to do with what we know about Doug? Is it even important?"

"Damned if I know. If what he was doing was on the up and up, he wouldn't have met that guy in an alley. Sounded like a drug delivery, plain and simple."

"I wonder if he saw us."

"Please, don't even think it." Sally slid up in the bucket seat, one elbow sticking out the window. She checked the mirror again. There it was, hanging several car lengths back, the same vehicle with the dark tinted windows she had seen near Evelyn's house. Sally said nothing. She felt a tingling sensation on the back of her neck. She massaged the spot. "What happens when bad weather hits the marketplace?"

"Should this storm bear down on us," Ruth said, "the buildings will be dismantled and stored somewhere. It's been done many times before. Overnight it disappears. Everything that isn't tied down is swallowed up like magic.

The smaller boats on the beach are moved to the highest ground possible, then buried under the sand so the wind won't destroy them, or worse yet, turn them into flying missiles."

"I get the picture. Lord, I hope that system doesn't become a hurricane, I need to work up to this kind of thing. I just got here and I'm not ready! And speaking of things I'm not ready for, are there any cases of dengue on the island? I heard you caution enough people today."

"I'm not convinced there is a problem," Ruth assured her. "Every case of fever and headache need not be dengue, but once there is the slightest rumor on the subject, everyone who catches a hint of a cold is convinced he has the fever." Ruth pulled off the road near the photo shop.

The car behind them stopped too, farther down the street. It was the final confirmation for Sally—she was being followed.

SALLY TOLD PETE about her day while she cut up chicken for dinner. He listened with half an ear as he sorted out the pictures she'd brought from town. He stopped and gave her his full attention when she came to the part about Doug.

"Are you sure Doug didn't see you?" he asked. "Damn it all! Now you've cinched it. I've done everything except beg you not to get involved in the criminal end of this boat dollie thing!"

"YOU'RE YELLING AT me, Pete. Stop it right now or I won't bother to tell you anything else!" She slammed the meat cleaver down on the cutting board. For sure, she was not going to tell him about the Latino at the marina or the person who was following her. "It started out as a lark, to see what weird thing Doug might be up to." She paced back and forth. "You would've done the same thing."

"The hell I would!" he rubbed his chin. "But I sure rather it had been me. I hope Ruth really does burn that bag of hers. If Doug fooled all of us as well as he has, then he's a whole lot smarter than we think he is."

Sally ran water. "We need to do something about him," she muttered under her breath, rinsing the chicken.

"What?" Pete asked.

But the question went unanswered because he jumped up. "Well, I'll be darned. Come have a look at this." He held a photograph out to her. "Looks like you were right, there was someone watching us on our last visit to Eremites."

"I knew it," she exclaimed. She dried her hands on a towel, took the picture gingerly and placed it on the table to study. Among the scraggly, green backdrop of Eremites, was the bearded face of the hermit.

"You said you needed a third present for him, well, there it is."

"I don't know," Sally shook her head. "Wouldn't it be like an accusation that he was spying on us?"

Pete's eyebrows raised. "Let me see that picture again," he joked. "You sure you're not related to this guy? You've both got spy blood in you."

"I think a picture would be a great third present for him," Sally said, ignoring his sarcasm. "But a picture of *us* on Sere Dina. I'll bet he'd like that since he knows us now."

"Knows us well, I'd say." Pete crossed his eyes. "Why, we're practically family."

Sally sighed. "So I'm exaggerating a bit."

Pete laughed. "My question is, how in blue blazes did he get up that cliff face." He scrunched up his eyebrows. "I'll bet he got there from up above, by that I mean he entered from the top by way of a cave. Makes sense. That whole island is one big labyrinth of tunnels and I'll bet he knows them all."

They glanced through the rest of the pictures eagerly, but there were no more glimpses of the hermit. Pete retrieved an earlier set of prints and selected a shot of them on Sere Dina for Sally to put with her gifts for Archie.

SALLY SLEPT FITFULLY. Her subconscious insinuated Doug into every dream. The message was clear, something had to be done about him. Her whole body felt stiff and anxious. Perhaps this should be the morning for her first joybath. She went topside with a towel, washcloth and soap.

She secured the little raft to the far side of the boat, facing the harbor entrance where no one could see her, then used the bailer to fill it with water. It only took a few squirts of liquid soap to prove that Mae was right about its ability to make suds in salt water. The result was a bubble bath as foamy as anyone could want. She reached up, placed her robe beside the towel on Sere Dina's deck, then slid into her first joy-bath. The first of many, she decided. There was something to be said for taking a bath and watching the sun rise at the same time.

Sally was sitting on the single wooden seat of the dinghy washing her feet when Pete appeared above her.

"Don't stop," he pleaded. "I'm enjoying this as much as you are, maybe more."

"What? No smart remarks? You must not be feeling well." She smiled up at him.

"Well…I was thinking that you probably have the cleanest little dinghy in the harbor."

"I have to admit that was pretty clever. And as much as I hate to change the subject, I see one small problem with this bath idea. Now I have to bail it out. If we didn't have the engine attached, however, I could just bail enough to flip it over. What do you think?"

"Does this mean you want to row back and forth to shore from now on, or that *you* plan to take the engine on and off every time you bathe?"

Sally gave him a snarl for answer and started to bail.

After rinsing on board with a little fresh water, Sally dressed in shorts and a tank top. She cut up fresh fruit from the new hanging basket, sliced the last of the homemade bread and placed it before Pete.

"I'll have to make some more this afternoon," she said. "I seem to be falling down on my end of things lately. And to think I had visions of lazing on palm-lined beaches when we came here. Hah! Mae and I are going over to Elaine's and see how the wedding plans are coming along. I really must get in some supplies too, in case of a hurricane."

"We have everything we need in terms of hurricane supplies," Pete told her. "For one thing, we would not stay aboard during an intense storm. You know as well as I do that if we haven't done everything for our boat that can be done before it arrives there is no way we are going to change anything in winds of more than one-hundred miles per hour." He paused. "I've been thinking about Doug. What are you going to do, report him? For what, roughing up some guy and using dirty words? You have no proof he was doing a drug deal."

"I'm not sure what to do."

"I think we need to work on this before you do anything rash. So, why don't you go listen to the wedding plans and enjoy yourself. When you're done you can help me with the check list for securing Sere Dina. While you were taking your bath this morning, I heard on the radio that Tropical Storm Brody became a hurricane this morning. Let's go

out to dinner tonight and then go to the Pot, talk it all over
and unwind a little. What do you say?"

"Sounds fine to me," Sally sighed. In the morning sunlight her fears about being followed seemed melodramatic.
She would watch more closely today. Why cause a scene
when she might be overreacting.

ELAINE WAS PROPPED up on the couch, notebook in hand, in
the main salon when the women arrived.

"We've decided to make a boat parade out of the wedding," Lyle said, entering from the galley with a tray of
coffee and rolls. He set it down and placed one hand affectionately on Elaine's shoulder.

"First we'll make a huge loop around the harbor. There
are only six boats concerned, so that's no problem," Elaine
said. "Then we raft up back here for the wedding, with our
boat in the middle."

Sally and Mae settled themselves comfortably in the
little nook that doubled as a dining area and navigation
table. "Sounds good to me," Sally said. "What about the
ceremony itself? Have you got a preacher or a justice of
the peace lined up?"

"Joseph is a notary. He's going to do it. Later we want to
have a religious ceremony, but we'll do that formally—for
my family," Lyle said. "And guess who's going to give the
bride away? Jake. He came by this morning to see how we
were doing and Elaine asked him. I think he was pleased."

"He's so funny," Elaine added. "You know what he said
in that smart aleck way he has of talking when he doesn't
want you to know what he's really feeling? He said, 'I'd
be glad to, I've always wanted to give some damn woman
away!'"

"Pete can oversee the parade and raft up," Sally said.

"Mae, why don't you and Jeff decorate the wedding vessel with lights and streamers."

"Consider it done, Sally." Mae tucked the hair behind her ears. "This is going to be fun."

"Lyle, if you pick up the champagne, we should have everything pretty much in hand," Sally said.

"Oh no! Boat Mama, you've forgotten something." Lyle grinned. "It's your job to get the bride ready, fix her hair, get her dressed and all that. And a few words of advice on her wifely duties might be neat while you're at it. Like, love, honor and obey, that kind of…." He ducked as Elaine threw a pillow at him.

"If we have this all wrapped up, I guess we should let Elaine get her rest," Mae said.

"Before we leave, I want to tell you all something. It has to do with Doug Wilson," Sally said.

Mae sneered. "Do we care?"

"I know you don't like him, Mae. I suspect your instincts are right, after what Ruth and I observed yesterday." Sally told them about the previous afternoon. She even told them about visiting Evelyn.

"Well, what do you think we should do about him?" Sally asked, surprised at their less than enthusiastic reaction.

They regarded each other questioningly, as though unsure of who should deliver the answer.

It was Mae who finally spoke her mind. "Look, no one likes Doug less than I do, believe me! And if anyone else had told me the story you just did, I wouldn't buy it. No one likes Doug…for a number of reasons." Mae hesitated.

"But not for selling drugs, that's what she wants to say," Lyle said under his breath. "How many boaters do you think have never smoked a joint or snorted a little coke, Sally?"

"You mean you've all been buying dope from Doug?" Sally dropped into the nearest seat, shocked to the core.

"No!" Elaine jumped into the debate. "I guess we knew someone had to be the big guy. We never questioned who. It's available on every corner for a price. And don't look at us like that, Sally. Lyle and I have an occasional joint when we have friends over. Maybe once a month."

"Don't defend yourself, Elaine," Mae pleaded. "Let me explain. You see, Sally, it doesn't matter if you're a light user like Rita was, a heavy one like Lisa is, or if you indulge once in a blue moon. The important point is, how do you get rid of Doug without bringing in an army of agents who will shred the insides of our boats like spaghetti?"

"You don't know what dangerous is until you've seen those guys in action," Lyle said. His hands were drawn into tight fists.

"So we do nothing, is that it?" Sally sighed.

"Now, don't be like that," Mae patted Sally's arm. "We'll do something, but amongst ourselves, no officials. Besides, you've jumped to the conclusion that the confrontation you witnessed had to do with drugs. I've never heard one person say they bought drugs from Doug."

The others remained silent adding authority to Mae's analysis.

"Talk to Jake tonight at the Pot," Lyle told Sally. "If anybody can suggest a clever plan, it would be Jake. He's been around a long time and he knows everyone in this harbor. I've seen Jake take bad situations and turn them into hilarious jokes. There's street smart under Jake's crust."

Sally searched the surrounding water as they boarded the dinghy to return to Sere Dina. Did she really imagine someone could tail her in a boat? She glanced at the seawall in search of suspicious characters, but gave up the effort when she saw more than a half dozen, all of whom fit that description.

TWENTY-NINE

PETE AND SALLY lingered over dinner at an outdoor restaurant above the harbor. A full moon reflected off the golden sand made the palm trees look like black cardboard cutouts against the blue gray sky. Sailboat silhouettes dotted the horizon and their elongated shadows cast hungry tentacles across the satiny surface of the bay.

"When I look out there," Sally said wistfully, "I find myself amazed that anyone would ever live anywhere else or any other way than on a boat. And then…I blink and try to imagine a hurricane."

"And what do you see?" Pete asked.

"Nothing," Sally shrugged. "I can't picture it, maybe I don't want to. It's really out there, isn't it?"

"Yes, it is, but nothing says it's coming here for sure. It's days away and can turn at any time."

"I have an ominous feeling," Sally said, "it's coming."

The crowd at the Pot seemed less animated than usual and there were more tourists on the scene. One rather large tourist couple had managed to move themselves up to the bar—beside Jake.

Not a clever move on their part, Sally thought.

Pete ordered Sally a drink, then went off to discuss the wedding plans with Lance and Lisa. Julia was still with them. The three appeared quite cozy.

Claudette welcomed Sally with a smothering bear hug. "I hear the news, Boat Mama. We going to have us a wedding party. Oh, yes!"

"Yes, yes, it is true. Isn't it wonderful? She's much better now. Not up and around yet but she was pretty sick. They're getting married Friday!"

Claudette clapped her hands thunderously. "Good, good. Then we have a big party here on Friday night, yes? I tell Joseph, we have the pig roast, all the people, they come, lots of food. The drum boys come, too. Here," she said, handing Sally a plastic container and a piece of paper. "You write on here, *pig money* and I pass it around."

Sally did as instructed. "Why not?"

The tourist seated next to Jake became progressively louder as the evening wore on. The only thing he talked about was himself. He introduced himself to anyone whose attention he could capture. He was Ed. Ed didn't introduce his wife.

"Nope, nobody ever helped me once," Ed explained to a less than interested audience. He was a heavy boned man, with a shiny bald head.

"Did it all myself," he continued. "Built the whole damn company. By God, not many people can say they've done that," Ed bragged.

Sally watched Jake turn to face Ed and his mousy wife. He reached over to give the man a congratulatory few pats on the shoulder. "Gosh," he said in an exaggerated tone. "What a guy you are, Ed."

"Why thank you, Jake," Ed replied. "It was just a little metal shop when I took it over, but it's a hell of a factory now." He looked to his wife, no doubt to see if she had caught Jake's compliment. She smiled, but her shoulders hunched slightly.

"Is that the little woman, Big Ed?" Jake asked, almost reverently. He leaned past Ed for a clear view.

Sally cringed. Others around the bar who previously ignored the couple now turned attentive. Jake was about to cremate somebody, you could feel the heat spreading, about to ignite.

Suspicion glinted behind Ed's wife's eyes.

"Ah…yeah, Jake," Ed answered. "Sure, this is my wife, Sugar."

"It is truly an honor, ma'am, to meet the woman behind the man." Jake said. "All those years you cooked and cleaned for Big Ed, how proud you must be." He reached out as though to shake her hand. Pulling it to his face, he kissed it instead.

The woman snatched her hand away as if it were burned. Big Ed was slow on the uptake but Sugar could see the underlying game plan and the rocky road ahead. If Big Ed noticed anything, it was only that he was no longer the center of attention.

"Yeah, Sugar's been a great little helper, Jake," he guffawed. "But it's a man's world after all, isn't it, Jake?"

Sugar plucked at Big Ed's arm and consulted her watch like they were suddenly very late for something. Anything.

Ed shrugged and brushed her hand away. "Twenty years. I built me an empire, Jake." He didn't notice that Jake twitched every time he used his name.

"Well gol…ly, Big Ed," Jake said, placing his hand to his heart. "You must be filthy rich! A goshdarned millionaire! We've got us an important man here, folks, a celebrity!" Jake announced to a rapt audience.

"Gosh, man," called a voice from farther down the bar. "And just to think, he's having a drink with us!"

"Hey, Big Ed," Lance yelled. "Do you give autographs? I just got to have me an autograph!"

Big Ed suddenly responded to his wife's tugging. He rose slowly and backed away from the bar as Sugar clawed at his sleeve.

"Ah…listen, Jake, we have to run, another time, huh?"

"Oh please, please don't go, Big Ed," one of the boaters pleaded, hands clasped in a prayerful manner. He pretended to cry and others joined him from around the bar as Sugar and Big Ed beat a hasty retreat across the sand.

Sally sipped her drink. This was definitely not an easy group to infiltrate. Although Sally admitted that Jake usually left the tourists alone if they left him alone.

Mae came up behind them and coaxed Sally. "Let's talk to Jake about Doug. I think Lyle was right, if anybody can come up with a plan to take care of him, it's Jake."

"No kidding," Sally said. They made their way to the two recently vacated bar stools.

For the third time in twenty-four hours, Sally repeated the details of the encounter with Doug in the marketplace. Jake listened without interruption.

"WELL, WHAT DO YOU think we should do?" Mae locked her fingernails together in anticipation.

Jake arched his eyebrows at her. "Just like that, you want the perfect plan. Give me a little time to weigh this over. There is one point we could address now though, and that's Ruth's bag."

"She really does only carry it when she goes to the market," Mae said. "It's her traveling medical kit."

"I know the one," Jake answered. "And I know where she got it, from one of the street vendors with the carts. You know, the ones along the seawall. They sell for peanuts. I suggest you get every boat girl in the harbor to buy one and carry it, starting tomorrow. In the meantime I'll work on what to do about Doug in the long haul."

"You're a genius, Jake," Mae said, then gave him a quick hug and left.

Jake gave Sally a sideways glance as though expecting her to move away. When she didn't, he fixed her with a concerned stare. "What's on your mind? Something in the diary you want to talk about? Let's hear it."

Sally hesitated, but only for a minute. She told him in a lowered voice about the Latino, the car at Evelyn's and even the gossip the woman had unloaded.

"Rita traveled up and down these islands for a while," Jake confirmed. "She probably reaped a boatload of gossip on the way. It's the stuff she didn't spread all over the island we should be most worried about. I've noticed your attachment to Mae. That little tidbit—Mae and Jeff being cousins—is worrying you if I'm reading you right. Forget it. You're probably the only person on the island who hasn't heard that one. Well…maybe Ruth too, until yesterday. And she's no doubt exorcized that evil knowledge from her memory. They're third cousins for Heaven's sake."

"Thanks, Jake," Sally said. "Mae does mean a lot to me. She makes me feel needed. She told me I reminded her of her mother, jokingly, but I can't tell you what that did to me. I wouldn't like to think of her in a close blood relationship because of the children that might result." She leaned her chin on her elbow. "Don't underestimate Ruth, however," Sally continued. "She's innocent more by design than lack of opportunity."

"If you say so, I'll accept it." Jake gave her a mock salute. "Now, how about the rest of this stuff, the Latino and the car at Evelyn's? What did Pete say?"

Sally stared into her drink. "I managed to leave that out of yesterday's report."

"Uh huh!" was Jake's only retort.

Sally looked across the bar at Pete. He and Joseph were in deep conversation. Then Pete frowned and wrote something down. Now what, she worried. Just then Pete raised his head and caught her glance. He held up the piece of paper and pointed at the telephone, then moved toward it.

"He doesn't want me to get involved. He thinks it might be dangerous since Rita was murdered."

"And now that you have two people following you, you can see how silly that idea is? Hah!" Jake snorted. "The man is right. Time to quit."

"You too? Actually I was hoping you would tell me I was crazy to think I was followed." She saw Pete coming their way. "And don't say another word on the subject."

Sally rose to meet Pete. "What's wrong?" she asked, nervous at his expression. "You look upset. Was it the phone call?"

"It's Barney. He's had a heart attack," Pete told her. "I need to go and be with Marla, she's hysterical. You know how she gets. I wish there were someone else I could send in my place, but there isn't." He shrugged.

"I understand. Marla is so…fragile, you have to go! I hope she called her analyst, she's going to need all the help she can get. How quickly can you get out of here?"

"Joseph said the last seaplane leaves at ten tonight." He glanced at his watch. "It's 9:15 now. I can make it if I hurry. It will only take me a minute to grab my things."

"I'll go to the boat with you." Sally turned to fetch her purse off the bar.

"It would help more if you called the airport and got me connections to Boston. Then call Marla and leave a message on her machine if you have to—tell her I'm on my way. I'll go get what I need and meet you back here. That will give us more time together before the seaplane leaves."

"Be glad to help. Take you to the airport. You name it," Jake offered.

"Thanks, Joseph has already volunteered. I won't be gone more than a few days, no matter which way it goes. Especially if Brody heads for the islands."

"Marla is his sister, and Barney is her husband," Sally

explained to Jake as Pete walked away toward the dinghy wall. "Pete and Marla's parents died when they were young and Marla always looks to Pete to solve everything when life gets tough. Even after she married." Sally turned to face Jake. "It's a fact Pete and I discussed when we were still dating. Marla would always be more like another child in our lives than a sister or sister-in-law."

Jake's eyes held Sally's for a moment. He nodded.

"I better go make that call," Sally said.

PECULIAR THINGS WERE happening, but from Armando's vantage point it was impossible to explain what instigated them. The boss told him never to enter the confines of the Pot again. Sit under a palm like a drunk, or swim up and down the frigging beach to watch them, he'd screamed at him. But he was never to get within spitting distance again.

So here he sat under a palm with a booze bottle full of some shitty soda, trying to figure what the hell was going on. He sure wasn't about to swim. He damned near quit the day he had to go on that charter boat.

Armando looked at the seawall. Sally's husband walked toward the bar. Things were improving, the husband carried a suitcase. He watched as Sally rushed over. They climbed into Joseph's car. Bad news? Good news? He took a long pull on his soda. He spewed it out onto the sand. It was lukewarm, having rested between his thighs for the last hour. When he glanced in the direction of the Pot again he saw the boss angle his way toward his palm tree. A change of plans was in the works. He hoped it didn't require boating or swimming this time.

"I HATE LEAVING you with a storm coming, Sally," Pete said. They sat on the hard benches near the ticket counter. "It's possible that Barney could die and I could be stuck there. God, it sounds like I don't care about Barney! I feel like I'm in a trap and no matter which way I turn I'll let somebody down."

Sally leaned her head on his shoulder. "I know that if you had choices here, it would be different. Barney and your sister need you desperately right now. I can take care of myself. This trip has done things for me. Being together again has been good for us, but we've both always been strongly independent. It's what makes us work. I know what you mean about the trap. I feel I should pack up and go with you, too, but I want to see to Sere Dina." Sally looked up. "Here comes your plane."

Sally stayed until she could no longer see the lights of the plane.

THIRTY

SALLY APPRECIATED MAE and Jeff's company as they walked along the seawall to where the dinghies were tethered. If someone were following her, keeping track of her whereabouts, he would be content to note her return to Sere Dina. However, he could hardly have missed Pete's untimely departure and would be aware she was alone on board. If someone wanted to accost her physically, there had been ample opportunities in the last few days. She felt reasonably safe as she boarded her dinghy.

The myriad of stars lit the heavens with a rewarding sparkle, but did little to illuminate the surroundings on her journey to Sere Dina's anchorage. Clouds were moving in and would soon obliterate what natural light there was. Mae and Jeff were ghostly shapes against the village lights as they escorted her across the water.

Sally refused their offer of a berth on Dream On. "I enjoy being alone," she told Mae. Some truth improved any excuse. She was used to being alone, with Pete's frequent escapades to bizarre haunts throughout the years, but self-sufficient or not, she was rabidly social at times. This just wasn't one of them. She waved goodbye and boarded Sere Dina.

The mess in the main salon took Sally by surprise. Pete must have been more upset than she realized, because it was not like him to leave things this out of place in his hastiest endeavors. The cabin looked like a tornado had hit it. Sally experienced a sudden chill, then the roots of her hair tingled at the scalp when she glanced toward the galley. It was trashed. Pete had not done this.

Sally backed toward the companionway and held her breath. Could the person who did it still be on board? She placed one foot on the step, then inched her way topside. What if there was someone on deck? She jerked her head around to make sure there was no one behind her. The dark opening to the night sky was empty. Sally let her breath out in a grateful gust, then ran for the lazarette on the stern.

Poised above the hatch, Sally divided her attention between the open companionway and the forward deck, her nerves on fire. She saw no one, heard no one. She raised the hatch, reached in and pulled out the lines and sailing harnesses. The compartment had a false bottom. Her hands clawed frantically for the tiny finger hole used for lifting purposes. She missed it on the first sweep. She forced herself to go more slowly and found it on the second try. The panel made a terrible screeching sound as fiberglass scraped against fiberglass when it came free.

Pete's gun was cold and heavy in her hand—but it felt good. It gave her purpose and strength. Her panic subsided slightly. She stood holding the gun in front of her with both hands, then walked the length of Sere Dina's port and starboard decks. Topside was clear. She scoured the surrounding blackness. Nothing. In the distance she could see Dream On's lights twinkle an invitation from her portholes. The smart thing to do would be to get in the dinghy and go over there for help, but she was too frightened to do the smart thing. There was some measure of protection to be gained by standing her ground on board. In the dinghy she would be doubly vulnerable to someone in a faster boat.

Perspiration ran down Sally's back and a cool breeze chilled it. A creaking noise made her start and she straightened to locate its source. The boom swung and bumped the side of her head. Sally let out a cry, then reached up to steady it. The lines were uncleated. She moved cautiously down the deck to secure them and nestled the boom in the gallows. Working with one hand was difficult but she dared not put the gun down. Her hands shook.

Sally took a deep breath then held it to hear better. No sounds came from the cabin. Sooner or later, she must go below. A slow seething anger began to take the place of her fear. The privacy of their home had been violated and if the bastard who did it was still on board she intended to rout him. She'd always wondered what she would do in a situation that required courage. Now she knew.

And she did have the gun.

The open hatch beckoned. Was this a robbery or had someone come for her? She entered the salon. "If there's anyone here, you had better come out now," she yelled. "I intend to search every inch of this boat and if I find you the hard way I promise you I will shoot."

Sally investigated every possible hiding place. She was alone and everything appeared accounted for. She looked at her purse on the table, then smiled. That's what they were after—Rita's diary. Why did she put it in her purse tonight? It was on the sink in the head when she fixed her face to go out and she'd scooped it up with her makeup. Fate. There was nothing incriminating in those pages, but someone might *believe* there was?

Since sleep was out of the question anyway, she busied herself with putting the cabin back to rights. It might take most of the night, but the exercise would keep her awake, and alert. She started in the galley.

HE THOUGHT EVELYN would never come out of the house. For the third time he reached to the inside pocket of his jacket and felt the knife. He had no choice this time, no handy neck would be offered for a noose. No, this one would be messy.

What had she told Sally? For that matter did she really know anything? If Rita ever told anyone—except her diary and he wasn't even sure of that—it would have been Evelyn. And if Evelyn ever wanted to talk, Rita's death provided the incentive to do so. Of course, it might scare her into silence too, but he couldn't take that chance.

His mind reached back across the years to Port Charlotte, to the day years ago when Rita appeared in court to face a drunken driving conviction. Why did it have to be the same day he was there? She actually laughed when they read the charges against him for statutory rape. Jesus, the kid involved had looked and acted twenty-five. She and her mother probably worked together. They took the money fast enough. Told the judge the kid had emotional problems and made things up all the time. That was the easy part. The court forgot him in a heartbeat. But Rita, no, Rita never let him forget that day. She'd been using the incident against him ever since. Well, not anymore.

He caressed the knife, his eyes glued to the back door. Rita's face crossed his mind once more. She had practically cheered when the prosecutor brought up his history of dropped molestation charges. If the mob found out about even one of them, they would drop him in a hole and fill it with cement. He was the money man. He had to be squeaky clean.

He thought about hiring Armando to kill Evelyn, but only for a second. He knew he had to do this himself, same as with Rita. Otherwise, he would just have someone else out there with something on him, someone else to worry about later. Besides, Armando was busy getting the diary, he hoped. Then he'd give the moron five-thousand bucks

to get out of the country for a while. That should be long
enough to finish everything. He'd take care of Sally once
Armando was gone, make it a clean sweep. He wanted
no more blabbering mouths, no more witnesses, no more
nosey dollies to worry about.

He focused on the screen door. Where the hell was
Evelyn?

EVELYN WAITED PATIENTLY for Julio to finish his dinner. She
wanted desperately to go to the back patio and have a cigarette as she always did in the evening. It wasn't that he
begrudged her smoking, it was his allergy problem. He suffered from asthma for one thing. He was allergic to dust,
smoke, cats and a million other things. She worried about
his health so much it almost made her sick. She couldn't
live without Julio. He'd been so good to her and she loved
him for his gentle ways, his forgiving heart.

Julio stretched, then pushed his chair back. He smiled
at her, blew her a kiss. "I'll watch television, *me amor*. Go
smoke your cigarette."

Evelyn blew him a kiss back, then went to the drawer
near the door and retrieved her pack and a lighter.

She lit up as she reached the steps. It was warm outside, comfortably warm to Evelyn. Julio kept the house too
cold for her. The air conditioner hummed day and night
to filter out all the dust and pollen that crept in when the
door opened. Any of those things could bring on an attack for him.

The first puff of the cigarette gave her a rush. She drew
deeply on it. Eventually she would have to quit for Julio's
sake. If she could quit drinking, she could quit anything.

Evelyn moved around admiring her flower beds. Working on them every morning made her feel alive. She considered each blossom a small miracle, a special gift for

her efforts on their behalf. The night blooming jasmine was one of her favorites. She wished now they were nearer the door, so the odor would assail her when she stepped out. No matter, she could always go to them, they would only aggravate Julio's allergies if they were too close to the house.

The leaves rustled behind Evelyn. For a minute she thought Julio had decided to surprise her by coming outside. She felt his presence. It wouldn't be the first time. She smiled as he slipped his arms around her. She could feel his breath on her neck.

It was his breath that brought realization. Julio's breath was always sweet. The breath behind her reeked of alcohol.

A huge arm reached around and clasped her across her breasts. Evelyn tried to scream, but another hand quickly covered her mouth. Something cut into her side. A knife, he had cut her open. The searing pain was more than she could bear. She struggled with renewed vigor to escape the agony, desperately wanting to hold her side, to stop the fire that consumed her very breath. She bit at the hand covering her mouth and felt her attacker cup his fingers. Her muffled screams could be heard now—on the patio—not in the air-conditioned house. The arm holding her loosened long enough to rake the knife deeply into her throat. She felt herself falling and with fierce determination turned toward her attacker as she went down. She wanted to see his face—to know. She clutched at him, then looked up into his eyes. It was too late, a soothing blackness enveloped her and the pain disappeared. Evelyn crumpled into her beloved jasmine, staining the delicate white blossoms a bright funereal red.

THIRTY-ONE

At three in the morning Sally put the finishing touches on their cabin. She picked up Pete's pajamas, folded them and placed them on the shelf behind his pillow. He had forgotten them. Sally sat on the bunk, Rita's diary in her hand. Dared she sleep? It had been hours since she'd returned to the boat. If someone were coming back for a second search, or for her, they would have done so by now. She read Rita's diary for a while. Perhaps drugs or alcohol accounted for the peculiar, introspective entries.

March

Well, here I am getting ready to go boat hunting again, the story of my life. What the hell, it beats living on land, I don't think I could ever go back to that, no matter what happens. I wish I could talk to Cynthia the way other people talk to their sisters. I can't tell her that the idiot I'm with gets violent when he drinks. She wouldn't understand. I will finish this charter, no matter what. I need to find a boat in a hurry or find another marina job. If we were anywhere near one of the big islands I probably would have left already. The people are real nice though and he won't act up until they've gone. Very bad for business. Had some rough weather today. One of the kids was sick most of the morning. The mother wanted to head back early. I hate to see a kid get sick, poor little

thing, but I almost wish they would all get sick, so
the mother would insist on racing for home. What's
wrong with me anyway, I don't mean these things.
Then I look at the father, he's very good looking and
I fantasize about having sex with him, even see him
leaving his family for me. I can't believe myself. This
is the most happily married couple I've ever seen.
They love their children and their children love them.
You can just see it, it's beautiful. I want to get away
from them and this boat. Soon, soon, soon!

Sally knew why Rita would desperately want to get
away from the perfect family. It was everything Rita ever
wanted and never had. She understood the girl's need to
fantasize herself into such a relationship. Rita didn't want
the father, she wanted to be the mother.

Rita mentioned the captain was rough. This must be
the man from whom she fled. Sally went to the next entry.

March

Thank you, God, for getting me off that boat alive.
That last night was so scary. He drank most of the
afternoon on the way in, to get himself a head start
for when the passengers got off. I could see him
watching me and I knew what he had in mind. He
likes rough sex, even when he's sober. And when
he's drunk he's dangerous. Every woman's worst
nightmare. I've managed to convince him to keep it
to an acceptable level so far, but there's no doubt in
my mind that there are more things than whips and
chains somewhere—for things other than anchor-
ing this boat. My God, the look on his face, it gives
me the shudders just to think about it. I packed all

my stuff as we were coming in. When I took the wheel while he went below for a minute, I just knew he would find my bag. I could hardly breathe the whole time. But he only went down there to have another drink where the passengers couldn't see him. When we tied up at the dock he was really nice to the passengers. Actually, he was just so glad to be rid of them. He was beside himself with anticipation. I know he wanted to kick me down the stairs when I came up leading those little kids with my bag over my shoulder. The father looked at me funny when I asked if I could get in the taxi with them. But I think the woman understood. She had a strange expression on her face. She was a woman, and she had been on that boat with us for a week. She must have sensed something was wrong. I know she could. I hope that's all she sensed.

April

Damn I'm scared. Found a boat going down the chain. I have to get out of here. I'm jumping at shadows all the time. Talked to Corene and she said to forget "him." He would have another girl in a week. He goes through them like clockwork. Few ever stayed more than a few months. She warned two other girls, but they wouldn't believe her. They thought she wanted the boat for herself. I can't wait to get on the new boat! I want the wind and the spray and endless horizon again. I'm miserable. I just want to get high and stay that way when I'm on shore.

There it was again, the mention of being high. Rita bared her sex life on paper, but was very careful when it came to mentioning drugs. Was the army of agents Lyle mentioned really that menacing?

Sally put the diary aside and reviewed her suspects in Rita's murder. First choice would be the cruel captain. But logic demanded she accept the same conclusion everyone else had, it was too long ago and the circumstances were not unusual in the boat dollie world.

That left her with Don, Tim and Doug. Of the three, she preferred Doug for the role. The entire population of the island would vote for him to be the bad guy. However, his only real claim to candidacy lay in the incident she and Ruth had witnessed. Did that make Doug a murderer? Did he have underworld connections? Being the obvious choice canceled one strike against him. She had to resist the tendency to wish it were him. Besides, she and Pete had pretty well ruled Doug out when they determined the killer was a boater—because of the knife. Not a concrete deduction, but of some merit in his defense.

Sally found it difficult to consider Don the murderer in view of Jake's undisguised respect for him. Although such a delineation was no fairer than the one with which she sought to condemn Doug. For all she knew Jake could be the murderer. No, that wouldn't play out in her head. But then, what about the woman he supposedly loved, who was killed suspiciously on the ferry. Had she turned on him, maybe had an affair? Laughed at him? A man scorned? Good grief, her mind felt dizzy with the suggestion. She sensed a goodness in him, and had experienced a bonding of sorts with him, too. But did she really know what made people kill? Did Rita have somethingn on Jake? God, she prayed not. When it came down to it, the only person in the whole wide world she trusted was Pete. And why hadn't she said *I love you* tonight when he left.

No time to think of that, it would only bring tears. Back to her suspects.

She was left with Tim. Tim came under suspicion only because he was such an enigma. He acted down-home for the most part, easy talking, humble, successful at running the marina, but he might have a past that would shock this quaint community. Sally conjured up the vision of Tim going out in a dinghy for a possible sexual liaison with Lisa. Of Tim, with the bedroom eyes looking into her own eyes. What did Rita have on Tim? If Sally had to make a guess, it would involve sex. Or maybe drinking. The story about his attendance at an AA meeting was revealing. Was Rita's treasured information about Tim that innocent? Like the fact that Mae and Jeff were third cousins?

Tim as a drug pusher did not fit Sally's mental picture of him. Did he have dealings with the underworld of crime in some other way? The marina would be a great front.

That brought up thoughts of the resort, a place reportedly run by a criminal organization. Tim could work for people at the resort and use the marina for cover in some nefarious business. Doug was employed there, too, or at least ran a restaurant that catered to the resort's guests.

And what about the resort itself? Why did movie stars and politicians frequent such a place? Silly question, Sally thought. Las Vegas, Atlantic City, in fact hot spots and hotels around the world were operated by such people. The famous and the infamous slept in the same beds and money was the integrator.

Sally stifled a yawn, her determination to stay up all night waned with the adrenaline dissipation in her body. She placed the gun on the countertop. It was still gritty in spots. Did the moron who trashed their galley really think she would hide a book in a sugar or flour tin?

She looked out the galley porthole. Sneaking up on

her boat would not be difficult. She opened the smaller ports and battened down the main hatches. The hell with it, let him come back. He would have to make a great deal of noise breaking through the hatches and she would be ready for him. But right now she needed some sleep. Sally poured herself a glass of wine and turned on the small fan over the couch in the main salon. She picked up the gun and tucked it under one pillow. It would be her constant companion from now on. She closed her eyes and tried to blank her mind.

ARMANDO WAS SICK of this job. Boating was for other people, not him. But here he was again in another stupid dinghy, twice in the same frigging night.

Tomorrow he would head for the mainland, maybe go to Atlantic City for a few weeks, visit some relatives and relax. Get away from the boss, that was the main thing. He was tired of his yelling all the time. What the hell, money was the important item. He had five-thousand extra dollars to blow and he was going to enjoy it.

A STIFF WIND arrived in the wee hours before dawn and swung Sere Dina to the west. At first the subtle change in the boat's position caused Sally mild anxiety, then soothed her jangled nerves as the boat rocked gently on its anchor. She drifted into a dream-ridden sleep.

A slight scraping noise on the side of the hull intruded on her subconscious and brought Sally to full alert. She reached up, turned on the small cabin light and retrieved the gun. She slipped off the couch in the main salon and made her way to the forward cabin V-berth. Knees bunched up to her chest, she waited, her weapon held ready.

The wind and slapping waves made it difficult to discern outside noises, but she would know the sound of a single footfall on deck. What she heard was more a thump than a footfall, like something had landed on the deck about mid-ship. Was someone out there? Had they come back to do her bodily harm? Fear returned like a hammering blow. Her heart raced and she felt faint. Then she heard the hum of an outboard. Was it coming or going? Should she charge the deck and face her attacker, or stay safe in the cabin and make him come for her? Her nerves drove reason from the questions, leaving her incapable of action, so she waited.

Finally, unable to bare the suspense any longer, she worked out a plan. If there was someone on deck they would expect her to exit through the center cockpit companionway. Wrong. She was smarter than that. She was going to slither out the small hatch above the V-berth, with a flashlight and her gun.

She cracked the hatch slowly. The cool air felt good after the stuffiness below deck. It revived her courage and her body. She surveyed the aft deck from a crouched position, but no unusual silhouette presented itself. She turned on the flashlight and conducted a finer search—one that included a sweep of the water immediately surrounding Sere Dina's hull. He could still be there.

Perhaps the sound she heard had been from a piece of debris borne on the wind and waves to scrape against the hull. A coincidence on one of the worst nights of her life.

She moved the flashlight carefully up and down the deck. Something lay on the floor of the cockpit. A small package delivered by toss from a passing boat. She'd had a visitor. She hadn't imagined it. Should she touch the package? Sally removed the mooring pole from the coaming and used it to poke the package from a distance. It didn't explode. She shone the flashlight on it. It looked like a book with a note wrapped around it. Someone had delivered a message.

The sun rose as Sally finally found the courage to reach for and inspect her gift. The package was flat and resembled a book, wrapped and tied with a string. She picked it up gingerly, as though afraid it might explode. She pulled the string and paper off to reveal a little red diary, almost a double for Rita's.

She opened the book. The wind ruffled the pages as she examined it. There wasn't a word written in it. She set it down and picked up the wrapper. There was writing on the inside.

How many people have to die before you learn to mind your own business? Guess who's next?

Sally's stomach churned. The killer *did* watch her. He followed her. He searched their boat for the diary. Although she was certain of these facts all along—now she had proof!

She set the wrapper down beside the book and covered her face with her hands. What should she do? Why had the killer singled her out? Because she was Boat Mama, that's why. And she'd been asking too many questions. Pete had it right.

Sally reached for the note again. It wasn't there. She stood quickly to search for it. The first rays of the sun lit the decks and she saw the wrapper float on the breeze. This couldn't be happening. She ran down the deck and grabbed for the paper. It hugged the gunwales in its journey aft, then rose into the air, out of reach. It crossed the boom and drifted downward toward the port deck. Sally leaped over the center cockpit coaming to fetch it and tripped. She rapped her shin bone sharply against the wheel. The pain made her gasp, but she sprang across to the opposite deck. The wind caught the wrapper once more and lifted it up and over the stern. It flew like a paper airplane for a moment, then settled on the sea.

Sally dashed for the aft starboard cleat to pull in her dinghy. The paper might float for a few minutes. The painter hung strangely slack. Her dinghy was not there.

The letter drifted on the waves for a few seconds, then sank. Sally slumped to the deck. Damn, how could she screw up so royally. She rubbed the rising lump on her leg. It hurt like hell. She cupped her face in her hands and surveyed the horizon.

Not far away, her dinghy bobbed on the choppy waves. Her visitor had probably cut it loose to send her another message, to demonstrate her vulnerability. She thought of the line that lay in the lazerette, the one with the wire center in it that Mae convinced her to buy. The one she had yet to put on the dinghy.

Damn it! She would not let this get to her. Sally stood, moved to the side of the boat, stepped over the rail, and cut the water in a clean dive. She stroked in the direction of her dinghy.

THIRTY-TWO

SALLY SAT ON the forward deck and drank cocoa. She watched the sun rise without actually noticing the event, her mind devoted to her dilemma. She resolved not to tell Pete. He had enough to contend with back home. And to involve Mae, Ruth or Jake might put them in danger, if the note was any indication. Besides, what would she divulge—that someone ransacked the boat? That she received a threatening letter? No…she had brilliantly removed the evidence of both incidents. She'd neatened the boat and lost the note.

Of course Mae, Ruth or even Jake would believe her. And there was always officialdom. She could tell Joseph. But what could they or he do? The best course was to isolate herself to whatever degree possible. Pete had been on target. She was out of her league in this mess. Well, it was time to improve. Who was doing this to her? This was a bad dream.

The drone of an approaching outboard interrupted her thoughts. A rubber dinghy headed her way. It bounced roughly on the morning chop and the spray masked its occupant's identity.

Sally stood to greet the unwanted company.

"Morning, Sally," Tim hailed as he pulled alongside.

Sally studied his face, searching for a clue. Was something wrong, something to do with Pete? Tim's expression didn't look so innocent anymore. "What's happened?"

Tim shrugged. "I get up early and scope the harbor out

every morning, and I couldn't help but notice your dinghy was adrift around sunrise. Everything okay?"

"Nothing serious, I didn't secure it properly," she lied.

"Let that be a lesson to you to be more careful. I warned you, remember?" He smiled up at her.

Sally felt her heart beat faster. What did he mean by that? Was he telling her that he'd sent the note?

"Strange goings-on last night, huh?"

Sally stiffened. She waited for Tim to say more.

"You haven't turned your marine radio on yet, I guess. The whole island is chattering with the news. There's been another murder. Evelyn, an old friend of Rita's. Somebody slit her throat last night. Very messy business."

Sally took deep breaths. "How horrible. Why would anyone kill her?" Her mind went to the note. She had taken it as a warning, not an announcement of another murder. Of course it was both. Sally crossed her arms across her chest and dug her fingernails into her arms.

Tim stared at her. "Sure is funny, you asked me about Rita. Then I tell you about Evelyn and now they're both dead."

Sally felt ill, unsure how to interpret his words. What in the world was happening? She shook her head, then stood up in dismissal. She ignored his last remark. She hadn't asked him about Evelyn, just about Rita. Jeff was the one who told her to talk to Evelyn. She would ignore the remark. "Thanks for checking on me," she said in dismissal.

"Well, you'd better be more careful in the future," he said, glancing at her dinghy. He guided his craft away from Sere Dina's hull. "Hope this doesn't ruin the wedding plans for tomorrow."

The wedding! Sally hadn't thought of it since last night. And she must guard against paranoia. Every remark need not be a threat. But it was time to stay away from Mae and Elaine. It would be difficult to put them off. The killer might harm them next. He'd warned her to back off on the investigation.

MAE RAPPED ON the side of Sere Dina ten minutes later. Sally hated to greet her. Being distant with Mae would be like telling Becky to get lost. This would be painful, but it was time to separate herself from the girl. To discourage Mae's company might prove the most difficult task ahead of her. She steeled herself for the encounter, then went topside.

"Permission to come aboard?" Mae rattled off the standard greeting and reached for the gunwale at the same time, as though permission was a foregone conclusion.

"Sorry," Sally raised a palm in refusal. "I spent a sleepless night and I don't feel much like company. Could you make it brief? What's up?"

The look on Mae's face told all—first confusion, then hurt, then understanding. "Oh. Any word on your brother-in-law?"

"No. Look, I have things to do, can we talk later?" It would be best to get the hard part over. "Aren't you supposed to be decorating your boat this morning? Well, I have a job to do, too, so let's both get on with it," Sally said as coldly as she could manage.

Mae said nothing for a minute. Then, apparently giving Sally the benefit of doubt, she smiled and sat down in her dinghy. "I hope everything will be okay, Sally." She made no move to leave, however. Standing once more she handed Sally a blue canvas bag. "Remember last night? Jake said we were all to carry one like Ruth's."

Last night seemed like months ago to Sally. She knew Mae was brimming with news about the murder. Again

Sally went for the jugular. "If you're here with gossip about the murder, I've already heard."

Mae blushed scarlet, then looked away. Still, she tried to be pleasant. "I better get to my decorating then, Boat Mama. Talk to you later."

Sally didn't answer, instead she turned her back on the girl and went below, afraid she would see the hurt or tears if she looked into Mae's eyes.

Today might be easy enough, the news of her brother-in-law's illness would cover her change in attitude. Needing to be alone in times of stress would not be thought of as unusual. She could even beg off on the wedding entirely if she chose, but she wouldn't. That would arouse too much suspicion on everyone's part. A crowded situation she could handle, being alone with Mae or the others was different. Sally didn't want the killer to single out anyone else for removal.

Remembering Evelyn, her quiet voice, her silky red braids and her trusting attitude made Sally ache with sorrow. She really didn't feel social. She felt responsible for the woman's death. The note had told her she was in no uncertain words. Sally felt a wave of nausea and ran for the head. Dear God, what had she done?

She splashed water on her face and dried it roughly to wipe away the guilt. It couldn't be done, but no one else need die on her account. She would attend to the wedding tomorrow, then move her boat to a private anchorage. Eremites maybe, or their hurricane hole until Pete returned. Then when he returned, she would tell him about the whole sordid mess, all her mistakes. They would leave, go down island and let the authorities handle the situation. Sally paced up and down the salon. She threw herself down on the couch and wept for Evelyn.

Sally managed to spend the entire day alone, although several people came by to check on her. She could tell by their attitudes, Mae had forewarned them of her mood. Jake came by. He was the easiest to handle, being stoical himself. Then Lyle arrived and looked too sympathetic. His departure sent her back to the couch. The real surprise was the visit from the ménage a trois. Even Lisa was strangely solicitous, reaching out to be friendly just when Sally was trying to separate herself from everyone.

Sally forced herself to stay below most of the day, worried that someone watched her every move. Whoever sent her the message would see she was properly disciplined. Her only foray from the boat was a dinghy trip to the seawall to call Pete.

She was grateful when he answered the phone. She didn't have the words to deal with Marla at the moment. "How's Barney?" she blurted out. "I've been afraid to call and ask. Is Marla holding up okay?"

"Everything is better on both counts, sweetheart. Barney will make it, but it was a close call for a while there. Marla has rallied with the improved prognosis."

"When do you think you'll be back? I...I miss you."

"Sally, I only left last night. You couldn't miss me, but that sounds nice. This situation reminds me how important you are to me. Is everything all right there? Your voice is trembling."

Hell no, everything is not all right she wanted to scream. I'm responsible for a young woman's death. "It's...." She couldn't speak. She closed her eyes and leaned back against the wall. She should tell him, why not? Barney was going to live. She needed him here. She took a deep breath and opened her eyes.

Doug stood before her, his eyes fixed on her.

Sally straightened. Was Doug eavesdropping? Or did he just need to use the phone?

"Sally, Sally? Are you there? What's the matter?" Pete asked.

"Sorry, I was overcome with emotion hearing about Barney." She stared into the cold empty depths of Doug's eyes again, then turned around to press herself tighter against the wall by the phone. She wished she could ooze through it into the other room. Doug was too close, he could hear her every word. First Tim had frightened her this morning with his strange choice of words and now Doug's presence prevented her from unburdening herself to Pete. Her preferred suspects were making her life a nightmare.

"I understand," Pete sympathized. "I'll be back no later than Saturday morning. That storm is picking up speed. I love you, Sally. Bye now."

"I love you, too," she told the dead phone. She walked around Doug, leaving him access to the phone. Screw the storm, Peter, she thought. There are more frightening things in this world than a hurricane—there's murder.

THIRTY-THREE

THE WEATHER FOR Lyle and Elaine's wedding turned out perfect. Blue skies oversaw the little palm-lined harbor and balmy temperatures promised a perfect atmosphere for the afternoon ceremony.

Sally arrived at the Lady Jane quite late, afraid her pursuer might think she was there to exchange confidences. Jeff, Mae and Ruth were already aboard.

Jeff gestured wildly while he explained to Sally about the water balloon launcher he had just mounted in his rigging. "Nobody has a boat parade without a balloon war," he exclaimed. "That's part of the fun, Sally. Even if it is a wedding, everybody will be expecting it."

Sally smiled. "If you say so, Jeff.

"How is the bride to be?" Sally asked Ruth.

"She looks pretty worn down, if you ask me. You look a little peaked yourself. Mae said you were out of sorts yesterday because of your brother-in-law. I meant to come and see you but Evelyn's murder put me in shock."

Ruth had been close to Evelyn, perhaps the only woman who was, after Rita's death. She placed her hands on Ruth's shoulders and gave her a gentle pat, then embraced her. "I'm so sorry about Evelyn, Ruth. I sensed how special she was to you when I watched you with her the other day. You did everything you could for Evelyn. You helped her get her life straightened out. Evelyn had a grasp of who she was and who she wanted to be. A lot of that had to do with your influence, I'm sure."

Ruth wiped at a tear. "Thanks, Sally."

Sympathy and guilt assailed Sally. My only contribution, she thought, was to make Evelyn a target. Sally tried to maintain distance from Mae's attentions without seriously wounding the girl. But Mae couldn't seem to take a hint, no matter how irritable an attitude Sally exhibited. Once the festivities were over, Sally decided, she would definitely do as she had resolved earlier, remove herself and Sere Dina from everyone's midst. If something happened to Mae, Sally would never forgive herself.

She brought her thoughts back to the task at hand as she pushed an iron across the cotton eyelet wedding dress. Elaine sat in front of a mirror in her robe, brushing out the short blond curls that encircled her delicate face. She wore green crystal earrings and a necklace, to match the green silk ribbon in her white straw hat. Mae clipped a small bit of ribbon to make a tiny bow for each of the bride's white, ballet-like slippers.

They heard the sound of other boats nearby. Through a porthole in the salon, Sally watched as the mast of one craft came alongside the Lady Jane. Whoever it was obviously planned to board. Sally and Elaine went topside to intercept the intruder.

To their surprise, the boat that nestled to starboard was Jake's sloop, Verity. The bride and groom would ride with Jake and Joseph.

"Verity is by far the prettiest boat in the harbor and Jake keeps her in pristine condition," Mae said as she dropped a fender between the two boats.

Sally studied Verity's highly varnished mast and rails that shone like glass in the morning sun. Her hull and sail covers were emerald green and her deck was unblemished teak. "Nice of them to bring a boat to match your ribbons," she told Elaine.

Elaine clapped her hands. "And would you look at the two of them," she cried. "Joseph is even wearing a tie!"

"What's the matter with the lot of you?" Jake said through clenched teeth. "Quit your goggling. Did you think we were coming as bums or something?"

"It's the long-sleeved white shirts and dark trousers," Mae said, her hands raised to her cheeks. "It's an unusual sight to see you two dressed like that!"

Jake glared at the women.

For all his bravado, Sally thought, Jake has a shy side.

Jake had drawn the line at a tie. And although Joseph probably begged to copy his example, Claudette firmly insisted that the man performing the ceremony would wear a tie.

"The boat parade begins in five minutes," Jake announced. "The bride and groom will sit on the bow of Verity as she leads the boats around the harbor."

JOSEPH LOWERED A pig into the pit over the bed of glowing coals before daybreak. Volunteers took turns at the spit— and drank rum-filled coconuts. Claudette opened the Pot early, much to the delight of the locals and tourists, who sensed the quickening tenor of coming events might soon affect them. "Don't dilly dally now, Evangeline," she ordered a black girl in her early teens. The girl fried meat patties and cheese-filled pastries over an open barbecue. "These got ta be delivered to the Lady Jane pretty quick."

Claudette sang as she worked, occasionally dancing her large bouncing body over to the open pit to deliver drinks to the men tending the pig. She had woven jasmine flower chains to be worn by Elaine and Lyle. Only a select few would celebrate the nuptials aboard the rafted-up boats. The real celebration would be at the Pot later that evening.

The blast of horns and the screams of the celebrants echoed across the water. It was time.

The parade approached the town slowly and waved at the vendors and tourists along the seawall.

The group rafted up around the Lady Jane for the vows.

"Okay," Jake said. He stood near the mast. "Joseph takes his official duties seriously, so let's have a few moments of order, you scalawags—long enough for him to perform the ceremony." He shuffled everyone into position.

Mae cried. "It's so beautiful," she sobbed. "They're such a perfect couple. Isn't this the most beautiful wedding you've ever seen, Sally?"

"Now, now," Sally consoled, sniffling herself. "Try not to be so dramatic, Mae." She moved away.

Jake strode forward with an air of dignity when it was time to give Elaine away.

He looks so proud, Sally thought, it could be his own daughter. Thoughts of Becky intruded. Sally pushed them away as Jake led Elaine to a position beside Lyle. Sally watched him give her a small hug before he stepped back. There was not a dry eye on board when Joseph pronounced them man and wife.

SALLY SAT WITH her feet dangling in the air above the deep green water of the bay. She drank champagne. Time to go. Soon the party would move to the Pot and she had no intention of participating in any further activities. Feeling a presence above her, she turned to see Jake standing behind her.

"I've been looking for you." He lowered himself beside her. Under one arm he cradled an unopened bottle of wine. He said nothing for a few minutes. The silence between them reached a comfortable level, a level their spiritual bond made possible. Then he draped one arm across her shoulders.

His concerned expression made Sally long to tell him her woes, all of them. There was his soul, exposed to her again, like that day on the dock when she'd been caught in the whirlpool of his eyes. Yes, he would understand her fear, her anger and all the rest.

"What's happened, Sally? You're carrying a brooding presence with you today. Is it your family? Or did you find something in Rita's diary? Something you didn't like?"

"I'll be damned," Sally swore. "You didn't read the diary, did you?"

"Of course not, woman! That's what I gave it to *you* for. Confound that Rita! Is it more gossip that's bothering you?" He reached into his pocket, removed a corkscrew, placed the bottle between his knees and extracted the cork. He took her champagne and spilled its contents into the bay. "Here, restore your sanity with a fitting elixir." He poured a hearty sample into her glass.

Sally couldn't believe she ever entertained the thought of Jake as the murderer for even a minute. But allowing for last night's circumstances, she forgave herself. Her world was chaotic to say the least, right now, and she would be foolish not to examine every *thing* and every *one* around her. But she didn't need to put those close to her at risk either. Time to retreat. She just wished she had more information to help her sort it all out.

Sally glanced up and down the deck and out to sea, looking for anything out of the ordinary. "Do you know what Rita had on Tim, by any chance?"

Jake drew back, suspicion written all over him. "You're acting real funny now, Sally. You still being followed?" He turned and looked around. "Out here? You think Rita's killer is somebody on the boat? If it's Evelyn's murder that has you spooked, I wouldn't worry too much. Joseph thinks someone local did that, not a boater. But to answer your question, no. I don't know what Rita had on Tim. Can't even guess; I haven't figured him out yet, myself."

Mae watched them from a distance, and Sally knew she was aching to join them and would at the slightest wave of welcome.

"Just thought you might know. And it's the situation at home that has me worried, that's all," she lied.

Sally finished her wine. She kissed Jake on the cheek and stood to leave. "I must go, Jake. That storm could be here as early as tomorrow and I can't wait for Pete's return to move Sere Dina."

Jake held her with his eyes. "You're running away, Sally. I'm disappointed you don't trust me enough to tell me what's wrong. It's not your family, I can see that. Let me at least help you secure the boat." He took her hand and held it tightly.

She felt strength flow through her with the contact. God, how she wanted to sit down with him again and make a clean breast of things. But the note intruded on her thoughts. Who's next, it had warned. She did not want it to be Jake. She pulled her hand free of his.

"No, I can take care of myself, I always have." She felt tears gather behind her eyes and worried he might see through her hasty departure as proof of his accusation that she was running away. "I really do have to go, Jake." Sally stood and moved away down the deck.

Mae approached when Sally pulled her dinghy alongside. It was inevitable that Sally face her before she could escape. This time she would have to firmly push the girl away. The thought of her ending up like Evelyn was not to be considered. She shuddered inwardly, picturing Mae as the body in the dinghy or lying dead somewhere with her throat slit. No, she had to get away from all of them. Mae would be the toughest.

"Sally, can I come over and visit later? I...I need to talk. Did I do or say something wrong? You're acting so different all of a sudden. Are you upset with me? I would hate it if you were."

"You haven't done a damn thing. You just need to learn how to take a hint. I would like to be alone for a few days. Got it?"

Sally saw Jake whip his head around at her words. If anyone would see through her, it would be him.

Mae paled. "I'm sorry, I just thought...well, if you feel better later, or you want help or anything, you know Jeff and I would be glad to do whatever we can."

Sally felt suicidal. First she'd iced Jake. But he was tough where Mae was fragile. She could feel Jake's eyes boring into her. Maybe she was overdoing it.

"Yes, Mae. There is something you can do."

Mae's face brightened, but Sally could see her brace for another blow. She felt sick inside. "I'm going to our storm anchorage." She gentled her voiced just a shade. "If you or Jeff wouldn't mind picking up Pete when he arrives and bringing him out to Sere Dina, I'd be grateful."

"Sure, where is it?"

Sally knew Mae might check on her every few hours if she told her, to see if her mood had improved. And for damn sure, Jake would hightail it out there. She dared not look at him. His stare was burning a hole in her heart. "Pete knows, he can direct you."

She tossed her purse into the dinghy below, horrified to hear it land with a resounding thump on the wooden seat. Damn, she kept forgetting the gun. She was lucky it hadn't gone off on impact. *Wouldn't that be clever?* Sally lowered herself to board the tender, anxious to depart now.

"I'll call on the VHF from time to time," Sally said, then pulled the cord on the outboard. She looked back and waved at Mae as she drove away, the only friendly gesture she would allow herself.

Mae's lingering expression pained her. Better a wounded heart, Sally thought, than a slashed throat. She faced forward, put the motor into high gear and headed toward Sere Dina.

The day's events had drained Sally physically and emotionally, but her anger had returned, reborn in the seething cauldron of her spirit, stirred by her growing frustration. She secretly hoped her enemy would come for her. A passion for vengeance emerged full bloom in her soul. Come and get me her voice cried from within.

THIRTY-FOUR

SERE DINA'S TRUSTY diesel coughed obediently to life at the turn of the key. Sally scanned the control panel to ascertain the status of the oil and temperature, then went to check the water output off the stern. She stroked the hull like the owner of a prize-winning pet who performed well on command. "Good girl, Old Tub," she muttered.

A quick glance at the harbor revealed no menacing dinghy following her course of departure. Most of the boaters were happily ensconced at the Pot for the evening, and probably until morning if Claudette didn't toss them out. The throbbing beat of steel drums reverberated across the bay. Sally recalled her first visit to the Pot, the night of Rita's wake. She went forward to haul in the anchor and hoped it wasn't set too deeply. She could manage it alone when she had to, but two made the task easy.

It finally came free when she was almost directly above it, the coiled line piled high at her feet. She dipped the chain several times to get the muck off the anchor, then hauled it aboard and temporarily secured it on deck.

Back in the cockpit, Sally settled behind the wheel, a glass of wine at her side, melancholy her company. The little harbor she recently called home was anathema now, a place where evil floated on the evening tide. Gazing back at the tropical landscape she found it perverse that her perceptions of this Shangri-la had changed so radically in the last twenty-four hours. Evelyn's death had tipped the scales.

An hour later Sally pointed Sere Dina's sleek bowsprit toward the entrance to her chosen hurricane hole. She scoured the shoreline for company and found it. Another sailboat lay at anchor at one end of the small bay. In the fading sunset, she studied the boat and recognized it as the one that rudely insinuated itself between Sere Dina and Dream On, a week ago. Just her luck. At least they were not to be feared. She hoped the old guy would keep his mouth shut. His verbal abuse of the woman made her heartsick.

She would drop anchor as far away as possible, which she prayed would be out of earshot. A ray of light shone like a beacon from the cockpit of the other craft. The old woman sat there spotlighted, involved in some peculiar task. Her forearms flailed in rhythmic fury. Why didn't she look up? Now Sally could see that the woman was knitting—like her life depended on it.

Good grief, she thought. Not even a friendly wave? *Whatever.* At least she felt certain these weirdos were not a threat to her. They didn't interact with anyone. And she doubted any other boats would arrive, the entrance to the tiny bay was too shallow for most sailboats.

At ten o'clock Sally crawled into her berth with Rita's diary, the link that bound them. But if Rita had known anything worth being killed for, she had not detailed it in her memoirs. Who was the creep she dealt with at the Pot one night? Why hadn't she named him? Who else had Sally heard called a creep lately? The memory escaped her.

Sally selected an entry at random. Rita often didn't make entries for extended periods of time and then would sometimes write several in a row. Without dates, it was hard to tell.

July

I'm shocked. Cynthia is divorced! Mother says it
was bound to happen, very few people are capable
of understanding Cynthia's sensitivities. Actually, I
think Mother is just thrilled to have Cynthia back
home again. Dad didn't say much on the subject, but
he hardly ever does. Don and I have been taking our
charters to this really neat place, we can get almost
up to shore with Summerswind and there's a super
beach. The diving is great, too. I like to go because
there is this incredible rock that sticks out over the
water, and I sit way out on the edge and meditate like
Paul taught me. Sometimes I get real weird feelings,
like spirits and things are passing through me. It's
wild. I hope I get to stay here a long time.

Sally put the book back on the shelf behind her head,
next to Pete's pajamas. She withdrew her hand suddenly.
Pete's gun? The one he kept loaded by the head of the bed.
Where was it? Was there anything else missing that she
hadn't noticed? Damn. Thank goodness the intruder hadn't
found the one in the lazarette. It lay beside her on the bed.

She got up and went to the salon to check the VHF for
traffic and scanned a few channels.

"Brody's picked up quite a bit of speed, but we expected
that," Sally heard a disembodied voice saying. "It's moving at fifteen miles per hour now and still heading our
way. Over."

"Oh boy," Sally said aloud in the airless confines of
the small cabin.

"I had hoped for a sudden turn, straight north, but we'll
take it as it comes," another voice assured its listeners.

"We're heading for cover at first light, how about you?" It sounded like Mae, this time. Sally rarely listened to traffic when they weren't under sail. She reached up to turn it off, but instead punched in sixteen, the hailing and emergency channel.

"Verity to Sere Dina on sixteen. Over."

Sally keyed her microphone. "Roger, Verity. Let's go to sixeight. Over."

"Verity's going to sixeight," Jake announced.

"Jake?" Sally dropped the formalities now that they had a channel. "Sally here, how do you read me?"

"Loud and clear, Sally. Got a message for you from Joseph. Pete called and will try to be here tomorrow morning, early. Joseph told me the airport authorities have doubled their flights in an effort to get the tourists out of here by midday tomorrow. Looks like Brody wants to give us a surprise party. Over."

Sally adjusted the volume on the radio and stretched the mike cord as far as it would go. She slid into the dining booth. "What's the soonest it could get here?"

"Well…she's a determined cuss. She could even arrive by sunset tomorrow. If Pete doesn't get here in the morning, you'd better batten down without him. The forecast right now is for the early hours of tomorrow night. But you never know with these damn storms. You put Sere Dina in the mangrove? Over."

"I will, come morning. Over."

"You got any company in your spot? They'll be your worst problem. You can protect against everything except the other guy's stupidity. Over."

"We chose this place because of the shallow entrance, I had to pull up the centerboard to get in here, so I don't expect a lot of company. I do have one neighbor already, however." Sally drew her legs up and wrapped her free arm around her knees. "I don't expect any more, but who's to say. How was the party? Has it finished already? Over." She deliberately changed the subject since they were on a public airway, the last thing she wanted was to announce her location.

"When Joseph put out the evacuation notice, it put a damper on things. Then Debra said she was coming down with something and promptly fainted, so half the female population volunteered to escort her to her boat. End of party. Before I forget, don't panic if the storm surge moves in tonight, it can be awesome to the uninitiated. I don't know how wide the entrance to your spot is, but believe me the surge will reach in and give you a long, undulating salute. Over."

"Thanks for the warning. Actually, I've felt a few strange movements in the last half hour and I noticed a current countering the wind. About Debra, I'm fond of her, keep me posted. Anything else I need to know, Jake? Over."

"I'll leave my radio on, so if you need me for any reason don't hesitate to holler. I wish you'd let me in on what's going on. I heard you with Mae today. What the hell was that about? Over."

"Nothing I want to talk about on the air. I'm fine, don't worry so much. I'll explain everything after the storm. But thanks for everything, for being a friend and especially for leaving your radio on, it makes me feel in touch. This is WYP8822 clear on sixeight."

HOURS LATER, Sally awakened at the insistence of a fresh breeze that forced its way through the forward hatch. The smell of the open sea reminded her of childhood trips to the beach. She took long, deep satisfying breaths.

The wave action followed the wind like a loyal puppy traipsing after its master. It lured Sally topside. She wanted to witness nature's appetizer to the entree named Brody.

The little harbor was aglow with an eerie moonlight that filtered through the high cirrus haze. She watched the silhouette of the other boat at anchor, as it gently rose and fell on the long slow swells. In the distance she could hear the sound of the waves crashing against the shore beyond the harbor entrance.

In the old days, this might be the only warning the natives would get that a storm bore down on them, barely enough time to gather their things and head for shelter on high ground.

Sally shivered slightly in the cool evening air. Hunger pangs struck. When she was nervous, she ate. Maybe the reaction was instinctive. When people lived off the land, food might have been scarce for some time after a storm. She read somewhere that birds and other creatures often stored up before natural weather catastrophes, warned by some sixth sense.

Whatever, Sally thought, on her way below. Food, she needed food. She piled a plate high with cheese, crackers and an apple for her health's sake, but then poured another glass of wine to tip the balance. Screw health. It might help her sleep tonight. She wished Pete were here. She wanted to wrap herself around him tightly. And she thought, she wanted to tell him she loved him, and always had. Finally, in the midst of her worst nightmare, she knew it was true. They were victims of grief and guilt and they had used them like weapons on each other. It was time to heal, to let Becky go. She willed it and felt a strange loosing sensation. Then, she felt the tears running down her cheeks and welcomed them. She cried herself to sleep.

SALLY HEARD ANOTHER sailboat enter the harbor at first light. It tucked into the mangroves. The occupants secured and departed in their dinghy before the sun was fully risen. She brewed coffee instead of her usual cocoa. A kick start for the work ahead. Going topside, she set her steaming mug on the cabin top, stripped the sail from the main and stuffed the jib into a sailbag.

Another boat approached. Sally's gun still rested among the cushions. She moved near to it and waited for her visitor.

The morning sunlight made her squint. Sally saw two passengers. One of them was Pete. All the pent-up anxiety of the past few days slipped from her consciousness like a veil.

Pete smiled and waved at her from Jeff's dinghy as they rode across the gentle swells toward Sere Dina.

"I need to get back and take care of Dream On," Jeff hollered to her as Pete boarded Sere Dina. "Mae's had me all over the harbor helping everyone else."

"Tell her to take care, and tell her I'm sorry about yesterday," Sally said. It wasn't much, but it was all she could offer at the moment.

Sally wished she could stop everything and tell Pete of her awful two days, but there was serious business to be taken care of first. She helped batten down for the storm. There would be plenty of time to tell him later.

"It's a good thing I caught that flight, it might just be the last one," Pete said. "The storm will be here before sunset. I can't believe it picked up so much speed and kept its strength."

"I would have been all right, Pete, you know that. I planned to hole up in the hospital once I secured the boat." Sally dropped the gun into her pocket on her way below. Pete hadn't seen it. There was so much to discuss, but this was not the time.

She made them a sandwich, then cleared the countertops for rough weather. She tied the hanging basket to a hook on the bulkhead and gave it a few test jerks. Finished in the galley, she went through the rest of the boat and made sure all the lockers were latched properly so they wouldn't disgorge their contents with an assist from the weather.

"About Barney and Marla," Sally said as they shared the sandwich, "do you feel like talking about it? I know how emotionally draining it is for you when things go wrong with Marla. How is Barney doing?"

Pete ran a hand across his brow. "It was rough I can tell you that. Marla indulged in her usual histrionics, more concerned what would become of *her* than Barney, I'm ashamed to say." He looked up at Sally. "You've been so patient all these years on the subject of Marla. I'm not sure I would have been so generous with your attention had the sibling problem been reversed."

Sally reached out and took Pete's hand. "Don't, Pete, it's not necessary. What does our future hold now? That's the question."

He bowed his head. "How would you feel about returning to the States? To Gulf Breeze? We could stay on the boat and I could help Barney for a while."

Sally sat up. "I could handle it. Gulf Breeze is where they have all those flying saucer sightings? I could get into that." She laughed as she took a bite of her sandwich.

"I can't live without you, Sally."

Now, Sally thought, now would be a good time to tell Pete about the events of the last few days, about the note and the murder.

Pete started to say something else, but was distracted by noises on the neighboring boat. "I see some of our favorite yachters have joined us." He relaxed against the coaming.

Sally turned around to look. She could see the man with

the paunch and the gray-fringed face. He wore the same
tank top. He was halfway up the mast. They too were strip-
ping down for the coming weather. The woman busily deposited things into an already overloaded dinghy.

"Have you spoken with them at all, Sally?"

"No opportunity, really." Sally washed her food down
with a long drink of milk. She glanced at their own lightly
laden dinghy, then across at the untidy pile of possessions
in the neighbor's craft. One good wave would create new
selections for them.

"Well, maybe they're just not the social type," Pete said.
He glanced up and down the deck. "I guess it's time to
wedge the old girl into the mangrove. You about finished
below?"

"Just about, but ready to tie her down whenever you are.
I can finish up later." Sally drank the last gulp of her milk
and gathered their plates to carry to the galley.

They wedged themselves as tightly in one of the canals
as they dared, then secured lines to the gnarled system of
roots. They couldn't make the lines too tight because the
water would continue to rise throughout the storm. Pete
stripped the deck of everything removable and Sally took
what she could handle to store below deck. Their V-berths
were stuffed with sails and sail covers. Fenders sat patiently in the dining booth, like guests waiting to be served.
Sally stuck Pete's hat on one of them. She removed everything possible from the floor in case they took on water.

She worked feverishly, aware that the storm might pick
up even more speed as it raced toward them. The leading
edge of Brody was less than two hours away. She looked
at her watch. It was 1:45. The latest report said it would
arrive at 3:30.

Pete came below with the last of the shackles from the
deck and deposited them on the floor of one of the hang-

ing lockers and moved to where Sally stood, staring at the barometer.

"What is it?" he asked.

"Isn't the mercury supposed to drop?"

"It dropped a little overnight, I'm sure," he said. "The problem with relying on a barometer is that it's not really as exact an indicator of an approaching storm as most people think. It doesn't accurately tell your position in regard to the storm until it's passing over."

"Oh great. In case you have nothing else to do in a hurricane, you can plot its course, once it's there. Helpful."

"You want to see an indicator, come topside for a minute and look at the sky. The haze is so thick it's almost like night out there."

Sally followed Pete to Sere Dina's deck again. The boat seemed alien after the strip-down and a strange atmosphere colored their surroundings. The swells, the gray haze, the skeletonized boat and the ominous, dark clouds that rose on the distant horizon to the southwest made the perfect backdrop for a sinister movie.

"Do you hear something, Sally? I could swear I heard the sound of an outboard, sounds as though it's somewhere back in the mangrove."

"I do hear it," she said. "Maybe it's Doug coming to offer his help," she joked. "I think his restaurant is on the back side of this bay."

"Thanks, but no thanks," Pete laughed with her. "We are better off without Doug's assistance!"

"Exactly!"

"I think it's time to close the old girl up," Pete said. He wrapped his arms around Sally.

"I just need to shut down the water pressure switch and check a few things. Five minutes max...and...I love you," Sally told him.

Before Pete could answer, they heard a resounding crash from across the water. The neighbor, who only minutes before had been halfway up his mast, now lay in a heap on the deck. They could hear him groaning. There was no sign of the woman. They waited anxiously for her to emerge from below deck to see what had happened. But she didn't appear.

Surely, Sally thought, she must have heard that crash, unless she was deaf.

"Damn!" Pete exploded. "Where the hell is that woman?" He turned to Sally. "I'm going to have to go over there and see how badly he's hurt. You go ahead and finish."

"I'll go with you," she insisted. "Maybe something happened to her, too. We still have time." She looked at the sky.

They climbed into the dinghy and started the motor. Sally freed the painter.

They could clearly see the man's leg was twisted as they pulled alongside.

"Thank God you're here," the man proclaimed as they approached. "Come aboard, please," he begged.

Somehow, he managed the strength to pull his leg out from under himself and straighten it.

"Where's your wife?" Pete asked. He bent over to examine the man's leg.

"Below. Emma's below," the man managed to say between gasps of pain. "Deaf, my wife is deaf! She probably felt the impact, but figured it was me dropping the boom."

Emma came topside at just that moment. She rushed to her husband's side, wringing her hands and emitting frantic squeaks of panic.

Sally caught Pete's hopeless expression.

"Whatever we do," Pete told the man, "it has to be done

now and we'll have to do it ourselves. There's no time to summon help."

"Okay by me," the man muttered. "Just strap this leg to an oar or something." He turned to shout at his wife. "Stop the damn whimpering, Emma."

Emma stopped abruptly.

"Does she read lips?" Sally asked.

"She don't read nothing, she just knows me is all," the man answered. "There's some canvas straps in the locker there." He pointed toward the cockpit. "You can use it to tie my leg to a splint."

Sally found the straps where he directed. Pete fetched an oar from Sere Dina's dinghy, placed it under the man's leg and strapped it down.

"My name is Fred," he told them as Emma wiped the perspiration that ran down his face and neck with the corner of her dingy shirt. "Can you at least close up my boat before we leave, it isn't much but it's all me and Emma got."

"I'll do it," Sally volunteered quickly.

Once below, she made sure all the through-hulls were shut off and that there was no drain on the batteries from lights or pumps. Sally dropped the wood slats into the door frame and slid the hatch cover closed.

Sally watched Pete and Emma lower Fred into Sere Dina's dinghy. "There's no way the three of us can get in their dinghy with all the stuff they have piled in it," Pete explained. "We'll wait while you close up our boat, then you can follow in their dinghy."

"Wouldn't it be easier if Emma rode with me?" Sally suggested.

"Forget it. I already tried that. Fred said she would be totally hysterical with a stranger."

"Okay," Sally sighed. "Go ahead and I'll be along in a few minutes."

THIRTY-FIVE

HE COULDN'T BELIEVE his luck, Sally was actually alone in the little harbor. Talk about getting away with murder. He stifled a laugh, it was time for business now. It was distasteful, but he knew the way to handle this one would be to drown her. The thought of having her touch him when she died, like Evelyn did, made him nauseous. He stared at the threatening sky. Yes, he could drown her without touching her. All he had to do was knock her unconscious and everyone would assume the storm was somehow responsible. She could be hit by flying debris, or have fallen on deck in the rain and slipped over the side. No telling where the storm might carry her body.

He watched Sally secure the other sailboat, certain she would return to Sere Dina because her cockpit door was still open. He would wait till she went below, then surprise her.

Sally climbed warily into Fred's dinghy, careful not to step on any of his or Emma's possessions. She pulled the cord to start the engine. Nothing happened. Again, and nothing happened. She played with the choke. Her heart beat faster. She pulled the cord over and over until the effort wore her down. Sally sat on the nearest box to catch her breath, not giving a damn about Fred and Emma's things anymore.

What if the engine never caught? The mangrove that blanketed the shore was a challenging maze. An attempt to navigate it might prove more dangerous than the storm.

She could easily get lost in there. Her options shrank with the passage of time. She stood and tried the engine once more. It suddenly caught. Sally twisted the gearshift with both hands to engage it. She headed for Sere Dina.

The incident with Fred and Emma had taken too long. It was almost 2:15. Sally left the engine in idle while she went below to finish closing up, afraid it might not start again.

A shadow alerted her when a boat passed the porthole and pulled alongside. Had Pete sent someone to make sure she got off all right? He probably had second thoughts about Fred's equipment. She moved to the porthole.

The face, not two feet from hers, smiled at her with familiar eyes. Tim. Sally clenched her fists and smiled back. The gun in her pocket gave her courage. She adjusted it to make sure the handle protruded and went topside.

The smile on Tim's face changed when he saw the gun. "So how come you're a pistol-packing boat mama today, Sally?" he asked.

"Didn't want to leave it on the boat, that's all. What brings you out here?"

"Just making the loop, covering all the holes to invite everybody to come to the marina for shelter. Safest spot on the island if you ask me. You want me to follow you? This dinghy doesn't look too reliable. Where's yours, anyway?"

"Accident on the next boat," she said, pointing at the neighboring sailboat. "Didn't you pass Pete on your way here? He took them to the hospital."

"I came from the far side of the island, remember? I'm making a loop, started at dawn, don't want to miss anybody. You sure you don't need any help with anything?" He gave a tug on one of the lines that held Sere Dina to the mangrove. "I promise not to make any knife knots." He laughed.

Sally took deep breaths, trying not to think what he

might mean. Had he tied the knot around Rita's neck, then tried to cut it with a knife? Was the game over?

"I think we're fastened in well enough, Tim," she said, her hand on the butt of the gun. "And thanks for the offer. I'll probably go to the hospital to make sure Pete's not still there." Sally stayed in the companionway until Tim exited the harbor. Was Tim the murderer? The agony of suspicion gnawed at her. She liked Tim, but she couldn't trust anyone.

Before leaving Sere Dina, Sally placed Rita's diary in two zip lock bags, then stuck it in the lined pocket of her jacket for safekeeping. Their real valuables were with Pete.

Sally emerged from below decks and boarded Fred's dinghy. The rain started, and by the time she reached the open water, it came down in sheets and a strong breeze slowed her progress. The ebony sky cast an eerie shadow over the earth and sea. High above her, birds skittered and dove, like confetti caught in the path of a rotating fan.

Fred and Emma's dinghy didn't ride the waves smoothly, it plowed into the boiling black swells. At least Emma had thought ahead enough to put everything in plastic bags for protection against the elements. Sally wondered what Fred and Emma might consider valuable enough to take ashore.

She didn't have time to ponder the subject long, because the little engine sputtered. "Oh, Lord. Please, please don't let this thing quit on me," she prayed. Sally's dripping hair fell across her eyes and she mopped away the water with one arm. She had traveled less than a quarter mile. She tapped the engine cowling with her other hand. "Come on, baby, you can do it," she said.

Giving one loud cough, the engine died. Sally adjusted the mixture and played with the choke. The engine would not start again. Frantic, she rummaged through the bottom of the dinghy. The effort failed to produce anything resembling paddles. What kind of boaters were these people? Her wet cotton clothing stuck to her back and legs. She shivered. One of the bags had to contain oars. She ripped one open, only to find an old half strung tennis racket and packages of instant soup. Tearing open another she unearthed a week's supply of gray tank tops for Fred and an assortment of rusted canned foods.

Decision time. Even if she found the oars, could she row to the safety of town before the edge of the storm hit? She could swim to shore with the dinghy in tow, or she could swim to shore without it and make her way across the land. Sally quickly opened bag after bag of Fred and Emma's treasures in a futile search for something she considered worth saving.

In the last bag she discovered a cache of Emma's treasures—jewelry, several broken hearing aids, a stack of ancient postcards and a solid bronze statue depicting the theme of see no evil, hear no evil, speak no evil. A gold ring graced the neck of the monkey representing the one who was to hear no evil.

Sally could not leave this assortment behind. It was clearly important to Emma. But she couldn't swim with it either, it would be like swimming with an anchor.

Sally put passports and other papers into the bag with Emma's treasures and tied the bag to the wooden seat. She placed the gun on the floor of the dinghy, then jumped in the water. She stroked toward shore. The rain slackened enough to see the island. Long high swells pushed her toward her goal. The land was closer each time she peeked from the top of a wave.

Coral reefs were exposed between the huge waves. She could be dropped on a reef by one wave and raked across it by the next. Sally decided to swim as close as she dared, then ride a wave over the reef. She would have to climb

back in the dinghy when she got close enough and then
brace herself across the seats.

Emma's sad treasures may have saved her from disaster,
for without them she would have abandoned the dinghy.

Above the roar of the waves, a new sound startled Sally.
The sound of an approaching boat.

Through the rain and sea spray she made out the shape
of a dinghy. The large figure Sally hoped might be a res-
cuer was Doug. Thank God. Obnoxious or not, Doug represented help. She was actually happy to see him. She
waved anxiously. He might miss her in the rain and surf.

She climbed aboard Fred's dinghy and stood up in the
raft almost capsizing it and yelled at the top of her lungs
for Doug to stop. She caught brief flashes of him when his
dinghy crested the giant waves.

Hand cupped above his brow, Doug scoured the immediate horizon searching diligently for something. Could he
be looking for her?

He wouldn't know she was out here alone and in need
of help. But what if Doug was the killer? Trust no one,
an inner voice reminded. She could make it to shore by
herself.

Sally jumped in the water again and kicked in the direction of the reef. Something tugged at her mind as she
swam. Tim kept saying knife knot, knife knot, over and
over in her head. Why? What was so important about
the term? All sailors were familiar with what were called
knife knots. They made jokes about them, because only
novices made them. No real sailor ever tied a knot he
couldn't undo. It took a knife to undo the work of an am-
ateur. That was it! The killer wasn't a boater, because he
couldn't untie his own knot. It was the clue that had eluded
her. The secret of knots was in their undoing. Doug didn't
know beans about boats. If he tied a noose around Rita's

neck, he probably did it with a knot he couldn't undo, except with a knife. He was the only true candidate related to that clue, all along!

The noise of Doug's dinghy drew closer. Sally kicked with all her might, but he quickly closed the distance between them.

Doug hailed loudly. "Sally, let me help you, you're very close to the reef." He reached out and grabbed a rubber handle on Fred's dinghy.

"I'm fine," she yelled, "I'm meeting Pete on the beach. Please, don't worry about me."

A wave broke over her head. When she looked again, there were two boats—Tim's and Doug's. She strained to hear their raised voices. The two craft collided. Sally grasped the side of Fred's dinghy and hauled herself up.

Doug brandished an oar. He swung it at Tim.

Sally heard Tim yell just before the oar caught the side of his head. She watched, horrified as he fell overboard.

Doug turned toward her.

Sally focused on his face when he approached. His eyes bored into hers. Eyes filled with hate. He swung the oar high when she came within reach.

Sally raised one arm in the air to fend off the weapon. The blow connected with her forearm, then struck a glancing blow to the side of her face. She felt dizzy from the impact. She treaded water and took deep breaths. Doug aimed the next blow, but Sally was prepared. She caught the descending oar in both hands and wrenched it from Doug's grip. She placed her feet against the side of his boat and pushed off as hard as she could.

Fred and Emma's dinghy drifted free, directly toward the breaking surf.

Doug lurched for the controls of his outboard. He

pushed it into gear, revved it to full throttle and made his charge.

Sally swam to avoid the racing propeller. At the last second she turned, then let go of the oar and sank beneath the waves. The oar floated broadside to the oncoming boat.

The engine made a thunk when it encountered the hard wooden obstacle.

Sally surfaced.

In the distance she took note that Tim's dinghy was empty. She looked in all directions and finally spied him as he struggled to hoist himself back into his dinghy. Good, at least the blow hadn't left him unconscious.

No sign of Doug, he must have fallen in when the prop hit the oar. She looked toward shore. Fred's dinghy had not breached the surf line. She made a beeline for it. There was no other way to cross the reef. She hoped Tim had drowned, but dare not approach his craft, in case he lay huddled in the bottom waiting for her to come to him.

She climbed aboard Emma and Fred's weary dinghy. The waves were monstrous now. Sally braced herself and sculled into position, her stern to the oncoming surf. She looked and saw the grand-daddy of all waves bearing down on her.

The leviathan lifted her craft like a feather. White knuckled, Sally held on with both hands. The roar of the breaking wave was deafening. It dropped Sally into space as it crested with her on its lip. She kept her forward position on the wave and rode the monster like a bucking bronco. Coral ripped a long gash in the canvas floor of the dinghy and one side of it deflated. The boat spun wildly in the surge, but finally slowed when it reached the long stretch of sandy bottom. She had conquered the reef!

Sally waded through the knee-high waves to shore on wobbly knees. She untied Emma's belongings from the wooden seat and used the painter to make a shoulder strap to carry them. Her hand unsuccessfully explored the bottom of the dinghy for the gun. It must have slipped through the slash made by the reef. If Doug were done for, she wouldn't need it now anyway. Relief washed over her.

She glanced at the violent sea and couldn't believe her eyes. Doug was coming. Like her, he braved the journey, perched on the tip of a wave.

Where was Tim?

Sally raced down the beach. It was three o'clock, but the dark sky made it seem like nine. She looked back again. Doug followed. He successfully crossed the reef. Unbelievable.

Giant rocks loomed ahead of Sally, rocks that came down to the sea. The water was up to the trees. She stopped to catch her breath at the foot of the rock pile, then climbed. The rocks were jagged and slippery in the rain. It would be easy to twist an ankle. It was like something out of a bad dream. For every two steps she gained, she slid back one. The more frantically she worked at it, the harder it became. Doug slowly gained on her. Her arm throbbed from where he hit her with the oar, making it difficult to clutch the outcroppings.

Doug grunted. He was not far behind her now. What fueled his efforts? she wondered. He was not the outdoor type. Then she knew. He had resources to provide the required push. Drugs. Drugs that could make him both powerful and insane. Her anxiety moved up a notch.

The wind took her advantage when she reached the top and almost threw her off her feet at times. Cactuses covered the dry islands. They raked her ankles and calves as she ran. A mass of vines entangled her legs. She tugged furiously at the stickers that clutched her pants. Her clothing held her captive.

Suddenly, Doug grabbed her by her wounded arm. He wrenched her free of the brambles and pushed her roughly back toward the cliff face.

"What do you want with me?" she screamed.

"Everything was fine till you came along and put your nose in. I know you saw me from your boat. And I know you read Rita's diary."

"Her diary didn't even mention your name," Sally said. "Let me go!" She fought to free herself. They neared the huge rocks that bordered the edge of the cliff.

"You went to meet her family and you followed me to the other side of the island."

"I didn't follow you anywhere. Did you kill Evelyn too? You're making a mistake!"

"Rita was going to ruin me. I gave her everything she wanted, but that wasn't good enough. Sooner or later word would get out. She talked too much. When you went to visit Evelyn, I knew I had to make it end."

"You're crazy! I don't know anything. Evelyn probably didn't either," she shouted above the wind.

"It doesn't matter now, does it?" he yelled, pushing her toward the slippery rocks.

A huge palm frond hit them across their backs, bringing them to their knees. Doug's grip loosened. He got quickly to his feet. Fear paralyzed Sally. Her throat tightened as though his hands were already on her neck. She tried to scream but nothing came out. He grinned down at her.

Sally's anger returned. Still on her knees, she butted him in the gut with her head. It unbalanced him. One moment he was there and the next he disappeared over the rocky precipice with a bloodcurdling scream.

Sally crawled to the edge. He was snagged on a jagged boulder ten feet down the hillside.

Doug clawed the ground for a handhold.

Sally fled, limping along the cliff top. Lightning lit the jet black sky and thunder shook her bones. The wind pushed at her from the very direction she wanted to go. Brody had arrived. She would never make it to the hospital, but she might make it to town, maybe even the marina. If only she had availed herself of Tim's offer. Dear God, Tim might be dead for all she knew. She had seen him climb back into his dinghy though. And he knew the sea as well as anyone. He would make it.

A fierce gust of wind slammed her to the ground. She broke her fall with her good arm, but landed with Emma's sharply pointed statue against her side. Searing pain radiated across her chest. She struggled to an upright position and slanted into the wind once more. It didn't hurt as much when she bent over, but she knew she had cracked a rib at the very least, if not broken it. Every breath felt like a stab wound. The wind and rain flailed at her. She could hardly see. A huge cactus plant torn from its roots and borne on the maddening wind struck her in the leg and she cried out in pain. There would be more. She had to find cover. She wrenched the cactus from her leg and cried out again. It hurt more when it came out than when it impaled her. The pain in her side worried her, what if the rib were broken and it punctured her lung? Best not to think on the worst scenario, she cautioned herself. *Just keep moving.*

The ground beneath her feet changed. She was on a road. On the island, all roads really did lead to town. She inched along with hope.

A raucous sound came to her through the howling tempest. She moved aside instinctively as a metal garbage can hurtled past, just missing her. Town could not be far. That would mean more debris, but it also meant shelter.

A large square shadow loomed ahead. It wasn't much of a building, but the absence of wind on the lee side provided some respite. Sally slid to a sitting position against the wall and rested her head on her knees. The stabbing pain in her ribs sapped her will to continue.

She stretched out her ravaged legs. Blood spread in circles on her rain-drenched, white cotton deck pants. She plucked large cactus needles from her thighs. Each extraction caused her to shudder. A dizziness overtook her. She had to find real shelter before the hurricane moved further inland.

Around the edge of the building, Sally spied another one, larger than the first. Arms tight against her sides, she made for it. Fear and pain came in alternating waves.

The wind grew stronger. Nearby trees were bent over. Strips of tin roofing flipped and clattered down the street. Every step became a victory over the last. She pressed on, convinced she was headed in the right direction. The next building was a row of shops she recognized. The beginnings of town. She tried door after door. All of them were nailed shut against Brody. She had to reach the seawall that led to the marina.

A stooped figure staggered in front of her. She ran forward, head knifed into the wind. The roar of crashing waves told her the jetty was close.

Sally recoiled when she recognized the stooped figure.

Doug jumped back in surprise, then recovered and grabbed for Sally. His clothing was tattered and blood streaked. He stumbled, but managed to grab her jacket when she tried to pass. A string of obscenities spewed from him above the maelstrom.

"Rotten bitch, you damned near killed me."

Sally spun violently to pull free of his grip. Emma's statue, still nestled in the sack hanging from her shoulder, swung with her and struck Doug full in the face.

Doug released her.

Sally stepped away, but tripped and fell to the ground.

Doug threw himself on top of her. Blood oozed from his nostrils and eyes. His weight forced the air from her lungs. Water and blood ran from his bloated face onto hers. She pushed against his shoulders and turned her head to suck in air. Doug's fingers closed tightly on her throat. Bright flashes of light blossomed behind her eyes. She passed out.

When Sally came to, the oppressive weight had lifted from her body. She could breathe again but she couldn't see. Rain and dirt assaulted her eyes. Everything was a blur as Doug dragged her along the ground by her feet. Her head scraped and bumped across the rough island terrain. She flailed at the ground for a handhold. Thorny vines tore at her fingers. The rocks and shells that bordered the road gouged her back. She screamed.

Giant waves broke over the jetty, sending torrents of water over them. Sally tasted salt water. Her vision cleared. She quit fighting his efforts to drag her, pretending to slip into unconsciousness again.

They gained the edge. He dropped her legs.

Sally squinted through the rain.

Doug squatted before her rocking back and forth unsteadily, hands resting on his knees, catching his breath.

Sally pulled her legs up and kicked out at Doug with all she had left.

Doug plummeted off the jetty.

Sally rolled over onto all fours, then fought to stand. The marina, she had to get to the marina.

THIRTY-SIX

SALLY CRAWLED THE last few steps up the stairway at the marina and beat on the heavy door.

It was Pete who opened it. She fell gratefully into his arms.

"Oh, my God! Sally." Picking her up, he carried her to the overstuffed chair in Tim's small office.

Sally put her face in her hands as Mae arrived with a dry towel. Mae patted her hair and back, ministering to her with a worried look. "Oh dear, oh dear," she muttered as she worked to wipe away the blood and water.

"I thought you were coming right behind me," Pete said. "When I looked back and saw you trying to start Fred's engine, I knew things were bound to go wrong. Town was deserted. I had to walk a mile for help with Fred and Emma. When I finally got them taken care of, Brody arrived. I waited at the seawall for a while, but decided you had more sense than to be in the water at that point. You would head overland for the marina. When you weren't here I tried calling the hospital thinking you had probably gone there. But the phone lines were already down."

"I.... So much went wrong, Pete."

She clutched at Mae's ministering hands. "Oh, Mae, I treated you so badly these past few days. Everything I did and said was for a reason, you have to forgive me."

"Sally, you're safe now." Pete touched her shoulder lightly.

"You can talk about it all later."

"No...no...I have to tell you! The boat we heard in the mangrove, the one we joked about being Doug's. Well, it was no joke, he was there." Sally buried her face in the towel Mac offered. "Doug tried to kill me, and he'll try again when he finds me."

"Doug?" Pete asked.

Sally took long gasps of air. "First he came after me in the boat, but I got away from him in the water. Tim was there, he tried to help. Doug hit him with an oar."

"It's okay, Sally," Pete assured her. "Tim's here. He got here about ten minutes ago. We've sent for an ambulance, he probably has a concussion. He doesn't know what happened to him, just remembers finding himself in the water next to his dinghy."

"Oh thank God he's alive. Doug chased me up the cliff. I pushed him. At first I thought I had killed him. I wanted to kill him!"

"He deserves worse than that," Mae declared, her fists clenched tightly against her chin.

Sally continued to dab at her soaked clothing with the towel. "He said I was responsible for everything going wrong. He believed I'd discovered whatever Rita had on him. I told him he was crazy. He thought I knew everything, especially after he found out I'd visited the other side of the island. He murdered Evelyn."

Mae gasped.

Someone handed Sally a dry towel.

Dozens of refugees tried to crowd into Tim's office to see what was going on, but Tim warded them off.

"I pushed him off the jetty," Sally continued breathlessly. "He's too evil to die though, I just know it. He may have been behind me the whole way here. Don't let him in here!"

"I hope he does come here," Pete said with fury. "I'll

finish him off myself if he shows up!" He brushed Sally's damp hair from her face tenderly.

"We thought the killer was a boater because he carried a knife." Sally reached for Mae's hand. "That was the something I thought I knew. Tim mentioned knife-knots today as a joke. The murderer intended to kill Rita with a knife, but at the last minute used the rope instead. The knife wounds were inflicted in an attempt to cut the line. Doug wasn't a boater, he couldn't tie a decent knot, one that can be undone. He tied a knife-knot! Don't you see. We should have known the killer couldn't be a boater."

Mae looked up, shaking her head. "The ambulance is here."

"I don't want an ambulance," Sally insisted.

"It's for Tim," Pete assured her. "Tim and you both need to have someone look at you. There's blood all over your pants." He held her hand. "You look like you've come through a war zone."

"I know I must look terrible. Pete, but I'm not leaving here and I'm not leaving you!" She clutched at his arm as she took a deep lung full of air. "I think some of my ribs are cracked, but I can breathe okay."

"Okay. But I want the emergency people to look at you just in case. Don't worry, I'll ride with you if they say you have to go."

"Debbie is going too, she's not feeling well," Mae added. "Remember Typhoid Mary? Well, we may have our own Dengue Debra."

Mae draped a blanket over Sally, while they waited for the ambulance attendant.

The young man checked Sally's vitals and examined the bump on her head. "Her eyes are dilating normally, no nausea. Some nasty scrapes and bruises. She's going to be sore for a while. But unless she can't stand up, she can stay here. The hospital is jammed. Come in after the storm though and have someone check out the head wound."

Sally sank back in the chair and closed her eyes. Now she could rest.

THE SOUND OF wood ripping woke Sally. She opened her eyes to see part of the roof lift at the corner of Tim's office. Pete and Mae were beside her in an instant.

"Come on, Sally, I'm afraid we can't wait any longer, the winds are worse."

Sally managed to get up. "I don't understand. Where can we go?" She leaned heavily on Pete.

"You're going to love this," Mae smiled. "Where you've been wanting to go since you first spotted it. Under that giant table in the center of the main room."

"I thought it was full of storage stuff."

"Tim emptied it out this morning, just in case. He figured it would serve as a last-ditch shelter if things got really bad," Pete said.

Sally insisted on going in last, knowing that her wounds would make crawling slower than a snail. She inched along behind Mae on hands and knees, but didn't go in far, she couldn't, so she just went in far enough for them to close the door behind her. At first it was pitch dark, but soon she could see others by the halos of their flashlights. Static coughed from a radio Lance held close to his face.

"You know," she confided to Pete, "I think I'll crawl for the next few weeks, it hurts less than walking." She settled herself on the sleeping bag he spread out for her.

In minutes Sally drifted off again. Time lost its frame of reference. Voices drifted into her dreams. A familiar voice woke her.

"I wonder who built this thing," Jeff said. He frowned

in the strange flickering light of the crossed flashlight beams. "It's some hurricane hole."

Sally sat up. "Pete, what about the islanders, Claudette, Joseph…the others?" She looked around. "Where are they?"

Pete put his arm around her. "They're okay. The islanders are used to storms. In a week, things will be back to normal. This wasn't a force five or anything. They've handled worse. I bet they'll be piecing the Pot back together by tomorrow."

Sally placed her hand on Pete's thigh and sighed. That's the way Ruth had described the scenario. The town would fold up, bury their boats, buildings and whatever else wasn't tied down and be back to normal in days.

"Hey, listen," Lance called from a dark recess. "The wind has stopped! We must be in the eye." He crabbed across the tightly packed space toward the small door.

The group exited like rats from a maze. Pete and Sally brought up the rear. "By the time I hobble out there it will probably be over," Sally said.

The first thing she noticed was the hole in the roof. The second was that they could see stars through the hole. Even though she knew the weather became ominously still in the eye of a hurricane, the reality of it shocked her.

"The balcony is safe." Jeff beckoned from the doorway. "You've got to come out and see this!"

Sally stared out at the surface of the bay. Waves danced upon waves, their meringue tips frothed over as they met and sliced through each other. "I thought everything was calm in the eye, even the sea," she said to Pete.

"No, the sea goes through real turmoil in the eye, it's pulled in all directions at once. Even this part is tough when you're riding it out in a boat."

"Is that Jake's boat out there?" Sally asked.

"For sure," Jeff said. "And he's on it. Don's riding it out too; diehards that they both are. They're keeping in touch by radio." He looked out at the water again.

He wanted to be out there too, Sally realized. They all did. "What about Don's new boat girl, is she out there with him?"

"Nah, she's here with us somewhere," Jeff said.

"I bet Rita would have stayed on the boat."

"Bet your life she would," Jeff agreed. "Hell of a boat girl."

Mae tugged at her arm gently. "Sally, what's that down there?" She pointed to a dark shadowy area at the water's edge. They hooded their eyes for a better look. Sally gasped when someone aimed a flashlight beam at it.

"It's a body!" Mae exclaimed. Her hands flew to her face.

Pete and the others directed their flashlights on the object.

The face-up body below them was Doug's.

"Oh, my God. I killed him!" Sally cried.

Pete extinguished the light. "No, I'm betting the storm probably did!"

Mae put an arm across Sally's shoulders. "It doesn't matter."

"Shouldn't we get his body?" Sally asked.

"No sense in losing someone else on account of Doug," Jeff hollered. "And I doubt you could get any of the boating crowd to volunteer now that they know he killed Rita and Evelyn."

A few voices put an amen to that.

"Brody is about to kick us with his other leg," Jeff announced. "We'd better get back inside."

Sally held back for a minute. She looked out to sea and thought of Archie alone on Eremites. He would be safe in a cave somewhere. She thought of Rita. She pressed her hand against her jacket pocket. Rita's diary was still there. She thought of Evelyn. Looking up at the quickly fading stars she said a silent prayer for Rita and Evelyn's souls. Then, like she had with Becky, she let them go with a blessing.

Pete slid his arm around Sally and led her back inside.

* * * * *

REQUEST YOUR FREE BOOKS!
2 FREE NOVELS PLUS 2 FREE GIFTS!

HARLEQUIN®

INTRIGUE®

BREATHTAKING ROMANTIC SUSPENSE

YES! Please send me 2 FREE Harlequin Intrigue® novels and my 2 FREE gifts (gifts are worth about $10). After receiving them, if I don't wish to receive any more books, I can return the shipping statement marked "cancel." If I don't cancel, I will receive 6 brand-new novels every month and be billed just $4.74 per book in the U.S. or $5.24 per book in Canada. That's a savings of at least 14% off the cover price! It's quite a bargain! Shipping and handling is just 50¢ per book in the U.S. and 75¢ per book in Canada.* I understand that accepting the 2 free books and gifts places me under no obligation to buy anything. I can always return a shipment and cancel at any time. Even if I never buy another book, the two free books and gifts are mine to keep forever.

182/382 HDN F43C

Name	(PLEASE PRINT)	
Address		Apt. #
City	State/Prov.	Zip/Postal Code

Signature (if under 18, a parent or guardian must sign)

Mail to the Harlequin® Reader Service:
IN U.S.A.: P.O. Box 1867, Buffalo, NY 14240-1867
IN CANADA: P.O. Box 609, Fort Erie, Ontario L2A 5X3

**Are you a subscriber to Harlequin Intrigue books
and want to receive the larger-print edition?
Call 1-800-873-8635 or visit www.ReaderService.com.**

* Terms and prices subject to change without notice. Prices do not include applicable taxes. Sales tax applicable in N.Y. Canadian residents will be charged applicable taxes. Offer not valid in Quebec. This offer is limited to one order per household. Not valid for current subscribers to Harlequin Intrigue books. All orders subject to credit approval. Credit or debit balances in a customer's account(s) may be offset by any other outstanding balance owed by or to the customer. Please allow 4 to 6 weeks for delivery. Offer available while quantities last.

Your Privacy—The Harlequin® Reader Service is committed to protecting your privacy. Our Privacy Policy is available online at www.ReaderService.com or upon request from the Harlequin Reader Service.

We make a portion of our mailing list available to reputable third parties that offer products we believe may interest you. If you prefer that we not exchange your name with third parties, or if you wish to clarify or modify your communication preferences, please visit us at www.ReaderService.com/consumerchoice or write to us at Harlequin Reader Service Preference Service, P.O. Box 9062, Buffalo, NY 14269. Include your complete name and address.

HIDIR13R

REQUEST YOUR FREE BOOKS!

2 FREE NOVELS
PLUS 2 FREE GIFTS!

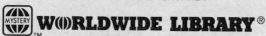

WORLDWIDE LIBRARY®
Your Partner in Crime

ReaderService.com

Manage your account online!

- Review your order history
- Manage your payments
- Update your address

---

*We've designed
the Harlequin® Reader Service
website just for you.*

Enjoy all the features!

- Reader excerpts from any series
- Respond to mailings and
  special monthly offers
- Discover new series available to you
- Browse the Bonus Bucks catalog
- Share your feedback

Visit us at:

ReaderService.com